The Red Veil

by

Donald Gorman

Bloomington, IN Milton Keynes, UK

AuthorHouse™
1663 Liberty Drive, Suite 200
Bloomington, IN 47403
www.authorhouse.com
Phone: 1-800-839-8640

AuthorHouse™ UK Ltd.
500 Avebury Boulevard
Central Milton Keynes, MK9 2BE
www.authorhouse.co.uk
Phone: 08001974150

First published by AuthorHouse 4/25/2007

ISBN: 978-1-4343-0406-3 (sc)

*Printed in the United States of America
Bloomington, Indiana*

This book is printed on acid-free paper.

Table of Contents

Chapter 1
Unpleasant Pictures

Brown and yellow leaves littered the urban sidewalk. A light breeze tossed a few more leaves casually past the corner to the next block. Trees were few and far between. Their branches were nearly bare.

Only a handful of sickly orange survivors clung desperately to the limbs from which they'd sprouted.

The sun hung with a hefty uncertainty in a pale blue sky. Still, it was warm for this time of year. A man in a jacket was walking his collie. Kids shouted playfully as they ran past him. Cars sped by the intersection.

Then, the church bells began to ring. It was a big, fine building with weathered brick walls. The sign outside read, "Cathedral of the Disciples of Christ." Well-dressed people chatted as they walked out through the tall glass doors. They waited on the steps for the guests of honor.

Even a pair of pigeons seemed to watch the doors with anticipation.

A growing crowd assembled outside on the stone staircase.

Church bells rang. Organ music played. Cameras flashed.

Then, the happy couple rushed out of the cathedral amid the cheers of the throng. The crowd parted as they ran hand in hand down the stairs together.

He wore a smart rented tuxedo.

She looked elated... and ravishing in white. Her long veil flapped about helplessly in the sharp breeze.

They hopped into the limo with the soap-painted back windshield. They drove off as the car dragged streamers and strings of cans behind in a noisy display.

Everyone cheered and waved as the car disappeared into the thickening traffic.

A man with a video camera complained, "I never got a good still shot of everyone in front of the church!"

An older gentlemen in a tailored suit replied, "Well, then try to catch up at the reception, will you?"

"It wasn't my fault!"

And, the hefty, uncertain sun hung just a bit lower in the sky.

The reception was held in a grand hall which was perfectly suited to such affairs. A five-piece band played a variety of music. Guests danced, talked and laughed.

There was plenty of food and an open bar. The happy couple did their best to get around to greeting everyone.

Two men sipped beer as they watched the newlyweds circulate.

"Karen looks absolutely breath-taking today," the heavy man observed.

"Yes," he said. "Well, she would today. Let's face it. Today is her day."

"Are you sad about losing your little girl, John?" his friend asked.

"Not as sad as I am to pay for this fiasco," John replied. "I can't wait to see the bills for this mess. Leave it to Karen to find a place like The Presidential Room in a hotel called The Classico Elegante. They think having a goofy name gives them the right to double the price on every dog biscuit they serve you."

"Don't you like the food here?" he asked.

"Oh, the food is wonderful," John admitted. "But, I know plenty of people that could have provided this same spread for half the cost."

"And, I'll bet that dress set you back quite a bit," he said.

"Don't get me started," John grumbled.

"But, she does look absolutely…"

"So you've said," John interrupted. "Still, I shouldn't let money get me down today. It's my daughter's big day. She's been planning for this her whole life. It's only been the past eight months that have been driving me crazy. I can only hope this is the only one of these I'll ever have to pay for."

"How's the groom?"

"Peter?" John said. "He's all right, I suppose. Not the sort of man I would've picked out for her. But, at least this one has a job."

"What does he do?"

3

John took a moment. Then, he said, "He's an exterminator."

"Are you kidding me?" he chuckled. "You're daughter's marrying a cockroach killer? How did she end up with a guy like that?"

"Beats me," John shrugged.

"Well," he offered. "At least, he's probably raking in the bucks just for spraying for termites. I'd just worry about what crawly things he brings home from work."

"I try not to think about it," John said. "So, when is *your* daughter going to take the plunge?"

"Chrissy?" he said. "Not for quite a while, God willing."

The two men shared a laugh.

A few minutes later, a member of the band announced the first dance as Mr. and Mrs. Peter Broderick. The newlyweds danced to their song. After a minute, other couples joined them on the dance floor.

Everything was going exactly as planned.

Nothing could possibly go wrong.

Another hour or two passed before someone asked, "May I dance with the groom?"

He turned away from his group of friends. "Sure," he said with a pleasant smile.

The band was playing a slow, romantic song when he took her hand. She smiled sweetly up at him as they began to dance.

"Did you choose this song on purpose?" he accused teasingly.

"Maybe."

"You little devil," he grinned. "I just got married this afternoon."

"You can't blame me for that," she said.

"Be a good girl," he said. "You're the Maid of Honor, for God's Sake."

"Believe me, I know," she said as she rolled her eyes. "Why else would I be wearing this hideous dress?"

"You look gorgeous tonight, Michelle," he said. "Not many girls could pull off that ruffly taffeta thing. What shade of purple would you say that is?"

"It's not nice to tease a girl about such things," she said.

"Sorry."

"That's okay," she said. "Dresses like this come with the territory, I suppose. That's what I get for letting my best friend get married. By the way, I never knew you were such a good dancer, Peter."

"Well, I do my best."

"If I'd have known…"

"Peter?" called a voice from beyond the dance floor.

He let go of Michelle and tried to look through the crowd.

"Peter?" she called again. "Where are you?"

The pudgy woman who approached appeared to be in her fifties. He smiled when he recognized her.

"Yes, Rachel," he said. "What can I do for you?"

"Where's your beautiful bride?" Rachel asked. "It's almost time to cut the cake."

"I'm not sure," he said. "She went off to the ladies' room about twenty minutes ago or so. And, I haven't heard from her since."

"I'd better go check on her," she said. "That cake won't wait forever."

"You do that, Rachel," he said.

When the old woman was gone, Michelle took his hand. "Now, where were we?" she asked.

As they resumed their dancing, he said, "You were telling me what a good dancer I am. You're not so bad, yourself."

"Thank you," she smiled. "It's nice of you to notice."

"Not at all."

"I took lessons when I was a kid," she said.

"You don't say."

"Oh, yes," she informed with a grin. "In fact, you're looking at a blue ribbon winner of competitions at The Millicent Grommschmidt Academy of the Dance three years running."

"Is that right?" he poked. "Millicent Grommschmidt, you say? Three years running? And, what did I do to deserve the honor of dancing with such a legend?"

"You're the groom."

"Yes. Of course."

"But, we're getting off the track," she said.

"What track is that?"

"Well, as I was saying before we were so rudely interrupted by Rachel and her cake," she continued. "If I'd have known what a good dancer you are…"

This time, she was interrupted by a horrified scream.

They stopped dancing. They looked around.

The band was still playing. People were still talking and laughing. The reception went on all around them.

Another scream rose up over the music.

The band did their best to continue. Some people checked around out of idle curiosity. Most of the crowd chose not to notice if anything was wrong.

"I'd better go see what's going on," Peter said.

He ran off toward the far side of the reception hall. A few people were gathering by the entrance to the hall leading to the rest rooms.

Rachel seemed visibly shaken.

"What's wrong?" he asked.

"I'm not sure," she said. "But, I think you'd better brace yourself, Peter."

"Why?" he asked. "What's the matter?"

"Cynthia first found the blood," she said.

"Blood?" he asked with alarm. "What blood? What are you talking about? Where's Karen?"

"I don't know," she said.

"I saw the blood over here," Cynthia said shakily. She gestured for Peter to follow her.

A few other people joined Cynthia and Peter as they hurried down the hall. They stopped just outside the door to the ladies' room.

They looked down at the trail that streaked the floor leading from the rest room heading toward the far exit.

"That looks like blood," a young man observed.

"Karen?" Peter called out with panic in his voice.

"In here," Cynthia said. She opened the door to the ladies' room.

Without thinking, Peter burst into the room.

Everything was still. No one was there.

However, there were puddles and spatters of blood all over the tile floor. And, the bridal veil sat in the center of one big pool of blood.

It almost appeared to feel uncomfortable in its unsanitary environment. It had once been a beautiful, immaculate white.

However, at this point it was mostly soaked through with a dark shade of red.

"No!" Peter shouted. "Karen! Where's Karen?"

"The trail of blood leads down the hall," Cynthia pointed out with tears in her eyes.

He rushed out of the room. Cynthia and four young men followed him as he hurried down the back hall in the direction of the bloody smears.

"It looks like someone was dragged bleeding toward the exit," one man observed.

"You're not helping, Evan," Cynthia said nervously.

Peter quickened his pace. He followed the broad smears that continued toward the back door of the building. The blood was as thick and frightening as it had been when their journey started.

When they reached the Exit sign, Peter pushed the door open.

"I can't go out there!" Cynthia averred in a trembling voice.

Peter ran outside. Three men followed him out to the landing. One man stayed behind with Cynthia.

It was late at night by this time. The reception had been going on for hours. The sky was almost an exaggerated shade of black. A pale half moon stood guard, and only allowed a handful of stars to come out and play in a darkness such as this.

A wooden fence shielded the back of the building from the parking lot. A scant set of lights barely illuminated the space allotted for workmen and staff. However, they could just about see what needed to be seen.

"The blood goes down the stairs?" Peter cried. "What the hell? Karen? Are you out here? Karen?"

There was no answer.

They ran down the stairs. They looked around.

"The blood trail is heading that way," Evan pointed out. "By the side of the building."

They followed the chilling streaks to the side of the building. They followed the trail until it stopped dead.

Peter glanced around. Then, he looked up.

"The dumpster?" he asked with panic. "You must be kidding! The blood stops at the dumpster?"

The lid was closed. However, there were a few drips of blood drizzling down the metal wall of the large receptacle.

"Oh no!" he whispered in a trembling voice. "It can't be!"

He took a few breaths for courage. Then, he grabbed the top of the dumpster with both hands.

He hesitated. He was afraid of what he might see.

"Please! No!" he whispered to himself.

He took another deep breath.

Then, he threw open the metallic lid. He gazed down in horror at the newest addition to the contents of the dumpster.

Her lifeless body had been tossed haphazardly atop the smelly piles of partially wrapped garbage and filth.

Her eyes were wide open despite the blood that lined their rims and leaked down her pallid cheeks. Beneath the crimson stains, her face seemed contorted in an expression of tremendous fear and pain. Her once beautiful white dress was torn and soaked through with broad, bright red blotches.

"No!" Peter screamed. "Karen! No!"

A few hours earlier, the sun was setting over a dreary urban skyline. It was just a little chilly and damp. A few clouds rolled in. They soaked up the pink and orange streaks over the horizon like billowy sponges hovering in mid air.

Still, the colorful stains in the sky retained their brilliance.

He slowly pulled into the parking lot. He was careful. He didn't want to be noticed.

He parked in the nearest space. Then, he sat. He didn't move.

He watched the couple who were walking by. They were laughing as they passed near his black Hyundai. She was a bleach-blonde in her middle forties. She was still very attractive. Her attire flaunted her bank account.

The man was younger. He was tall, dark and boyishly pretty. It was no secret what he was after.

They were absorbed in each other's company. They laughed again. They didn't notice the man in the black Hyundai as they entered the restaurant.

He just sat in his car. He waited a minute or so.

Luckily, the happy couple appeared in the window. They took a table with a view. Apparently, discretion was not a priority for them.

However, it was a top priority for the man in the parking lot.

His video camera was small and silent. It was easy to catch the couple in the restaurant on film. They held hands in this romantic venue. There was even a kiss or two as the delightful sunset provided the perfect backdrop to their intimate dinner.

He caught it all on tape. Or at least, he caught enough to matter.

Kissing, hand-holding, the way they looked at each other...

It was all there.

Finally, he put the camera away. He parked across the street. He opened a bag of corn chips. He ate while drinking coffee from a Styrofoam cup.

He was glad that entering the restaurant had not been necessary. He listened to the crunching of the chips as he chewed.

Being patient was never a problem. He just ate and watched.

About an hour later, they came out. The young man helped his companion into the passenger's seat of a shiny, blue car. Then, he sat behind the wheel of his brand new Mercury.

They drove off without a care.

They had no idea that a black Hyundai was behind them.

He knew where the blue Mercury was headed. He'd been there before. Still, he kept the car in sight as he drove.

Every twist and turn was predictable. He stayed out of sight while following them to their inevitable destination.

Finally, the Mercury parked near the curb. There was a Laundromat on the corner and a small park across the road. The happy couple hurried into a stone building.

It was dark outside by this time. The darkness seemed shallow and empty in this part of town. It was a darkness with no soul, conscience or intent. Streetlamps cast their beams upon the street as if trying to light a dismal stage before another monotonous performance of the repetitive drone of nightlife in this city.

It was not really a bad part of town. There was a certain amount of money here.

However, much of that money was as dirty as the decaying leaves which lined the roads and clogged the sewer drains.

You would be well advised to watch your back around here.

Lights came on in the second floor window of the stone building. The curtains were partially drawn. But, there was still a clear view of the happy couple from his seat in the black Hyundai.

He took a few still shots with a camera just for fun. Then, he got some quality video footage of the two of them as they kissed and undressed each other.

When he got what he needed, he stopped filming.

There was such a thing as discretion. He didn't want to cross any lines.

He watched with only a fleeting interest for a minute.

Then, he drove off into a darkness that had no soul, conscience or intent.

The following morning was cool, crisp and partly sunny. Clouds were populating more of the sky than they had the previous day. However, they were still white and friendly. It promised to be a pleasant day.

Still, everyone was hard at work in the office.

A young woman walked across the large room. A sandy blonde ponytail rested against her back as she carried a series of folders between long rows of cubicles.

When she reached the private office at the far end, she knocked on the door.

"Come in," said the muffled voice.

Everything in the private office was set up to appear professional. The matching desk and chairs looked sturdy and functional. Every "In" or "Out" basket and pile of papers on the desk was neat and tidy. Even the tall plants set against the back corners seemed to serve a purpose.

The man seated in the leather chair had earned every gray hair on his balding head. Each wrinkle on his pudgy face was a badge to the hard work that he had performed at that very desk.

"Ah, Miss Pierce," he smiled as she entered. "You didn't take long."

"I aim to please, Mr. Callahan," she said. "Here are those files on the Davis-Kromsky merger you asked about."

"Thank you, Miss Pierce," he said. "Just put them on that table, will you?"

"Yes, sir."

"And, I keep telling you," he reminded. "You can call me Steve."

"Thank you... 'Steve.'"

"You've been here for a whole week, Angela," he pointed out. "And your work has been exemplary so far. I think you'll do fine with us."

"Thanks, sir," she smiled shyly. "That's nice to hear."

"Just stop calling me 'sir' and 'Mr. Callahan'," he said. "We don't rest on formality in this office. We're all one big, happy family here at The Blue Arrow Agency."

"I'll try to remember that, Steve."

"Although I must admit," he said with a suddenly sullen tone. "It's hard to be happy at the moment. Not after what happened to Karen Ryland from over in Payroll this past weekend."

"Why?" she asked. "What happened?"

"She got married yesterday," he said. "To some guy named Broderick."

"She did?" she asked. "That's wonderful! Good for her. Why would anyone be unhappy about that?"

"Didn't you hear?" he asked. "She was murdered during her own reception. She was stabbed 22 times and left in a dumpster behind the reception hall."

"That's terrible!" she gasped. "Who would do such a thing?"

"The police are investigating," he explained. "Last I heard, they had no solid suspects."

"Oh, the poor girl," she said. "And, what about her husband? This has got to be really hard on him."

"I take it you didn't know Karen that well," he surmised.

"No," she shook her head. "We met a few times, but I didn't pay much attention to her personal life. I didn't even know she was engaged."

"Well, you missed your chance to get to know her," he said. "Some folks are passing the hat around along with a sympathy card for the family."

"I'll look forward to giving a few bucks," she said. "Her parents must be devastated."

"I can only imagine."

"It's just so sad," she said. "And on her wedding day, too. I can't think of a worse way to go."

"She left here Friday night as Karen Ryland," he said. "And by the time she was murdered last night, she was Mrs. Karen Broderick."

"Who would even think to kill a bride on her wedding day?" she queried. "I mean, what sort of sick person would do such a thing?"

"There are all kinds of crazy people in the world, Angela," he said. "Try not to take it too hard."

"I have to tell you, Mr. Callahan," she said. "I was in a good mood when I came in this morning. But, this is going to ruin my day."

"Don't dwell on it, Angela," he recommended. "As you said, you hardly knew her. Life still goes on for the rest of us. And, I'm sure you have a lot of work to do."

She simply nodded.

"You'll be fine," he said. "You have a bright future here, Miss Pierce. Keep looking forward. And, call me Steve."

"Okay… Steve."

She tried to smile before leaving the office. Then, she slowly walked back to her desk. She couldn't get Karen out of her mind.

She stood near her chair. She stared at her computer screen. There were two new emails in her mailbox. She didn't feel like reading them.

"Hi, Angela," said a happy voice behind her.

She turned to face the well-dressed young man who was leaning on her cubicle.

"Hi, Neil," she said.

"Why so glum?" he asked. "You look like you're having a bad day. Did Callahan give you some monstrous project to do or something?"

"No," she said. "I just heard about Karen Ryland."

"Oh," he sighed. "I heard about that. Poor girl. Such a tragedy. Did you know her well?"

"Not very well," she shook her head. "No. I wish I had known her better. I wish I had taken the time to talk to her."

"You can't be friends with everybody here," he offered. "This is a big place with a lot of people. Some people you actually want to avoid. Speaking of which, here comes that creepy Dylan Zeblonsky from Contracts."

She looked over at the hefty young man who was carrying an armload of large paper files. They were rolled up with rubber bands. They almost looked like blueprints.

"I don't know what scares me more," she whispered. "His clothes or his hair. What garbage dump did he get that suit from? I hope he didn't pay money for it."

"We probably shouldn't talk about him," Neil whispered back. "But, I wouldn't want to bet on the chances of getting a comb through that rat's nest on his head, either."

They tried not to snicker.

Dylan's face lit up as he approached. "Hi, Angela," he said with a nervous smile. "How are you today?"

"Fine, Dylan."

"Where are you off to, Dylan?" Neil asked politely.

"I have to get these plans…" he began.

However, a few of the rolled papers slipped out of his grasp. Neil and Angela tried not to wince as the plans bounced on the carpet.

Dylan quickly bent down to recover the files.

"I just have to get these to, uh…" he tried to say. But, he dropped a few more files.

"Would you like some help, pal?" Neil offered as he knelt down.

"No!" Dylan averred. "I got it!"

17

He quickly scooped up the files. After dropping a few more, he scooped them up again as quickly as possible.

"Are you sure I can't help, buddy?" Neil offered again.

"I told you I got it!" Dylan snapped.

He hoped his face wasn't too red as he jumped back up to his feet. He tried to look at Angela with a bit of dignity.

However, he couldn't even glance directly at her face.

"I have to get these..." he indicated with a nod. He clung tightly to the files as he concluded, "... Over there. I have to go."

"'Bye, Dylan," she said.

She struggled to keep a straight face as he ran off.

"That was a sad display," Neil finally said. "I don't like to pick on the 'competently challenged', but that guy makes my skin crawl."

"He's not so bad," she said. "He just needs help with his social skills."

"And his hair," he added.

"And his fashion sense," she snickered.

They shared a laugh.

"You know he's got a thing for you, don't you?" he informed.

"Oh, he's like that with all the girls," she said. "He's just shy. I've seen him do that with every decent-looking girl in the place. In fact, I've seen him act like that around Karen once or twice."

"Well, it's still in your best interest," he advised. "To stay as far away from him as you can."

"Don't worry," she said. "I have no reason to go near that guy. To tell the truth, I do find him a little scary."

"Good," he said. "Keep it that way."

After a pause, he said, "Well, I should get back to work. See you around, Angela."

"Take it easy."

She watched him walk away. A sense of melancholy returned as her mind wandered.

"He *is* kind of cute, huh?" said another voice from behind.

She spun around to face another girl in her twenties. "Who?" she asked awkwardly. "Neil? Yeah, I guess. Sort of."

"You can't fool me, Angela," she poked. "I know you like him. It's written all over your face."

"Cut it out, Jennifer," she demanded. "I have no interest in Neil Worthington."

"Then, why do you keep looking at him that way?" Jennifer asked.

"I don't!"

"If you say so, honey," Jennifer prodded. "It's just a shame he's already seeing somebody. You two would go great together."

"That's enough, Jennifer!"

"In fact," Jennifer confided. "I wouldn't mind getting some of that myself."

"You can have him, then."

"I told you," Jennifer reminded. "He's already seeing somebody. In fact, his girlfriend Cynthia was the first person to find Karen's bloody veil at the wedding reception. You heard about Karen, right?"

"Neil was at the wedding?" she asked. "We were just talking about Karen. I wonder why he didn't mention he was there."

"He didn't?" Jennifer asked with surprise. "What did he say?"

"He said he 'heard about that,'" she explained. "But, he didn't say anything about being at the wedding or the reception."

"That's odd."

"Of course, we were interrupted by Dylan Zeblonsky," she reasoned.

"Yes, I saw," Jennifer said while rolling her eyes. "That was a pretty picture."

"But still," she continued. "That was afterwards. He could've said he was there. I wonder why he didn't."

"Maybe he didn't want to bring up his girlfriend in front of you," Jennifer suggested with a smile.

"I said that's enough, Jennifer!"

"Oh well," Jennifer shrugged. "I have to get back to work, anyway. Good luck with Neil, honey. You'll need it."

"I don't need any luck," she insisted. "I don't have any big thing for Neil Worthington!"

She watched Jennifer leave.

Then, she sat down at her desk. She thought about Neil. Questions kept running through her mind.

Was he at Karen's wedding? If so, why didn't he mention it when the subject came up? Could he possibly be hiding something? If so, what could it be?

And, why?

"Sergeant Diaz?"

"Yes, sir?"

"I'm Detective Sumaki," he informed while flashing a badge. "This is my partner, Detective Reynolds. We've been assigned to this case."

"Of course, sir," Diaz nodded. "The victim was a Mrs. Karen Broderick. She was stabbed 22 times right here in the Ladies' Room. She had just gotten married a few hours earlier. That's her bridal veil in that pool of dried blood."

"Oh!" Reynolds grimaced. "That's a nasty picture!"

"Lovely," Sumaki grumbled.

"Then, she was apparently dragged out into the hall," Diaz explained. "We're guessing she was already dead. She was dragged down the hall to the back exit."

"Let's take a look," Sumaki said.

The three men stepped out into the hall.

"You can see the blood stains leading toward the back exit," Diaz pointed out. "The body was dragged outside, down a flight of stairs and around to the side of the building. The groom was the first person to actually see the body. She was left in a dumpster."

"Somebody didn't want that marriage to last," Reynolds said. "Somebody with a score to settle and a mean temper."

Sumaki watched the floor carefully. He slowly led the men along the dried blood-streaked path to the back door. He stared at the door handle.

"No prints on the door?" he asked.

"We dusted everything for prints," Diaz said. "The Ladies' Room, the hall, the door, the alley, the dumpster… even some garbage and toilet paper. There were thousands of prints on everything, of course. But, there's nothing that we can specifically pin on a murderer. Nothing with anything incriminating like blood or anything."

"No bloody fingerprints?" Sumaki asked. "No bloody footprints? Nothing we can use to nail the little bastard?"

"Nothing obvious so far," Diaz said.

"Well," Sumaki smiled. "This should still be an easy case to solve. I notice they have security cameras in the hall. All you have to do is look at the tapes."

"That's just it," Diaz said. "We looked at the tapes already."

"And?"

"We could see the victim walk into the Ladies' Room," Diaz explained. "We thought we were home free. Then about a minute later, all the cameras went black. It was like a computer glitch or something. The cameras came back on about eight and a half minutes later, and it was over. You could see the blood stains on the floor, but everything was done. It was the damnedest thing."

"Are you kidding me with this?" Sumaki asked angrily. "They all went black at the same time?"

"It's like I said," Diaz reminded. "It looked like a computer glitch or something."

"Were there any shots from the main room of anyone entering the corridor?" Sumaki asked.

"There were no clear shots of anyone leaving the main room," Diaz said. "It was a wedding reception. People were everywhere. Camera angles were insufficient. Plus, those cameras were having glitches then, too. We got nothing from the main room."

"What a stroke of luck," Reynolds said sarcastically.

"It looks like our friend really had his act together," Diaz continued. "That's why we decided to call you guys."

"How many people were at this shindig?" Sumaki asked.

"The hotel manager told me there were 250 guests," Diaz said.

"250 guests?" Sumaki wondered impatiently. "And, nobody saw anything? Not even someone dragging a bloody body down a long corridor? 250 people at a party with an open bar, and nobody needed a bathroom?"

"There's another set of restrooms at the other side of the reception hall," Diaz explained. "They're closer to the action. It's not hard to believe that this corridor wasn't used all that much."

"Our killer still had a lot of balls," Reynolds commented. "It's awful risky pulling a stunt like this in the middle of a huge party."

There was an uneasy pause.

"All right," Sumaki finally commanded. "I want to see the dumpster. I want a better look at that Ladies' Room, and a better look at that veil. And, I want to see those tapes. Something's awfully fishy here. And, I'm going to find this scumbag, if I have to tear this place apart!"

"Oh," Diaz added. "The hotel wants to know when they can clean the blood off the floor. Apparently, they have more receptions coming up."

"To hell with the hotel!" Sumaki growled. "We have a murderer to find! We'll be done when we're done! If they want something to do, tell them to fix their computer glitches and camera angles!"

"And, they can line up their entire staff," Reynolds added sharply. "Evidently, they will be the first in a long list of potential suspects and witnesses we have to question."

🌿 🌿 🌿

The lighting was subtle. It was an elegant establishment with a circular bar in the center of the large room. There was a small stage for nighttime entertainment. A pop radio station played softly in the background.

The bartender was chatting with the three patrons seated at the counter. Not many people came here before the lunch rush. The place was nearly empty.

However, one man sat in a distant corner booth. He toyed with his tie while nursing a martini. He ran his fingers through his graying hair.

He checked his watch nervously. He sipped his drink.

Finally, the younger man stepped up to his table.

"Good morning, Dr. Freitag," he said with a professional smile.

"Mr. Polopous," Freitag said. "I was starting to wonder if you were going to show. Have a seat."

"Sorry," he said. He sat opposite the doctor in the booth. "I'm running a little behind today."

"I take it you have some news for me," Freitag said.

"Yes I do, Doctor," he said. "But, I'm afraid it's not happy news."

"So, my suspicions were correct?"

"Yes, Doctor," he said. "Your wife is indeed cheating on you."

Freitag braced himself with a deep breath. "I knew it!" he muttered. "There were signs. Okay! Give me the details."

"Not so fast, Doctor," he said. He held out his hand.

Freitag rolled his eyes. Then, he reached into his coat pocket. He pulled out a stuffed envelope. He handed it across the table.

"It's all there, Polopous," he said. "Feel free to count it."

"That's okay, Doctor," Polopous said as he stuffed the envelope into his overcoat. "I trust you."

He pulled out a thick, padded envelope of his own. He set it on the table.

"There's a video in there for you," Polopous said. "I even threw in some still shots for good measure. The guy's name is Grant Langley. He's 31, and a real pretty-boy type. He works as a salesman for T.F.I. It's an insurance company on Essex Blvd. He's notorious for dating rich, bored widows and housewives. He loves having women spend other men's money on him."

Freitag grabbed the envelope impatiently.

"I've got to warn you," Polopous said. "You're not going to like what you see in there. I used discretion, but there is serious evidence of infidelity. Enough to keep you on top in the divorce. You're going to find some of those pictures very unpleasant."

"Maybe I'll wait," he muttered. "Can I buy you a drink, Polopous?"

"No, thanks," he said. "I should get going. Everything you need is in the envelope, Doctor. Should I assume our business is concluded?"

"For now," said the doctor. "If I need anything else, I'll call you."

"Fair enough," he nodded. "So, what are you going to do about your wife?"

"I haven't decided yet," Freitag said. "I'll have to see the tape and pictures first. I guess I'll just have to find my own way to deal with it."

Polopous gave him an uncertain glance. "Well, be careful," he advised. "Don't do anything rash."

"What I decide to do is not your concern, Mr. Polopous," he said. "You have your money. Now kindly leave me to my grief."

"Good luck, Doctor."

Polopous quickly left the building.

The doctor finished his drink as a warm female voice asked, "Is your friend gone? Are you going to want another martini?"

"'Yes' on both counts, dear."

She ran off to get his drink. A few more people walked into the bar.

"Oh, Madeline!" he muttered. "How could you do this to me? To yourself? To *us*! Haven't I always given you everything you ever wanted, you little slut?"

He stared angrily at the envelope on the table for a minute.

"I can't wait to see this tape," he whispered to himself. "Then, I guess I have some decisions to make!"

Chapter 2
Somewhat Disturbing

The television was on. He was watching a real judge hear a small claims case. He wasn't really listening. It hurt too much. Wads of tissues filled an overflowing waste basket and littered the living room carpet.

Yet, he still wasn't done crying.

He yanked another tissue from the box. He wiped his eyes.

He was sobbing into his hands when the doorbell rang.

He was expecting company. Still, he dreaded the thought of getting up to open the door. He was in no mood to talk to anyone. He heaved a heavy sigh before rising to his feet.

When he opened the door, he appeared startled by the men on his porch.

"Sorry, sir," said the man as he flashed his badge. "We didn't mean to scare you."

"That's all right," said the host. "I was expecting someone else."

"We'll try not to take up too much of your time," he said. "I'm Detective Sumaki. This is my partner, Detective Reynolds. Are we addressing Peter Broderick?"

"Yes."

"We're investigating the murder of your bride," Sumaki explained. "May we come in for a minute please?"

"Sure."

The three men stepped into the living room.

"First," Sumaki said. "May I offer my sincere condolences on the death of your wife, sir? I'm sure it's been very rough on you."

"Thank you," he said. "We were supposed to be in Jamaica on our honeymoon right now. Four days and three nights. There's no point in me going alone. I've been crying all day. Who would kill a sweet girl like Karen on her wedding day?"

"That's what we're here to find out," Sumaki said. "Do you know of anyone who would want to harm her?"

"No," he said. "Everyone loved her. She was a sweetheart, without a care in the world."

"No ex-lovers or jealous old boyfriends?" Reynolds added.

"Not that I'm aware of," he said.

"Where did she work?" Sumaki asked.

"Some place called The Blue Arrow Agency downtown," he said. "I understand they handle corporate PR and legal matters from all over the area. They have a lot of clients in Pittsburgh. She worked for their Payroll Dept."

"And, what do you do for a living?" Reynolds asked.

"I'm an exterminator," he said. "I work for the No Pest Extermination Company on Sterling Blvd. That's how I met Karen. Blue Arrow had a serious ant problem almost two years ago."

"What a romantic story," Reynolds said.

The doorbell rang.

He opened the door. A beautiful girl with long, black hair offered him a sympathetic smile. "Hi, honey," she said. "How are you holding up? Come here."

She took Peter into her arms.

"Is there anything I can do?" she asked.

"No thanks, Michelle," he said as he held her. "I'll be fine."

"Anything you need..." she began.

Then, she saw the detectives standing near the coffee table. She immediately let go of her host.

"Oh, excuse me," she said as she glanced nervously down at the carpet. "I didn't know you had guests."

Sumaki made the necessary introductions. Then, he asked, "And, who might you be?"

"I'm Michelle Dorsett," she said. "I was the maid of honor at the wedding yesterday. I just came here to console Peter."

"You were the maid of honor?" Sumaki asked. "Then, I can ask both of you at the same time. What happened last night? Did either of you see anything suspicious?"

"No," she said. "We were dancing together when we heard something was wrong."

"You were dancing together?" Reynolds asked.

"Sure," he said. "As the groom, I have to dance with everybody. Plus, Michelle is a friend. She's been best friends with Karen since high school."

"That's true," she agreed.

"I suppose it was around 9:00 last night," he explained. "When Karen told me she was going to the Ladies' Room. I was talking with friends and making my rounds. It didn't bother me too much when Karen didn't come back, because it was a big place and it was full of people."

"I asked him to dance around 20 after 9:00 or so," she said. "After all, it was a wedding and he was the groom."

"It was almost 9:30 when a friend of Karen's family," he expounded. "Rachel Carver asked me where she was. She said it was time to cut the cake. I pointed her toward the rest rooms. Five minutes later, we heard screams."

"Screams?" Sumaki asked.

"A friend of Karen's named Cynthia starting screaming when she found the veil," he explained. "Cynthia Trott. I don't know her very well. We only met a few times. I went to investigate. And, we followed the trail of blood out to the dumpster."

"You were the first person to see the body?" Reynolds asked.

"It was a sight I'll never forget," he said. "It was… It was…"

He began sobbing uncontrollably. Michelle took him into her arms for comfort.

The detectives allowed a respectful pause.

After a minute, Reynolds asked, "And, what about you, Miss Dorsett? Do you know of anyone who would want to kill Karen?"

She was still holding Peter as she said, "Of course not!"

"Do you know where we can find this Cynthia Trott, Miss?" Sumaki asked.

"I think she lives across the road from Karen on Becker St.," she said. "I don't know the exact address. It's a big, red stone building."

"And, how can we reach you if we need you, Miss?" Sumaki asked.

"I work at The Jolly Shopper Supermarket on Cardinal Ave.," she said impatiently. She was still clinging to her weeping friend. "You can reach me there all day any day of the week. Monday through Friday. Now, can't you leave us alone? Hasn't this poor man been through enough?"

The detectives shared a glance.

"Okay," Sumaki allowed. "I guess we can come back at a more convenient time. I'm sorry to have bothered you. I'll leave a few of my cards on your coffee table, sir. If either of you can think of anything, please give me a call."

"We'll let ourselves out," Reynolds added.

When they were out in their car, Reynolds commented, "He seems pretty shaken up. I don't think we'll get anything out of him."

"I don't think he saw anything," Sumaki agreed. "The poor bastard. You got to feel sorry for him. That Dorsett girl is a nice place to find some solace, though."

"Yeah," Reynolds nodded. "She's a mighty fine-looking girl. And, I don't like the way she was looking at him. His wife just died. But, she seemed interested in offering more than a friendly shoulder to cry on."

"She was unhappy to see us in the beginning," Sumaki said. "And, she seemed awfully anxious to get rid of us."

"How long do you think the maid of honor had her eye on the groom?" Reynolds asked. "Maybe they had something going before the wedding."

"I doubt it," Sumaki said. "He was too upset about his wife. But, who knows how long Miss Dorsett has been watching Broderick?"

"Do you think she's our killer?" Reynolds asked.

"No," Sumaki replied. "She's not big enough. She never would have been able to lift that body up into the dumpster."

"Could she have had some help?"

"It's possible," Sumaki said. "But not likely. Still, up until now, I was sure that the culprit was jealous of *him*. Now I see that it's very possible that the murderer may have been jealous of *her*. We'll have to keep watching in both directions."

"And, we should keep our eyes on the maid of honor," Reynolds suggested.

"I heartily concur."

Back in the apartment, she helped the sobbing widower over to the sofa.

"Sit down, honey," she said. "You should rest a while. You've been through so much. Did you get any sleep at all last night?"

33

"None at all," he said. He wiped his eyes as he sat beside her.

"Would you like me to get you something?" she asked with her arm around his shoulders. "You should probably have a drink. Maybe some fruit juice or water?"

"No, thanks," he said. "You've been very sweet."

"It's the least I can do," she said as she held him just a bit more tightly. "I can't even begin to imagine what you're feeling right now."

He felt a certain comfort in her embrace. Suddenly, it made him feel awkward.

"Michelle?" he finally asked. "Why exactly did you insist on coming over today? Shouldn't you be at work now?"

"I thought you could use a friend," she said.

"You're being extremely attentive," he said. "And frankly, it's starting to scare me a little."

"Why?" she asked. "You just lost your wife. You're going to need a lot of support to help you through this rough time. I'm just here to give all the support I can offer."

She kissed his cheek.

A certain sense of anxious suspicion began to churn in his stomach.

🌱 🌱 🌱

"So, your girlfriend is the person who actually found the veil?" he asked.

"Yes," he confirmed. "Do you believe it, Joe? Even though I work in the same office as Karen, my Cynthia is really the only reason I got dragged to the wedding.

I hate weddings. But, you know how girls are about those things."

"I sure do," Joe chuckled.

"I actually met Cynthia through Karen," he said. "They're good friends as well as neighbors. They live across the street from each other."

He stopped with a solemn contemplative pause.

"... Or at least, they used to," he corrected himself.

"Yes," Joe said respectfully.

He ran his fingers through his thick, white hair. Then, he nervously adjusted his tie.

"How long have you been seeing this girl?" he asked in order to change the subject.

"The better part of a year," he said. "It's going okay, sort of. I just hope that wedding doesn't give her any ideas."

"I hear you," Joe smiled. "We were just talking about 'women and weddings.' That can be a scary combination."

They shared a laugh.

"Exactly," he agreed. "And from what her mother tells me, the Trott women are famous for getting carried away with those occasions."

"Her mother's already dropping hints?" Joe poked. "Run, boy! Run as fast and as far away as you can!"

"Don't think I haven't thought about it," he chuckled. "We've had our problems. But, she's a nice girl, for the most part."

"Trott?" Joe asked. "That's the family name?"

"Yes..." he began.

But, he was interrupted by a nervous man with messy hair.

"Excuse me, Mr. McMahon," the intruder said.

"Yes, Dylan," Joe said as he turned. He struggled to maintain a polite expression. "What can I do for you?"

"I went to get those quarterly reports you asked for," Dylan said. "But, they're down in Accounting. Apparently, we're being audited."

"Okay," Joe sighed. "That's fine. I think Mr. Callahan had some work for you anyway. Why don't you go see what he wants?"

"Yes, Mr. McMahon," Dylan muttered.

Joe turned back to his seated friend. He was on the phone.

"If you think you remember something," he said into the receiver. "Call the cops. I'm sure they'd love the help. I'll call you before I leave work. 'Bye."

He hung up.

"What was that about, Neil?" Joe asked.

"I was checking my messages while you were talking to Dylan," he explained. "My girlfriend must have called around lunchtime. She said she remembered seeing something at the wedding reception that made her suspicious. She sounded a little scared on the phone."

"Cynthia?" Joe asked. "What did she say?"

"She didn't say much," he replied. "It was just a short message. She just said that she remembered seeing something suspicious and she wanted my advice. I just called her back and left a message on her machine telling her to call the cops."

"I wonder what she saw," Joe said.

"Who knows?" he said. "I'm glad I get to go home in a couple of hours. I didn't like how she sounded."

"I'm sure she's fine, Neil," he said.

"You're right," he sighed. "But, I worry about her sometimes. She tends to get a little too overanxious."

"Well…" Joe began. Then, he stopped and turned. "Why are you still here, Dylan?"

"I'm sorry, sir," Dylan said nervously. "I guess I got distracted by Neil's phone call. I heard about what happened yesterday, and I…"

He stopped talking. He cowered beneath the glares of Neil and Joe.

"I'll just go, sir," Dylan sputtered. "Sorry."

He scurried out of the office.

Then, Joe turned back to his friend. "Don't worry, Neil," he said. "I'm sure your Cynthia will be okay. Do you think she went to the cops yet?"

"I hope so," he said. "But if she's scared, she might be waiting for me to see her first. It's hard to tell with her."

"Well, I should get back to work," Joe said. "And as your boss, I suggest you do the same."

"Yes sir."

He turned back to his desk. He managed to get a minute's worth of work done before he was interrupted by a female voice.

"Neil?" she said. "Can I ask you something?"

He looked up from his files and smiled. "Yes, Angela," he said. "What's up?"

"I was just curious," she said. "When we were talking about Karen earlier, why did you say you *heard* about that? Why didn't you admit that you were at the wedding?"

"I don't know," he said. "I suppose I was just trying to avoid long explanations. I went with Cynthia and the groom into the Ladies' Room. I saw the bloody veil. I even went down the hall to the exit. But, Cynthia was too scared to go outside, so I stayed with her. I never went outside. I never saw the body. I just don't like talking about it all. So, I just try to avoid the whole subject all together."

"That's okay," she said. "Sort of. But, I wish you wouldn't lie to me, Neil. We're supposed to be friends."

"I'm sorry, Angela," he said. "I'll try my best to improve."

"Thank you," she said. "Have a good day."

"You too."

He watched her leave. He had to admit she had her appeal. However, he had Cynthia. And at the moment, Cynthia gave him plenty of reason to wonder.

He was just a bit concerned.

"When was this parking lot painted?" Sumaki asked.

"Thursday and Friday."

"Do you think it matters?" Reynolds asked. "This is a hotel. Those tire tracks could have been caused by any one of a zillion customers or staff."

"That's very true," Sumaki nodded. "But just to be safe, I want to get a possible make on the kind of vehicle that could leave those tracks. If someone was playing with the computerized security system, they may have been casing the joint a few days in advance."

"That's quite a long shot, Tom," Reynolds said.

"Maybe," Sumaki said. "But if we catch the right type of car with white paint on the tires, you'll thank me."

"I can tell you just from looking," said the hotel staff member. "Those look like they came from an SUV. You can tell by the tread and the spacing."

"Thank you," Sumaki said. "I figured that as well. But, I'm hoping our experts can give me something a little more specific."

"Fine," Reynolds said impatiently. "But, can we please get out of here, Tom? We still have thousands of wedding-goers to question."

🌿 🌿 🌿

She took a sip of fruit juice. She sat on her sofa. She ran her fingers nervously through her long, dark hair.

She thought about calling the cops. Should she?

That's what Neil had suggested in his phone message. It made sense. Did she really remember anything worth mentioning?

Why did she suddenly feel frightened?

She glanced around the apartment. Everything was quiet. Everything seemed fine.

She allowed herself to laugh. She knew she was just being silly.

The television was on. However, she could barely hear it. The news was playing. It was a story about a local politician. She was glad that the sound had been turned down.

Neil would be leaving work soon. It was the end of the workday. He said he would call before he left. She looked forward to hearing from him.

She was only home because she was still rattled from the day before. Seeing something like that was enough to make anyone a little edgy. She would be okay soon. She would probably go back to work in the morning.

She was still depressed about Karen, though.

Karen had been such a good friend. How could this have happened?

Who could have…?

Could it have been…?

She stood. She walked to the bathroom. She looked in the mirror.

Her face looked a bit pale and drawn. She hadn't slept well the night before. Her eyes were red from crying. She still didn't feel right.

The mirror served as a door to the medicine cabinet. She pulled it open. She fished around for something to calm her nerves. She closed the cabinet.

She looked in the mirror.

Perhaps she should make an early night of it. Perhaps she should just get some sleep. She wished Neil would call. She would feel better if she knew he was on his way home.

She opened the plastic container. She poured two pills out into her hand. She put the lid back on and opened the medicine cabinet. She put the bottle back and closed the cabinet.

She looked in the mirror.

She gasped with shock.

The mirror showed something that was not there earlier. It was a shape. It was almost more of a shadow. It was the shadow of a person. She couldn't make out who it was. However, the person was wearing a veil. It looked a lot like the veil Karen had worn at her wedding.

However, the veil was almost entirely red, as if the white garment had been covered with a thick coat of blood.

She spun around to face the shadow.

But, it was gone. So was the veil.

She was breathing heavily. She was still frightened.

She leaned back against the sink until her breathing returned to normal. The pills were no longer in her hand. She must have dropped them.

She didn't care. She was not going to turn her back to the door again. She didn't want to face the mirror. She knew it was silly, but she refused to turn around.

Carefully, she made her way back to the living room. She inched along slowly and silently. Her eyes darted back and forth in all possible directions. Her heart was pounding with fear.

She kept moving slowly toward the living room. She remained silent and vigilant.

The living room was much brighter than the bathroom. It made her feel more safe and secure. She knew there was nothing to worry about. It was just a figment of her imagination. It was a delayed reaction to the gruesome experience at the reception.

She smiled as she came back to her senses. How could she have seen that image in the mirror? How ridiculous!

Then, her face froze.

Why was the television off? She hadn't turned it off. It was still running the news when she left the room.

Who turned off the television?

She started glancing around the room again. Fear was growing as her body became tense. She rushed over to the sofa. She looked behind every piece of furniture that could possibly conceal an intruder.

Everything was in order.

Once again, she laughed at herself. She must have turned the TV off and just forgotten. She picked up the remote from the coffee table. She was about to turn the TV back on when she noticed something.

There were two or three red spots on the coffee table.

They looked like blood.

She gasped.

Then, she looked around. There were a few more small red stains on the carpet. They were new. They hadn't been there before!

Her heart leapt up into her throat. Her heart started pounding again. She looked around the room. Nothing was out of place.

Still, she reached over to the coffee table again. She pulled her cell phone out of her purse. She quickly dialed and waited for a response.

"Hello? Cynthia?" the voice on the other end finally replied. "How are you, honey?"

"Listen, Neil," she said nervously. "I need you to come to my house right away. Something's not right around here."

"What's wrong?" he asked.

"I went to the bathroom to get some pills for my nerves," she explained. "And, I saw a shadow in the mirror. I couldn't see who it was, but the person was wearing a veil. It looked like Karen's veil from last night. It was white, but it was caked with some red... it looked like blood! It looked like the bloody veil from last night!"

"Calm down, Cynthia," he said. "You're probably just hallucinating. You're still upset about what you saw last night. It's perfectly understandable. You had quite a scare. Did you call the cops today like I told you?"

"Not yet," she said. "I wanted to see you first. I wanted to talk to you. I'm not sure what I could say to the cops. Are you coming home soon?"

"Yes," he said. "I was just about to call you. I'll be leaving in five minutes or so."

"Please hurry, Neil," she begged. "I didn't tell you everything yet. I also saw some bloodstains on the floor and the table."

"What?" he asked. "What are you talking about?"

"I also saw..."

The phone suddenly fell silent.

Then, Neil heard a blood-curdling scream on the other end.

"Cynthia?" he called into the phone with alarm. "Are you there, Cynthia?"

There was no reply.

"Cynthia?" he cried. "Speak to me!"

Still, there was no reply.

He quickly hung up the phone. He grabbed his coat. He told the nearest person he could find, "I have to go! I think my girlfriend is in danger!"

Then, he ran out of the building.

❦   ❦   ❦

A cool breeze blew by. The clouds that invaded the sunset were as gray and heavy as his mood.

He stood on the doorstep. He took a breath to steady his nerves before entering.

Then, he took the keys from his pocket and opened the door. He walked into the parlor with a measured stride.

A voice called from the kitchen. "Joshua?" she asked. "Is that you, dear?"

"Yes, Madeline," he said in an even tone. "It's me."

He carried his briefcase to the beautiful new glass table. It complimented the freshly decorated living room ensemble so nicely.

She had insisted on redoing the whole room. She refused to settle for anything that didn't cost a fortune. The décor was a simply gorgeous reminder of what a fool he had been.

She came out of the kitchen. "How was your day, sweetie?" she asked with a smile.

She scampered over and gave him a kiss. He was less than receptive.

He looked up at her from his seat in the top-of-the-line recliner.

"Interesting," he said. "My day was interesting and informative."

"That's lovely, dear," she said. "You'll have to tell me all about it when I get back. I was just getting some food for you. I have to leave. I'll try not to be too late."

"You're leaving, Madeline?" he asked.

"You know I have my pottery class on Mondays," she reminded.

"Pottery class?"

"Honestly, Joshua," she said. "We go through this every week."

"That's an awfully beautiful dress to be wearing if you're going to have your hands in a lump of clay all evening," he observed.

"Well, I have to look my best, darling," she replied nonchalantly.

"And, what class did you have last night?"

"I told you," she said impatiently. "I had to see my friend Samantha. We were going shopping and out for drinks because her husband left her."

"Is that right?" he asked. "Did he leave her because she was cheating on him?"

"No," she said. "Listen. I don't have time for this. I have to get ready for my class."

She turned to leave. She started to walk away.

"Who's teaching your class tonight, dear?" he called after her. "Is it Grant Langley?"

She froze.

"What?" she asked calmly.

"I thought that would get your attention," he said. "Is that who's teaching your class? Is that why Samantha's husband left her? Was she having an affair with Grant Langley?"

She spun around to face him. "Where did you hear that name?" she questioned.

He reached over to the glass table. He opened his briefcase and took out a large envelope.

"Someone supplied me with some interesting information concerning you and our Mr. Langley, Madeline," he said. "Apparently, you two have become rather close."

"What are you talking about?"

"Oh, I've suspected for some time," he continued. "But, I've only been having you followed for about two weeks."

"You've been having me followed?"

"My friend was very expensive," he said. "But, he was very thorough. He did an excellent job. He was well worth the money, and I'd highly recommend him."

"What's in that envelope?" she asked.

"Everything I expected to pay for," he said. "I probably know more about Grant than you do. I have dates, addresses and all sorts of information. I have a video and lots of unsettling pictures."

"Videos and pictures?" she asked. "What kind of a pervert are you?"

"Oh, relax," he said. "There's nothing pornographic in there. My friend has a sense of decency. But, some of those pictures are somewhat disturbing. In fact, the pictures of last week's pottery class are downright scandalous. I didn't see a kiln anywhere in any of those shots."

"I don't believe you did this, Joshua!" she snipped. "How could you disgrace me like that?"

"*I* disgraced *you*?" he scoffed. "That boy is a full 15 years younger than you are!"

"Yes," she said. "And, you're seven years older than me. What's your point?"

"He's a gigolo, Madeline," he asserted. "He makes his living by making fools out of women like you. He's famous for it!"

"That shows what *you* know," she averred. "He told me all about his past. He assured me I have nothing to worry about. Grant really loves me!"

"Is that what he told you?"

"It's true!"

"If he loves you," he asked. "Why are you spending all the money? *My* money?"

"It's not your money," she corrected. "It's *our* money! And, I have the money to spend. He's an insurance agent, for God's sake!"

"I'm the only one bringing home a paycheck in this house, Madeline," he said.

"Don't you dare throw that up in my face, Joshua!"

"And, I'm not bringing money home for you to throw away on prepubescent gigolos," he continued. "And, I won't have you running off to that piece of filth and leaving me home alone with a can of tuna and a bowl of store brand potato salad! I want you to end it, Madeline. I want you to tell him you're leaving."

"And, if I refuse?"

"Don't drag us through divorce court, Madeline," he warned. "You can't win. I have tons of proof that you've been unfaithful."

"I dare you, Joshua!" she argued. "Go ahead! See if I care! I don't give a damn what you have in that envelope! I'll get everything! You know I will! And, I'll laugh while I'm doing it!"

"Why are you doing this, Madeline?" he asked. "You know how much I love you. I've given you everything. And now I find you're giving everything I hand you to slimy little boys who go through women like you more often than they change their underwear! What's wrong with you?"

"Don't start, Joshua!" she warned. "Don't you analyze me! You do it every time we have an argument. Every time I spend too much money on shoes, you have to drag out your Harvard diploma and tell me all the clinical reasons about how my excesses are a way of dealing with my psychological shortcomings! It's demeaning!"

"I'm only trying to help you."

"You're only trying to talk down to me," she corrected. "You're only trying to be superior! Well, I'm not a page in your college Psychology text book, Joshua! I'm a person! And, I'm your wife! And, I'm sick of it! That's why I'm with Grant now, sweetheart! He doesn't act like he's too good for me! He's not condescending! He loves me for what I already am! Not because I'm a test case that needs to be squeezed into some preformed Freudian mold!"

"It's impossible for Grant to look down on you," he said. "The boy's a parasite! There is no life form that's lower than him! Besides, I've never looked down on you! I have always held you in the highest esteem."

"That's a laugh!" she scoffed. "You analyze everything I do! If I serve meatloaf on a Tuesday, it's because my mother stifled my creativity when I was a child!"

"I've never said anything like that!" he argued.

"That's how I know you'll never divorce me," she pointed out. "Your reputation as a Harvard-educated psychiatrist will look awfully tarnished if your marriage falls apart. 'The Great Dr. Joshua Freitag!' How can you fix anybody else, if you can't even fix your own mentally defective wife?"

He stared at her in shock. The silent pause grew heavier as she glared at him.

"How long have you been feeling this way, Madeline?" he finally asked.

"I don't have time for this now," she said. "I'm late."

She grabbed her purse. She turned to leave.

"Please don't go like this," he said. "Let's talk."

She didn't even turn to face him. "I have to leave now," she said. "If we talk any longer, I'm afraid you might send me a bill."

As she marched toward the door, he called out, "Why would I send you a bill? I'd be the one who has to pay it! Just like I've been paying for your little gigolo!"

She didn't respond. She just kept walking.

And as she opened the door, he shouted, "I won't lose you to him! You tell him it's over, Madeline! You'll regret it, if you don't! I swear you'll regret it!"

She just slammed the door behind her as she left.

🌿 🌿 🌿

She walked into the room. Just as she suspected, the television was on. And, you couldn't mistake the back of that head for anyone else.

"Dylan?" she asked. "Are you just getting home now?"

"I got home about five minutes ago," he said.

"Where have you been?" she asked. "Your dinner is stone cold."

"I had to go see some friends after work," he said.

"What friends?" she asked. "Who are they? Why don't I ever get to meet any of them?"

"Get off my back, Mom," he grumbled. "I'm 24 years old!"

"I know, dear," she said. "I don't care if you see your friends. But if you're not going to come straight home from work, I wish you'd call me and let me know."

"I'm a grown man, Mom," he insisted. "I don't need your permission to have a life!"

"I never said that you did," she told him. "I'm just asking for a little common courtesy. That's all."

"I had something to do, okay?" he snipped. "God! I can't wait 'til I save up enough money, so I can move out of here! I need a place that doesn't come with its own nagging babysitter!"

"If you want out of here so badly," she said with growing impatience. "Then, why did you waste money on that big, gas-guzzling SUV?"

"I need a vehicle with power," he said. "Can you please stop nagging me?"

"Your tone is beginning to irritate me, young man," she said. "Now be a good boy and come help me with dinner. We'll have to start fresh, since you were so late."

"I'm watching TV."

"Dylan!" she snapped. "Get your worthless little ass in the kitchen before I box your ears! I'm trying to be nice, but you're testing my limits!"

"But, Mom…"

"Get in the kitchen, NOW!" she shouted.

He sat up straight. Then, he rose to his feet as if pretending he was too tired to obey.

"Go on!" she shouted. "I don't care what that no-good shrink says about you! Your only problem is your attitude problem! Spoiling you rotten will never fix what's wrong with a lazy good-for-nothing like you! Now, get in that kitchen!"

"Yes, Mom," he mumbled.

He was intentionally slow as he ambled off toward the kitchen. She slapped the back of his head as he shuffled past her.

"Ow! Mom!"

"Just get in there!"

When they were in the kitchen, he stood by the counter. He watched her chop carrots and onions with a long knife. He listened to the *clomp, clomp, clomp* of the blade striking the cutting board again and again.

"Don't just stand there," she ordered. "Get some soup out of the cupboard."

He walked to the cupboard without a word.

"Are you supposed to see that shrink tomorrow?" she asked.

"Yes."

"Tell him I'd like to talk to him," she said. "Honestly! I want to know what could possibly be gained by indulging your uncooperative behavior."

Clomp! Clomp! Clomp!

He took a can of soup over to the counter.

"Well, open the can," she said. "I swear! I'm glad your father's not alive to see what a weasly little disappointment you grew up to be! It would just kill him!"

Clomp! Clomp! Clomp!

He took a can opener from the drawer.

"Out with friends?" she scoffed. "As if you ever had any friends! Am I supposed to indulge your lies, too?"

Clomp! Clomp! Clomp!

"On top of everything else," she continued. "Does your shrink know what a little liar you are?"

Clomp! Clomp! Clomp!

"Well, answer me!" she demanded. "Does he?"

Clomp! Clomp! Clomp!

"Ow!" she screamed. "God damn it! I almost chopped my finger off! Get me something to wrap my finger before I bleed all over the place!"

He just stood there. He watched the blood run down her hand. She used a small cloth to blot the blood. But, he just stood there and watched.

"Are you deaf, boy?" she asked. "I told you to get something to wrap my hand in. Can't you see I'm bleeding?"

"Yes," he whispered slowly. "I see."

Still, he didn't move. He just watched the blood run over her hand.

"Dylan!" she shouted with a touch of panic. "What's wrong with you? Get some kind of bandage! I'm bleeding!"

He just stared at the blood. It was as if he was mesmerized as the blood flowed over her flesh.

He just watched her bleed. And he smiled with an eerie grin.

"Dylan!" she yelled. "Get a bandage! Dylan! Dylan!"

He just stared… and grinned.

Chapter 3
Once Panic Begins

Earlier that evening, the sun sank down into a rich, thick bed of dark clouds that cushioned its gentle fall behind the horizon. It turned sharply colder by the time he pulled his car up beside her building.

He jumped out of his car. He bounded up the stairs to the front door. Thankfully, he had his own set of keys. He let himself into the building. Then, he raced up to her apartment on the top floor.

Caution and discretion made him stand outside for a moment. He took a breath for composure.

He knocked on her door while calling out, "Cynthia? Are you okay?"

The door fell open just a crack.

He gasped. He stared with dread. His heart began to pound.

Then, he burst through the door.

"Cynthia?" he called out while glancing around. "Cynthia? Are you here?"

Everything was silent and still. He carefully stepped into the living room while surveying his surroundings.

"Cynthia?" he shouted. "It's Neil! Answer me!"

There was still no reply.

Then, he noticed her purse on the coffee table. And her cell phone appeared to have been carelessly tossed on the carpet. A folded piece of paper was half falling out of her purse. Actually, he couldn't tell if the paper was falling out or if it had been just sloppily stashed in the leather pocket.

However, there was a spot of blood on the paper.

There were more blood stains on the table. And as he looked around he noticed a few more on the carpet. It wasn't much blood. Just a few drops and small splotches were spread haphazardly about the floor.

It could have been easily missed.

Still, it added to the tension that was mounting throughout his entire body.

He called out her name again. There was still no response.

He carefully made his way over to the kitchen. He looked inside.

The room was empty and unsettlingly silent.

He quickly moved over to the walk-in cupboard. He took a breath for courage. Then, he opened the door.

Everything was in its place. Nothing was wrong.

Hastily, he walked over to the short hall that led to the bath and bedrooms. He called her name again.

It drove him mad when he still received no reply.

He checked the bedroom. He searched through her closet. He checked the bedroom.

There was no sign of her anywhere.

He was growing frantic.

Why would she leave her apartment door open? Why would she leave her cell phone on the floor? Why would she leave without her purse?

Why would she call him, tell him she was scared, scream into the phone and then leave suddenly without a trace?

Something was obviously very wrong.

He didn't even want to consider the possibility of kidnapping. But, how could he ignore it?

There was a knot in his gut the size of a basketball. He was nearly trembling when he reached for her cell phone. He intended to use it to call the police.

Then, he looked down at the coffee table. The paper with the red spot was practically falling out of Cynthia's purse.

He stared at it.

Had it moved since he'd left the room?

After a few moments, he felt compelled to pick up the paper. He thought it might offer a clue. He slowly unfolded the page.

He read the contents.

As he read, his eyes grew angrier and angrier.

When he finished, he dropped the page into his lap. "You bitch!" he muttered to himself. "How could you do this to me?"

He grabbed the paper out of his lap. He crumpled it up with his hand. He threw it down on the floor.

Then, he got up and stormed out of the apartment.

She clicked her fingernails on the table of the restaurant in which she sat. She had a nervous twitch in her leg when she was tense. Usually, she didn't even realize she was doing it.

But at this moment, she could feel her leg rattling like a jackhammer.

She stirred her Sloe Comfortable Screw. She only drank those when she was really upset. She even slurped as she took a big sip.

Where was he? He was seldom late. And of all the nights to break his routine, this was definitely the wrong night!

She slurped at her drink again.

Finally, she heard him say, "Sorry I'm late, honey. It's been a long day."

He leaned over and kissed her.

"Where have you been?" she asked with a tone.

"I got caught up at work."

"Work?" she asked as she watched him slide in across from her in the booth. "Who the hell buys insurance at 7:30 at night?"

"I do more than just sell insurance, Madeline," he said evenly. "Why? What's your problem?"

"He knows, Grant!"

"What?"

"Joshua," she said. "He knows about us. He's been having me followed for the past few weeks."

He was silent for a moment.

Then, he asked, "What did he say?"

"He wants me to leave you," she said. "He told me I'd regret it if I don't. He mentioned divorce, but I doubt he'd go through with it. But, I can almost guarantee he won't take this lying down."

"So, what's our next move?"

"I don't know," she said. "I'm certainly not going to leave you. I love you, sweetie. And, I don't want that bastard husband of mine standing in our way."

"Is there anything I can do?"

"Oh, God," she said. "I don't know! I haven't had time to think. He sprang this on me when I was on my way out the door this evening. The whole thing hasn't sunken in yet. I need time to calm down and relax. I need to weigh my options."

"Well, I'm here for you, Madeline," he said. "Whatever you need, just say the word."

"Thank you," she said. She finished her drink. "You know, Joshua brought up your past reputation with women. Apparently, he's done some research."

"I told you, darling," he reminded gently while taking her hand in his. "I did a lot of things I'm not proud of when I was younger. I was a young fool. But, those days are behind me now. I've matured. And, I'm glad I found the love of a wonderful woman like you to lead me to a new and better life. I won't throw that away. I promise."

She smiled as she looked into his eyes. She squeezed his hand for reassurance.

Later that evening, they found themselves back in his apartment.

"I'm still worried about Joshua," she confided. "He's usually mild-mannered. I've never seen him as angry as he was when I left."

"Don't let it bother you," he said.

"I'm just not sure what he's capable of," she said.

"What's he going to do?" he asked. "I can take care of myself. I'm half his age. And if he hurts you, I'll kill him."

"Let's hope it doesn't come to that," she said.

Then, she seemed nervous as she glanced down at the carpet. "Do you think I'll really get everything if I divorce him?" she asked.

"You can't lose," he assured her. "He's a rich doctor. You're the housewife who's supported, nurtured and taken care of him for nearly twenty years. You've done everything. And, you deserve to be duly compensated."

Her fragility was evident as she kept her gaze on the carpet. "Should I divorce him, Grant?" she asked.

"Why not?" he said. "Frankly, I'm glad everything is finally out in the open. Now you can get rid of him, and we can stop hiding out all the time. We can get a brand new start together."

She looked at him with that same fragility.

"Do you love me, Grant?" she asked.

"Of course I do," he said. "I tell you often enough, don't I?"

"I mean, do you *really* love me?" she persisted. "Would you love me even if I didn't have Joshua's money?"

"What a silly question," he smiled. "You know I'd love you no matter what. It's just that if we had his money, we could get out of Thorn Ridge. Hell! We could leave Pennsylvania all together and start a whole new life in a much better place. Maybe we can go to California, or even the Bahamas."

"But, what if we didn't have his money?"

"That's not even a possibility," he said. "So, why bring it up?"

"But, I…"

He stopped her with a kiss. It was a long, passionate kiss. It was a kiss that offered all the promises she needed.

Then, he lifted her up in his arms.

"If you need proof of how much I love you," he said. "Then, let me show you in a more positive way."

He carried her into the bedroom. He stretched her out in the bed. He kissed her again.

Then he lavished her with all the solace and reassurance she needed to get her through the night.

❦ ❦ ❦

The following morning was dark and dreary. The thick gray clouds had made a home for themselves over the town. A cold, steady rain was dousing the streets with a gloomy shower that was sure to dampen anyone's spirits.

Inside, he sat at his desk. His mood had been soured by more than just the rain.

"Hi, Neil," said a cheery female voice. "How are you today?"

He looked up. He tried to smile. "Good morning, Angela," he said. "What's up?"

"What's wrong?" she asked with concern. "You look terrible."

"I had an awful night," he said. "It's Cynthia."

"What happened?"

Before he could answer, he was interrupted by two men who were displaying badges.

"Excuse me," said the first man. "We're looking for a Mr. Neil Worthington."

"That's me," he said. "Can I help you?"

"I'm Detective Sumaki," he said. "This is my partner, Detective Reynolds. We're investigating the murder of Karen Broderick. We understand you were at the wedding reception where she was killed."

"That's right."

"We also understand," Sumaki continued. "That you are dating Cynthia Trott. She was the person who discovered the bloody veil in the restroom."

"Yes."

"And we have just been informed," he went on. "That you filed a missing persons report on Miss Trott last night around 8:00."

"That's true."

As best he could, Neil recounted the events of the previous evening to the detectives. They listened intently as the story unfolded.

After he finished, Reynolds asked, "When exactly did she call you?"

"A few minutes after 5:00."

"And, you just rushed right over there?" Reynolds continued.

"I had to," he said. "You should have heard the sound of her voice. And, then she screamed as if she was being attacked. Then, the phone went dead."

"And, you say she claimed to have seen a shadow?" Sumaki asked. "And, the shadow was wearing a bloody bridal veil?"

"She told me it looked like Karen's bridal veil," he said. "But, it was all red. As if it had been covered in blood."

The detectives shared a glance.

"So, if you rushed right over there," Reynolds proceeded. "When did you arrive at her home?"

"Around 5:30."

"And, the reason it took you so long to call the police," Sumaki said. "Had to do with the letter you took out of her purse."

"I didn't really remove it from her purse," he corrected. "It was falling out anyway."

"So, you're telling me," Sumaki said. "That she left a letter falling out of her purse for you to find that she received from Peter Broderick."

"I don't think she intentionally left it there for me to find," he said. "I don't know how it got there. I don't even know why I felt the need to open it up and read it. I guess I was confused, scared and looking for clues about Cynthia's whereabouts."

"What exactly did the letter say?" Reynolds asked.

"Peter took the blame for initiating a short affair they had about a month before his wedding," he explained. "He admitted they slept together twice. He apologized to my Cynthia for everything. He told her it would never happen again. And he said he still loved Karen and still planned on marrying her."

"And, according to you," Reynolds continued. "That's supposed to be your reason for why it took two and a half hours to report your girlfriend missing even after the blood and the phone calls with shadows and bloody veils and screams. Is that right?"

He could hear the tone in the detective's voice.

"You don't understand," he defended. "That letter hit me very hard. I thought I had a great relationship with Cynthia. I thought everything was going perfectly."

"So perfectly," Reynolds pressed. "That you figured two and a half hours with a kidnapper who has shown violent tendencies is not a problem for her?"

"I wasn't thinking straight," he argued. "That letter caught me completely off guard. It's hard to…"

Suddenly, his attention turned to the man lurking behind the detectives.

"What do you want, Zeblonsky?" he asked angrily.

"Oh… me?" Dylan stuttered. "Uh, nothing! Sorry. I guess I got distracted by your story. I didn't mean any harm."

"Well, move along and mind your own business," Neil ordered.

"Uh… sorry."

"Maybe you think the kidnapper put it there," Sumaki said. "Maybe you think Karen's ghost came back wearing a bloody veil, kidnapped Cynthia, and conveniently left that letter for you to find. Maybe Karen's ghost wants you to know why she kidnapped your girlfriend. Is that what you want us to believe, Mr. Worthington?"

"I don't care what you believe," he snipped. "I don't know what to believe myself. You asked for the facts, and I'm giving them to you."

"Facts?" Reynolds grinned. "Those are the facts, are they?"

"Yes!"

"I'll tell you what, Mr. Worthington," Sumaki offered. "Let's go back to the wedding reception. Exactly what happened Sunday night?"

"Zeblonsky!" he scolded. "Why are you still here?"

"I don't know," Dylan said. "Sorry. I'll go now."

"Just a minute," Sumaki said. "What's your full name, sir?"

"Dylan Carleton Zeblonsky."

"Were you at the wedding or the reception?" Sumaki asked.

"No," he said. "I wasn't invited."

"But, you do work here?" Sumaki continued.

"Oh, yes," Dylan said. "I work in the Contract Division."

"We may want to talk to you later," Sumaki said. "But for now, why don't you allow us to talk to Mr. Worthington alone?"

"Yes sir," Dylan said. "Of course, it can't be this afternoon. I have an appointment."

"Well, don't let us keep you," Sumaki said. "Run along and we'll talk to you later."

"Thank you, sir," Dylan said. He scurried off.

Everyone watched him leave. Then, Sumaki turned and asked, "And, what's your name, Miss?"

"Angela Pierce," she said.

"Were you at the wedding?" Sumaki asked.

"No," she said. "I hardly knew Karen."

"So, you wouldn't know of anyone who would want to hurt her?" Sumaki asked. "Or Cynthia Trott, for that matter?"

"As I said," she reiterated. "I hardly knew Karen. And, I never even met Cynthia."

"In that case," Sumaki asked. "Would you mind if we had some privacy please?"

She glanced at Neil. Then, she said, "Not at all."

When she was gone, Sumaki requested, "So, tell us about the reception, please."

Neil recounted the story to the best of his recollection.

"So, you were more concerned about staying with Cynthia throughout most of the ordeal," Sumaki said. "Is that right?"

"Yes."

"You didn't even see any blood until Miss Trott and Mr. Broderick led the way down the hall?" Sumaki continued.

"That's right, sir."

"And, you never saw the body?" Sumaki went on. "You stayed inside with Cynthia."

"She was very shaky," Neil said. "As you can understand. I thought it would be in her best interest if I kept her company."

"Were you acting in her best interest last night?" Sumaki pressed. "When you failed to call the police? Even though her door was open and there was blood on the floor?"

"That letter really tore me up," he defended. "It was all I could think about after I read it."

"You do realize," Sumaki advanced. "That everything you've told us seems highly questionable, Mr. Worthington. Don't you? Of course, our main focus is the murder of Mrs. Broderick. I have no immediate reason to tie you to that. However, your story about your girlfriend's disappearance is a bit flimsy."

"I know it sounds kind of weird," he said. "But, it's true."

"Phone calls about shadows wearing bloody veils?" Sumaki listed. "Screams? You go over there, and she's already gone. But you 'accidentally' go rifling through her purse and find a love letter from our murder victim's husband. Then, it takes you two and a half hours to report that Cynthia is missing. That's quite a story."

"Listen, Detective," he began. "I…"

He stopped. His expression changed to one of wonder.

"Wait a minute," he said. "Come to think of it, Zeblonsky was lurking around my desk when I got the first call from Cynthia. The call where she told me she remembered something about Karen."

"Dylan Zeblonsky?" Sumaki said. "The guy who was just here a minute ago?"

"He does that a lot," he said. "He's a creepy little jerk. He may have had a thing for Karen. He seems to have a thing for a few girls around here."

"He does seem to express an interest in this case," Reynolds observed.

"If he killed Karen," Neil surmised. "He could have gone after Cynthia to cover his ass! He probably even planted that letter to throw everyone off the track. Cynthia probably never even had an affair with Broderick! He heard me tell Joe McMahon that Cynthia remembered something. This is all his doing! If that little bastard hurt my girl, I'll kill him!"

"Stay away from Zeblonsky, sir," Sumaki advised. "Don't do anything you're going to regret. If he has any connection to this case, we'll take care of it."

"It is an interesting theory," Reynolds said. "We had a definite feeling these two incidents were related."

"What do you know about Zeblonski, Mr. Worthington?" Sumaki asked.

"Not much," he said. "He's just a very creepy, nervous little dude. He almost seems to be in love with whatever girl he's talking to at the time. I'm sure he's a virgin. And, he drives this big, custom-painted SUV."

"A custom-painted SUV?" Reynolds asked.

"Yes," he said. "It has dark blue doors with stars painted on and a big, robotic bird. It says 'Space Eagle' on the hood."

"Space Eagle?" Reynolds scoffed. "He sounds like quite a character."

"I'm telling you," he averred. "The guy's a nut! He's even seeing a psychiatrist."

"He sees a shrink?" Sumaki asked.

The detectives shared a glance.

"That's probably what his appointment is this afternoon," he said.

"It's easy to picture a guy like that playing with bloody veils," Reynolds postulated. "He seems to have a flair for the dramatic."

"Okay," Sumaki said. "I think that's all for now. I'm looking forward to having a chat with our friend, Mr. Zeblonsky. We'll probably like to speak with you again too, sir."

"I'm always easy to find," he said.

"May we speak with this Joe McMahon you mentioned?" Reynolds asked.

"I think he's in a meeting right now," he said.

"We'll catch him later then," Sumaki said. "In the meantime, keep your hands off Dylan. And, don't tell anyone about your theories. And, definitely don't tell anyone about shadows wearing veils. Those stories circulate and get exaggerated too easily because people eat them up. They can start a panic. And once panic begins to spread, it becomes impossible to stop. And, that makes our job a lot harder."

"You can count on me, Detective," he said.

As they made their way to the front door, Reynolds asked, "So, what do you think about this Zeblonsky character, Tom?"

"He's certainly worth looking into," Sumaki allowed. "I definitely want to talk to him a little more. If he's our man, it would make it easier to wrap up both cases. But, I'm not done looking at Worthington, either. His little ghost story combined with the fact that he waited two and a half hours to place a missing person's report makes him look awfully fishy. Besides that: Dylan supposedly overhears a conversation at the office. Then, he goes out and buys a bridal veil, paints it red and then writes a phony love letter to plant in a purse? That's a little hard to swallow."

"I guess you're right," Reynolds agreed. "We still don't have a lot of time to mess around. Cynthia Trott's life may hang in the balance."

"Believe me," Sumaki announced. "We don't have to worry about Cynthia Trott. Whichever one of those clowns got his hands on her, she's dead already. Even if someone else did this altogether, there's no way we'll find her alive."

"From a professional standpoint," Reynolds said. "We can't afford to live by that assumption. We have responsibilities here, Tom."

"I know all about our responsibilities, Dave," Sumaki said. "But no matter how you slice this case, Miss Trott was dead before Worthington ever called the police. You can bet on it!"

"Michelle?" he asked. "Why did you insist on coming over here again today?"

"I told you, Peter," she said. "I realize what a difficult time you're going through. You shouldn't be alone at a time like this."

"I'm fine, Michelle," he said. "Sure, I'm depressed. It hurts like hell. But, I have to work this out on my own."

"Well, what about me?" she asked. "I'm depressed, too. She was my best friend. I miss her terribly. I need comforting and companionship also. This can be best for the both of us."

"Well, if it's all the same to you," he said. "I'd rather be alone right now."

"Please don't shut me out, Peter," she said. "Karen was your bride. And, she was my best friend. I can't be alone today. And, you shouldn't be alone, either. It's unhealthy. We need to stick together to get through this trying time."

"If you were at work like you should be," he said. "You'd have lots of company."

"I couldn't possibly face work today," she said. "I took a few days off. Besides, it's not the same. I need to be with someone I care about. Someone who cares about me. You do care about me. Don't you, Peter?"

"Of course I do."

"Good," she said. "Because that's what I need right now."

"I just don't know what I..." he began.

Then, he stopped when she began sobbing into her hands.

"Oh, please don't do that," he begged. "If you start crying, you're going to get me started. It took me all morning to stop."

"I can't help it," she wept. "Who could do this to Karen?"

A new wave of tears overcame her. She wept uncontrollably into her hands beside him on his sofa.

He could only watch for about fifteen seconds. Then, he said, "Come here."

He took her into his arms. She practically felt limp against his body as he held her tightly. She flooded his shoulder with tears.

And as she clung to him in desperation, he began to cry as well.

Together, they formed a virtual fountain of despair.

After a minute or so, they stopped. They looked at each other.

Then, they kissed.

It was a long, meaningful kiss with the power to soothe if not heal. It filled great, gaping voids, if only for the moment.

When it was over, they looked at each other. Luckily, the phone rang.

He jumped up and answered it.

"Hello?" he said into the phone. "Hi, Mrs. Ryland. Oh, yes. Yvonne. I'm sorry. How are you feeling? Yes, I know. It will be a long, slow process for all of us. What can I do for you, dear?"

His smile vanished as he listened to her reply.

"Uh... dinner?" he said. "Tonight at 7:00?"

He glanced over at Michelle.

Then, he said, "Thank you. That would be wonderful. Yes. I'll be there at 7:00. Thanks again. See you then."

He hung up the phone. He walked over to Michelle.

"You're having dinner with Karen's family?" she asked.

"It's the right thing to do," he said. "I think you should go."

"I understand," she said. "We can talk tomorrow."

"There's no need," he said. "That kiss was a big mistake, Michelle."

She stood. "You don't believe that any more than I do," she said. "That kiss happened for a reason."

"Yes," he said. "Mutual grief for Karen."

"We're both grieving," she said. "There's nothing wrong with grieving together."

"I don't think this is what she would have wanted," he said.

"If she were here to argue the matter," she said. "There would be no matter to argue about."

He looked at her with confusion.

She strode over to the door. "Besides," she added. "We both know there was more than grief in that kiss. There was something deep that goes back a long way."

"You were her best friend," he reminded. "How can you even think that?"

She opened the door. "Go have your dinner, Peter," she said. "I'll call you tomorrow."

"I wish you wouldn't."

"Good night, Peter."

He watched her walk confidently to her car.

Then, he closed the door.

❦ ❦ ❦

"So, Angela," she said. "You're telling me that Neil's girlfriend is missing?"

"Do you believe it, Sarah?" she said. "When I first saw the cops, I expected them to ask about Karen. But, that story of Cynthia's disappearance really freaked me out."

"Do you think it's true?"

"I don't know," she said. "Neil sounded awfully serious when he told the cops what happened."

"Sure," Sarah nodded. "But, shadows wearing bloody veils? Love letters lying out for anyone to find? It all sounds a bit staged. Don't you think?"

"You should have seen Neil," she said. "He was really shaken up about the whole thing. I can't say what happened, but it really gave me the creeps."

"So, you don't think Neil did something to his girlfriend?" Sarah asked.

"He couldn't have," she said. "He's not the type. I think there is a connection to her disappearance and Karen's murder."

"If you're right," Sarah said. "At least Neil is free and clear, so you can go after him now. You can console him in his misery."

"You too, Sarah?" she asked with surprise. "Jennifer Cibello was trying to say I had a thing for Neil only yesterday."

"You do have a thing for Neil," Sarah insisted. "It's no secret, Angela. Everybody knows it. Well, everybody except Neil."

"I don't have feelings for Neil," she argued. "And, I wish everyone would stop saying that I do! I've only been working here a week. How is it even possible?"

"Love strikes instantly," Sarah poked. "And, without warning."

"Cut it out!"

"Are you talking about how Angela is in love with Neil Worthington?" a third party chimed in.

"Yes we are, Jennifer," Sarah laughed.

"Well, let me get in on this," Jennifer teased.

"Don't, Jennifer!" she averred. "You're the one who started the rumors in the first place."

"I didn't start anything," Jennifer said. "Anyone can see how your eyes light up whenever he's around."

"They do not!" she insisted. "My eyes never light up!"

"At least, his girlfriend is gone now," Jennifer said.

"She's missing," she corrected.

"That leaves Neil out in the clear for you, Angela," Jennifer teased. "Go get him, girl!"

"I'm not going after anybody!"

Sarah and Jennifer shared a laugh.

"Ssshhhh!" Sarah whispered. "Here he comes. Hi, Neil!"

"Good afternoon, ladies," he said.

"I hear your girlfriend disappeared," Sarah said with genuine sympathy. "I'm surprised you even came to work today. How are you doing?"

"About as well as can be expected," he said. "I'll be climbing the walls until I find out what happened, though."

"Is it true what we heard?" Sarah asked. "Did you really find a letter from Peter Broderick after getting a phone call from Cynthia about seeing a shadow wearing Karen's veil?"

He glared at Angela.

"Don't blame Angela," Jennifer defended. "Those detectives talked to a number of people here in the agency. People overheard things. The word got spread around pretty quickly."

"I know it sounds strange," he admitted. "But, that call from Cynthia was a bit scary. She sounded so frightened on the phone. At first, I thought she was just seeing things as a result of what she went through at the wedding reception. But then, she screamed and the phone went dead."

"What do you think happened?" Angela asked.

"I'm not sure," he said. "But, I'll never forget the sound of her voice during that call. Or, that scream!"

"You're giving me the willies just by talking about it," Jennifer said.

"You can't possibly believe it was Karen," Sarah said. "Do you?"

"I hate to even think about it," Angela added.

"Can you girls keep a secret?" he asked.

"Sure," Angela said.

The other girls nodded. And when he leaned in, they all leaned in as well.

"When I first told Joe that Cynthia called to say she remembered something," he whispered. "Zeblonsky was hovering around and listening."

"Dylan?" Jennifer gasped. "Really?"

"Do you think he's involved in all this?" Angela whispered.

"Think about it," he whispered. "If he killed Karen, he would have the perfect motive to keep Cynthia quiet."

"But, why would he kill Karen?" Jennifer asked.

"Who knows?" he said. "He's a weird little freak. Maybe it was jealousy. Maybe he was more in love with her than we thought."

"So, you think Dylan killed Karen out of jealousy?" Sarah whispered. "Then when he heard Cynthia remembered something, he got a veil and painted it red to scare Cynthia? Then, he wrote some bogus love letter to frame you?"

"That's a bit of a stretch," Jennifer whispered. "Even if he was bright enough to dream all that up, how would he have the time?"

"So, what do you think happened?" he asked. "Do you think Karen's ghost is going around looking for revenge?"

"Can we please stop talking about that?" Angela asked.

"I don't know," Jennifer said. "But, I don't have time for this. I have to get back to work."

"Me too," Sarah said.

"I know it's kind of unlikely," he admitted. "That's the only reason I haven't hunted Dylan down yet. But, if I get any proof that little shit had anything to do with Cynthia's disappearance, I'll slaughter him!"

"Cool your jets, pal," Jennifer advised. "Don't do anything you'll regret before you get some real proof. Believe me. I'm the last person to stick up for Dylan Zeblonsky, but I don't want to see you get in any trouble."

"You're right," he agreed. "Don't worry. I'll be good."

"I'm glad to hear it," Jennifer said.

"Now, if you'll excuse us," Sarah said, "Jennifer and I have to get going. We'll leave you two alone to talk."

"'Bye," Jennifer grinned. She even waved in a way that Angela found annoying.

When the girls were gone, Neil asked, "What did Sarah mean by that?"

"I'm sure she meant nothing at all," Angela said.

"Well, I should be going, too," he said.

"Neil?" she asked. "Do you really think Dylan is behind all this?"

"It's either him or Karen."

"I wish people would stop saying that!" she insisted.

"Why?" he asked. "Do you believe in ghosts?"

"Not usually," she said. "But this whole matter with Karen and Cynthia scares me."

"Try not to worry about it," he assured her. "I'm sure there's some logical explanation."

"I hope so."

"By the way," he added. "Do you think it was safe for me to tell those two my theory about Dylan? The cops wanted me to keep quiet. They don't want to start a panic."

"Are you kidding me?" she laughed. "Jennifer Cibello and Sarah Krause are the two biggest gossips on the planet. You might as well have broadcast the whole story on a global satellite network."

"Damn!" he said. "Oh well. It's too late to worry about it now."

"It sure is."

"Have a good day, Angela."

"You too, Neil."

"I'll do my best under the circumstances," he said. "And, steer clear of Zeblonsky."

"I will."

She watched him walk away. Then, she turned to her computer screen. An image of a shadow in a bloody veil crept into her thoughts.

It made her tremble. But just for a moment.

Two men walked briskly through the parking lot. The sun was out. The puddles were beginning to dry.

And, the clouds were slowly clearing like bad actors being rejected from an audition.

"This has been a hell of a day so far," he said. "I'm almost looking forward to going back to the office to face some paperwork."

"Not so fast, Dave," his partner said. "We still have some people to question."

"For God's sake, Tom," he said. "We've questioned almost everyone in The Blue Arrow Agency already."

"Not quite everyone," Tom said. "We never did catch up to our little friend Dylan Zeblonsky. And, I really wanted to speak to him."

"Me too," Dave admitted. "He is a slippery little weasel, isn't he? Wait a minute. Isn't that his SUV?"

The detectives stared at the vehicle.

"It fits the description we got from Worthington," Tom nodded. "That's a beautiful paint job on that baby."

"It looks like our friend is quite the artist," Dave commented.

"It looks like our friend is quite the nut case," Tom corrected. "'Space Eagle', huh? That's one strange kid."

"Like it or not," Dave said. "He could make a fortune doing that kind of work."

"Hold on," Tom said.

His face grew serious as he knelt down. "Check out the left front tire," he said.

Dave squinted as he looked. "White paint!" he finally gasped. "Is it possible that he was staking out that hotel a few days before the wedding?"

"The tread on those tires is a fairly close match," Tom observed. "And, look at the paint on the other tire. At a glance, I'd say we found the SUV we were looking for."

"Well, look at that," Dave chuckled. "Who would've thought your little hotel parking lot theory would work out?"

"Suddenly," Tom said. "I feel an increased urgency when it comes down to finding our pal, Mr. Zeblonsky! Let's go!"

The two men hurried back into the building. They crossed the lobby and hit the button for the elevator. By the time one of the six elegant carriages arrived, they were muttering, "Come on! Hurry up!"

They jumped aboard and pushed the button for the ninth floor. One or two people either boarded or exited the elevator on nearly every floor.

"Damn it!" Tom said. "I knew we should have taken the stairs!"

"Nine floors?" Dave scoffed. "Are you crazy?"

When they reached their floor, they hurried into the agency lobby. Tom asked the receptionist, "Where can I find Dylan Zeblonsky?"

"Dylan?" she asked with surprise. "I just saw him leave about two minutes ago. He had a doctor's appointment. You just missed him."

"Damn!" Tom spat as he punched her desk with frustration.

She jumped with a start.

"I'm sorry," he said. "I just really wanted to catch him. Do you have his doctor's name and address?"

"No," she said. "I'm sorry. We would have no way of knowing that information."

Tom flashed his badge. "We're detectives with The State Police," he said. "I'm Sumaki. This is Reynolds. And, we need to speak to him. Can we at least get his home address please?"

"Sure, Detective," she said. "I'll get it for you right away."

She picked up her phone and dialed a number.

Tom leaned over to his partner.

"With a little luck," he whispered. "We just might bag us a killer before we clock out for the night."

"I'll keep my fingers crossed," Dave replied.

He tried to get comfortable in his chair. These visits always made him nervous. The pastoral setting was intended to put people at ease. It didn't matter to him, however. He always felt as though he just didn't belong here.

"Hi, Doctor," he said. He struggled to sound almost polite.

"How are you today, Dylan?" the doctor asked calmly.

"Fine, I guess."

"Where would you like to begin today?" the doctor asked.

"I don't know," he shrugged. "Where would you like to start?"

"Have you had a pleasant week since our last visit?" the doctor asked.

"Well," he said. "The last few days have been eventful."

"How so?"

"Some girl where I work got married over the weekend," he explained. "But, she was murdered at her reception."

"That's terrible."

"Yeah," he said. "The cops were crawling all over the place the past day or two. It's been kind of a blast. It's been disruptive, though."

"Did you know the girl well?"

"Not really," he said. "I try not to get close to people at work. I don't really have anything in common with any of them. Her name was Karen. She was okay. She was very pretty. Kind of hot-looking."

"Did you have feelings for her?"

"Like I said," he repeated. "I thought she was hot-looking. That's about it."

"Does it bother you that she's dead?"

"Not really," he shrugged. "It don't matter to me what happened to her. It's a shame, I guess. But, it's no skin off my nose."

"Is there any girl you have strong feelings for?"

It took him a few moments to say, "Not particularly. There's one girl, kind of. But, I don't feel like talking about it."

"Okay," said the doctor. "Have you been cutting yourself?"

"Not too much," he said. "I've been trying to keep it to a minimum. I know it can't be too healthy."

"Have you come to terms with why you enjoy it at all?"

81

"Well," he said. "The initial sting is kind of a rush. The pain is pleasant. But, what I really enjoy is bleeding."

"You enjoy bleeding?"

"I like to watch the blood squirt out of the wound," he explained. "Do you know what I'm saying, Dr. Freitag? The way it oozes out of the hole and just runs over the skin like raindrops on a window, or a new river being born in a fertile valley. It's positively exhilarating!"

"Is that right?"

The doctor jotted a few notes down in his book.

"I'm sure it's not normal," he added. "But, it turns me on. At first, I thought I just got a rush from watching my own blood."

"At first?"

"Yeah," he said. "But, last night my mother was cutting vegetables for dinner."

"Your mother?" the doctor asked. "How is she?"

"Okay, I suppose," he said. "She'd like to see you, by the way. She doesn't think she should have to be nice to me. Apparently, she thinks I deserve to have a mother who's nothing more than a useless, screaming bitch."

"Well, if your mother would like to talk to me," the doctor said. "I would be happy to oblige. You still don't like her very much, do you?"

"As much as a guy could like any useless, screaming bitch, I guess," he shrugged.

"So, what happened when your mother was chopping vegetables?"

"She was yelling at me," he said. "You know, Dr. Freitag? Just being her usually bitchy self. And, she almost chopped the end of her finger off."

"Is she all right?"

"Sure," he said. "She's fine now. But at the time, she was yelling at me to get a bandage. But, all I could do was watch her bleed. It was such a rush! The wound was exquisite! And, the blood was just gushing out of her like Old Faithful! It was so cool! I just couldn't look away."

"And, this turned you on, did it?"

"More than anything I can think of."

"Do you think it's because it was your mother?"

"I don't know," he said. "I doubt it. Like I said, I just like watching blood. I guess I'd get turned on watching *anyone* bleed. Does that make me sick, Dr. Freitag?"

"Well," Freitag said. "'Sick' is such a strong word. There are psychological reasons for your unusual fascination. We just need to find out what those reasons are."

"I wish I knew more about it," he said. "I wish I knew what to do. I can't go around watching people bleed. Too many people already think I'm crazy."

"You're not crazy, Dylan," Freitag said. "You just need a little help and guidance."

"Do you really think so?"

"Oh, yes," Freitag said. "It may take some ingenuity, but I'm sure we can find a way to help you."

"I'd appreciate it, Doc," he said. "I don't want to be crazy. I'd do anything!"

"I'm glad to hear that, Dylan," Freitag said as he stared at the wall. "Because, I'd just love to help you. I really would."

Chapter 4
Blood Fetish

Sunsets in this part of town seemed a little more pink and violet than in other parts of town. Trees stayed green and held their leaves longer into the season. Pittsburgh was a thin trace of building tops along the horizon to the east. And the proud, tall mountains to the west seemed to eat the sun at dusk like the very mouth of civilization.

He made a point of getting home on time. He walked through the front door at the time she would expect.

She wasn't there.

He called her name a few times. There was no reply. He felt a wrenching pain in his gut. He knew where she was.

He knew who she was with.

He sat down. He waited for the pain to subside.

It didn't. He would have been more surprised if it had.

He gave himself another minute to regain his composure. Then, he dialed her cell phone number.

When she answered, he said, "Hello, Madeline. It's Joshua."

"Oh," she grunted with disappointment. "Hi. What can I do for you?"

"What can you do for me?" he replied. "You can come home. That's what you can do for me. I thought we were going to talk tonight."

"I can't right now."

"Is he with you?"

"No," she said. "I'm shopping. I'm supposed to meet him in about an hour. Why?"

"What do you mean, 'Why?'" he said. "We need to talk."

"What would be the point?"

"I can't believe your attitude," he said. "You're my wife! *That* would be the point! You didn't even come home last night. You always used to at least come home."

"That was before you knew about Grant," she said. "That was before I knew you were paying some guy a fortune to follow me."

"I wish I never had to do that," he said. "But, you can't blame me for your infidelity. Oh, excuse me. You already did!"

"I'm not going to use up all my minutes on this phone with this inane conversation, Joshua," she said. "Wait 'til I get home."

"And, when will that be?"

"I'm not sure," she sighed. "Maybe tomorrow."

"*Maybe* tomorrow?" he snipped. "What the hell, Madeline? Does our marriage mean anything to you at all?"

"It'll mean more to me if you let me end this call, Joshua," she argued. "You're wasting my cell phone minutes!"

"Fine!" he shouted. "Get off the phone! I'm glad that damned phone is more important than our marriage! You called me condescending? Maybe by the next time you can be bothered to talk to me face-to-face, I can tell you all the text book Freudian reasons for why you're such an insufferable ass!"

He slammed the phone down into its cradle.

He stewed silently for a minute.

"That's right, Madeline," he finally muttered to himself. "Don't waste any of my money on that fucking phone. Save up my money, so you can spend it on your worthless little gigolo. I won't let you destroy our marriage, you little whore! I won't let it happen!"

He sat silently for a minute longer.

Then he slowly repeated, "I won't let it happen!"

"This is a beautiful home you have here, Mrs. Zeblonsky," he said as he glanced around.

"Thank you, Detective," she said. "My late husband built most of it himself. He was a carpenter by trade. He always took pride in his work. He died on the job eleven years ago. He fell off a scaffolding. Dylan's never really been the same since. Neither have I, for that matter. I guess you never fully recover from something like that."

"I guess not," he agreed. "Is Dylan an only child?"

"Yes," she said. "We didn't try to avoid having more kids. But, we didn't push for more either. We figured God's will would be done either way. Maybe if he'd had a few siblings, he may have adjusted to life better."

"Would you say your son is maladjusted, Mrs. Zeblonsky?"

"Oh, heavens no!" she said. "He's a good boy. He's just a little shy."

"Is that why he's seeing a psychiatrist?" Reynolds asked.

"Mostly," she said. "He does have a few behavioral problems."

"What sort of behavioral problems?"

"Back talk," she said. "He doesn't always listen."

"Does he have a problem with his temper?" he asked. "Or even violence?"

"Violence?" she scoffed. "I should say not! He wouldn't hurt a fly."

"Is he always this late getting home from work?" Reynolds asked.

"I must admit," she said. "He's been doing this more often the last year or two. That was one of the reasons I thought he should see a shrink."

"Do you think it's doing any good?"

"I haven't seen any difference," she said.

"When did your son get home last night?" Reynolds asked.

"It was almost 8:00."

The detectives shared a glance.

"Where was he between say 9:00 and 10:00 Sunday night?" he asked.

"He told me he was out with friends," she said. "He didn't get home 'til nearly 11:00 Sunday night."

The detectives shared another glance.

"Don't you believe him, ma'am?"

"As I said," she reminded. "He's kind of shy. He doesn't have many friends."

"I see," he replied. "What happened to your finger, ma'am?"

"I was chopping vegetables for dinner last night," she explained. "I guess I should've been more careful with the knife."

"I guess so," Reynolds agreed.

Just then, they heard a noise. The front door opened and closed with a series of thuds and bangs.

"Dylan?" his mother called with a polite voice. "Is that you, dear?"

"Yes."

He stopped in his tracks when he saw the two men in the living room.

"Aren't you those two detectives I saw at work today?" he asked.

"That's right, Dylan," Sumaki said. "We never got the chance to talk."

"What do you want to talk about?"

"Where were you this evening?" Sumaki asked.

"Just driving around," he said. "I like to do that sometimes. I like to be alone. It relaxes me after work."

"Is that what you were doing last night?" Sumaki asked. "Your mother said you got home around this time last night."

"Yeah. So?"

"Cynthia Trott disappeared last evening," Sumaki reminded. "If you had something to do with that, you would have had ample time…"

"What are you talking about?" he interrupted. "Do you think I kidnapped somebody? Why would I do such a thing?"

"Kidnapped?" his mother asked in shock. "Disappeared? What is all this, Dylan?"

"Nothing, Mom!"

"You didn't get home 'til 11:00 Sunday night?" Reynolds added. "Where were you then, Dylan?"

"Out with some friends," he said. "Why?"

"Can your friends back you up on that?" Reynolds said. "Because we'd really like to know where you were when Karen Broderick was getting murdered."

"Murder?" his mother asked. "Who got murdered? What did you do, Dylan?"

"I didn't do anything!" he insisted.

"Tell me who you were with Sunday night," Sumaki said. "We'll need to check your alibi."

"I was at a place called The Atomic Avenger most of the day Sunday," he said. "That's a store that sells lots of computer games, comic books and stuff. And they hold gaming tournaments for games like Dungeons and Dragons. I was there rooting for my friend Reese Karnikov, who was in the Andromeda Death Boxing Cyber Tournament."

"How long were you there?" Sumaki asked.

"They close at 8:00."

"That doesn't help you any," Sumaki pointed out. "Karen Broderick was killed between 9:00 and 9:30. Where were you then?"

"After Reese lost the match," he explained. "I went for a drive up to a secluded spot on Ginger Hill to watch the foliage after sunset."

"So, you were alone," Reynolds summed up. "And, nobody can account for your whereabouts during the murder."

"I'm sorry I didn't know I was going to need witnesses," he said sarcastically. "I never got the memo telling me somebody was going to get killed."

"Dylan!" his mother scolded. "This is not the time to have an attitude!"

"What are you going after me for?" he said. "I hardly knew Karen. Why would I want to kill her?"

"Word around your office," Reynolds said. "Is that you had a bit of a crush on her."

"A crush on Karen?" he scoffed. "I don't think so! I mean, she was attractive and all, but I don't fall to pieces over every pretty girl I meet. She meant nothing to me."

"Why are you seeing a psychiatrist, Mr. Zeblonsky?" Sumaki asked.

"I have a few things I need to sort out," he said. "Is that a crime now?"

There was a brief, unnerving pause.

"In fact," he continued. "I saw him today. And, he wants to see me again tomorrow. He told me we're making some real progress."

"Tomorrow?" his mother complained. "This quack is going to send us both to the poor house!"

"You know my insurance covers most of the cost, Mom," he reminded.

There was another awkward pause.

"What brought us to you," Sumaki calmly explained. "Is the white paint on your tires. It matches paint smears at The Classico Elegante Hotel where Karen was murdered. The parking lot was painted a few days before the wedding. Since the security cameras were on a computer link, and you just practically told us yourself about your affinity for computers, we have to wonder why you were scoping out the murder scene. The cameras malfunctioned during the murder."

"Are you suggesting I scoped the place out because of the security system?" he scoffed. "That's stupid! If I wanted to hack into their security system, I wouldn't have to go there a few days ahead of time. I'd just do it."

"So, you admit that you know how to hack into their system?" Sumaki pressed.

"Well," he said while growing nervous. "I'm sure I could figure it out if I wanted. But, so could any one of ten thousand other people in this town."

"But, none of them work with the murder victim," Reynolds pointed out.

"I didn't have a crush on her," he insisted. "And, I didn't kill her!"

"So, why were you at the hotel last week?" Sumaki asked.

"Sometimes when they're not booked, The Victorian Room has a really nice lunch buffet," he explained. "We went there once for an office retirement party. That's how I know about it. That might even be how Karen first heard of that hotel. I go there sometimes, if I know the buffet will be open."

"We'll check your story with the hotel," Sumaki warned.

"Be my guest!"

Dylan's sudden confidence left the detectives at a disadvantage. Sumaki excused himself and his partner for a private conference in the hall.

"I don't like this kid," Reynolds whispered.

"I know how you feel," Sumaki agreed. "But, we don't have enough to hold him on."

"I know," Reynolds replied. "And, it's really pissing me off."

"We'll have to cut him loose for now," Sumaki whispered.

"Alright," Reynolds sighed. "Let's just do it, then."

As they turned to enter the living room, they heard the mother yelling at her son. They also heard, "Ow! Quit it, Mom!"

"Excuse me," Sumaki said. "I guess we have all we need for the time being. But, we will probably be talking with you again. We'll definitely check your buffet story with the hotel. I strongly suggest you don't leave town."

"Don't worry, Detective," the mother said. "He will cooperate with you in every way possible."

"See that you do," Sumaki advised. "Good night."

A staunch darkness had settled over the town by the time they left the Zeblonsky residence. As they got into their car, Reynolds commented, "I still think he's the guy to watch."

"I agree."

"There's just something about that kid that doesn't sit right," Reynolds continued.

"Unfortunately," Sumaki added. "You can't lock someone up just for that. Besides, with a mother like that, it's no wonder the boy has issues."

"Yeah," Reynolds nodded. "She was a prize."

"Let's keep digging 'til we get something a little more solid," Sumaki said. "I'm glad his mother gave us his shrink's number and address. That's a good place to start tomorrow."

"I'll bet you five bucks the shrink doesn't like him either," Reynolds said.

"No thanks," Sumaki chuckled. "I don't think I'll take that bet."

❦ ❦ ❦

"Are you sure nothing's wrong, sweetheart?" he asked. "You've been kind of distant all evening."

"Well, what do you think is wrong?" she replied. "It's my husband. He called me when he got home tonight. He wants to talk. That's the main reason I made a point of being out. But, I'm going to have to talk to him, Grant. Sooner or later, we're going to have to hash things out."

"So what's the problem?" he asked. "You're in the right. He's been keeping you under his thumb all these years."

"He really wasn't so bad," she said. "I really loved him once. But, I got bored. He always got to go out and have a life. I got stuck staying home. Of course, I had friends. There were outings and shopping or whatever.

But, there was no passion, and nothing to hold on to. We never had kids."

"Why not?"

"I don't know," she said. "It just wasn't in the cards, I guess. And, I never got a job because I didn't need one. That's why I married a doctor. So I wouldn't have to work. It was great in the beginning. But after twenty years, it just wasn't enough."

"You said he treated you like shit," he reminded.

"I may have exaggerated a little," she admitted. "Sure, he's a bit over-analytical. It comes with the territory, I suppose. But, he's always tried to be a good husband."

"So, what are you saying?"

"I don't know," she said. "My feelings for him are gone. I wish there was something I could do, but there just isn't! It's over."

"That's good news for us," he said. "Isn't it?"

"Sure it is, honey," she smiled. "Sometimes, I wish I didn't love you so much, though."

He took her in his arms. "What kind of thing is that to say?" he asked reassuringly.

"This was more fun when it was a secret," she said. "It was exciting. It was an adventure. Now, it's just frightening. Joshua scares me sometimes, Grant. He never did in the past. But now, it's a different story."

"You have nothing to worry about, my darling," he said. "Our love will get us through this. Our love will get us through anything."

He kissed her. It was a long kiss meant to comfort and placate.

It worked to a certain extent.

However, it was growing difficult to forget about her husband.

🌿 🌿 🌿

Wednesday morning started out well. She had been busy. She got all her copying done for Steve.

She was filing some paperwork away in the Archives Room in the back. It was a dirty, dreary, secluded little room at the far end of the hall. It was full of dusty cabinets with musty drawers. The ancient files in the drawers left the entire room smelling of decay. The lighting was insufficient.

However, she didn't care. The work kept her mind occupied.

She closed one drawer. She opened the bottom drawer to the next cabinet to her right. She looked for a folder marked, "White List Acquisitions."

Then, a voice behind her said, "Hi, Angela."

She spun around with an instinctive smile. Then, her smile vanished.

"Oh," she muttered. "Hi, Dylan."

"You had stuff to file, too?" he asked anxiously.

"Yes," she said. "But, I'm done now."

She stood.

"What do you mean you're done?" he asked. "Judging by that pile you're holding, you didn't even reach September's reports yet. I used to have to file that stuff once. I know how that crap works."

"Oh," she muttered. "You're right. Silly me! Well, that's okay. I just remembered I have to do something for Steve Callahan right away. I can do this later. Excuse me."

"Please don't leave."

"Why?"

"What's your hurry, Angela?" he asked. "Why are you so nervous?"

"I don't know," she said. She stared at the floor. "No reason. I'm not nervous. I, well I…"

"Look at you," he observed. "You're shaking like a leaf. Are you frightened? Are you scared of me, Angela?"

"W-what?" she stammered. "Scared of you? N-no. I'm not scared of you. Why would I be scared of you?"

"You tell me," he said. "Why are you scared of me, Angela?"

"I'm not," she insisted.

He took a cautious step or two toward her. She took a step or two backward.

"Why are you backing away from me, Angela?" he asked.

"I'm not backing away from you."

"Why do I scare you, Angela?" he asked slowly. "You don't think I'd hurt you, do you?"

He took another step toward her.

She took another step back.

"Of course not, D-Dylan."

"Then, why do you keep backing away?"

"Why do you k-keep approaching me?" she stuttered.

"To show you that you have no reason to be afraid," he explained softly. "I would never hurt you, Angela. Never!"

He took another step forward.

She took another step back.

"Please, Dylan," she said. "You're starting to freak me out a little. The lighting in here sucks. It makes things look a bit spooky. And, you're s-starting to make me a little bit n-nervous."

"There's no reason to be nervous, Angela," he said. "I'm perfectly harmless."

He took another step.

She took a step backward.

"Please stop, D-Dylan."

"You know, everyone here has always treated me like I'm some kind of freak," he said. "But, I'm not!"

"I know, Dylan."

"And since Karen got murdered," he said. "Everyone's been looking at me extra funny. Everyone's been making a special effort to avoid me."

"I'm sure you're mistaken."

"Everyone acts like they think I'm the murderer," he said.

He took another step.

She took a step backward. She was really starting to tremble. She realized she was backing farther into the archive room. Her chances of escape were slowly dwindling.

She began to feel trapped.

"N-no, Dylan," she said. "I'm sure nobody thinks that!"

"Why does everyone act like I'm a murderer, Angela?" he asked.

The sound in his voice made her even more nervous.

"No one thinks it's you," she insisted. "Murder just naturally makes people jumpy. Everybody wonders who's to blame."

"But, why does everybody naturally blame me?" he asked in a quietly disturbing voice. "Do I *seem* like a murderer?"

Perhaps the way the shadows accented his facial expression in this dim light made him look more frightening.

"N-no," she said. "Of course not."

"Then, why is everyone always so afraid of me?" he asked.

"What makes you think…?"

"Don't play games with me, Angela," he interrupted with an impatient tone. "I know everyone's afraid of me. I just want to know why. Why are *you* afraid of me, Angela?"

"Right now," she said as she took a step backward. "You're scaring me because you won't let me leave."

"I'm not keeping you here, Angela," he corrected. "I'm just trying to talk to you. Why are you afraid of me?"

He took a step toward her.

"Don't come any closer, Dylan," she warned in a trembling voice. "I swear I'll scream if you don't back off."

"Why would you scream, Angela?" he inquired. "I'm harmless. You can see that, can't you?"

"I mean it, Dylan," she averred. She tried to seem strong as she took a step backward. "I'll scream if you don't leave!"

"Why are you acting this way, Angela?"

"I'm deadly serious, Dylan!" she insisted. "I'll... AAHH!"

"What happened?" he asked.

"The corners on these metal file cabinets are razor sharp," she said. "I think I cut my arm. Oh, my God! It's bleeding!"

She held the wound with her hand. A trickle or two of blood ran down her arm.

Dylan froze. He watched intently as another trickle of blood oozed out between Angela's fingers.

"Dylan!" she scolded. "What are you doing? I'm bleeding! Go get help."

He stood there as if paralyzed. He stared at the blood that slowly dripped down over Angela's arm. The dim light cast eerie shadows across his face. His expression frightened her as she winced with pain.

"Dylan!" she shouted. "What's wrong with you? I need a bandage for my arm!"

He was transfixed. He watched her arm with a mesmerized glee.

"Help me!" she screamed. "Somebody! Help me! Please! Help!"

The door burst open. Neil ran into the room.

"What's wrong?" he asked.

"I cut my arm on a file cabinet," she explained. "I need a bandage."

"Let me see," he said. He pealed her hand away from the wound. After a quick look, he continued. "It's not too bad. It needs to be cleaned. And, a small bandage with some gauze should do the trick. What's Dylan doing here?"

"I don't know," she said. "He was going on about people being scared of him. Then when I cut myself, he just stood there staring. I asked him to get help, but he kept staring at me. It was like he got some cheap thrill out of watching me bleed!"

"What?" Neil asked. He spun around to face Dylan.

"What's the matter with you?" he asserted. "Can't you see she's hurt?"

"I… I…" Dylan stammered.

"She asks for help, and you just stand there?" Neil interrogated. "Were you just watching her bleed?"

"Well, I…"

"What's wrong with you, you little freak?" Neil pressed. "Do you have some kind of demented blood fetish or something, you warped little psychopath? Get out of here!"

"B-but, I didn't…"

"Did you hear me, you babbling idiot!" he threatened. "Get out of here before I bash your fucking brains in!"

Dylan gawked at Neil. Then, he glanced at Angela. His gaze slid down to the wound on her arm.

Then, he turned and fled the room.

By this time, a few people had gathered by the door.

Neil turned back to Angela. "Come on, honey," he said. "Let's get you out of here and get something for that cut."

"Thanks, Neil," she smiled.

"What exactly would you say is wrong with Mr. Zeblonsky, Doctor?" he asked.

"I'm not at liberty to discuss his complete file with you, Detective," Freitag explained. "There is a doctor/patient confidentiality clause that pertains here. Of course, he does have his issues. There are certain social inadequacies you may have noticed."

"I'll bet his mother had something to do with that," Reynolds deduced.

"Oh," Freitag said. "You've met his mother, have you?"

"Yup," Reynolds nodded. "She's one for the books. I'm guessing she could've turned Gandhi into another Charlie Manson."

"That's an interesting analysis," the doctor allowed. "And, I understand the urgency of your murder investigation. Still, all I am obliged to tell you is that Dylan is incapable of murder."

"Are you sure of that, Doctor?" he asked.

"Reasonably sure," Freitag nodded. "Yes."

"You don't sound too certain," he observed.

"Well, *anyone* is capable of murder," Freitag pointed out. "Under the right circumstances. The will to survive can drive a person to do extraordinary things. But, this was not a case of survival. I don't know that Dylan had a crush on this girl. But even if he did, he would not have killed her because she married someone else. I surmise this is the theory you're working with."

"Yes."

"Then, Dylan is definitely not your killer," Freitag said. "It doesn't fit his profile. He fears women in a way you wouldn't understand."

"We met his mother," Reynolds poked. "Believe me. We understand!"

"This is not a joke, Detective," Freitag said. "I've been following the story about this murder in the paper. Dylan may fear women, but he doesn't *hate* them. Your killer is a misogynist, gentlemen. Dylan may be maladjusted, but the level of severe rejection reaction you're looking for in this case goes beyond any level Dylan has reached."

"That's a bold speculation," he said.

"Of course, it's mere conjecture," Freitag admitted. "Based on just a few newspaper articles. There's no guarantee that the murder was even related to her marriage. For all we know, it could have been a simple argument with any of the wedding guests. Perhaps a bridesmaid didn't like her dress. Who knows? But if you're going under the theory that a jilted or rejected would-be suitor did this, then you're looking for a man with severe inner conflicts. Someone whose love for this woman was set off against his hatred of all women. And when mixed with a deep rejection reaction syndrome, it made for a volatile emotional cocktail."

"As evidenced by his overkill tactics and the dumpster?" Reynolds suggested.

"Precisely," Freitag nodded. "Dylan's 'insecurities' are just not that complex."

"Really, Doctor?" he asked.

"You sound disappointed, Detective."

"Frankly, I am."

"I know it's easy to look at someone like Dylan," the doctor said. "And think, 'he's not wrapped too tightly.

He's our killer.' But, believe me. He's not the man you're looking for."

"I hear you'll be seeing him today," he said.

"Yes I am. Why?"

"Keep us informed if anything changes," he said. "Or if you think of anything that might help us."

"Of course."

"Thank you," he muttered. "We may need to speak with you again."

"Anytime, Detectives," the doctor said. "Have a nice day."

He waited until they were outside before asking, "Do you think the doctor was lying to protect his patient?"

"I doubt it," Reynolds said. "He doesn't seem the type. He's too ethical. It's certainly possible, though."

"I don't think Zeblonsky is responsible for Cynthia Trott," he said. "Since the lab confirmed that letter really was a month old, I think Worthington took care of his girlfriend out of jealousy."

"You do?"

"You don't believe the guy's story about phone calls with shadows wearing bloody bridal veils, do you?" he asked.

"No."

"Then, there's your answer," he said. "These are two separate murders. Zeblonsky is still a suspect in Mrs. Broderick's murder. Maybe the doctor was right. Maybe it was an even bigger screw ball. But, I think Worthington has to be the man behind Trott's disappearance. It's the only explanation for his bullshit 'veil-wearing shadow' story. It's pretty clear he doesn't like Zeblonsky. Maybe he's trying to set the guy up to take the fall for him."

"All right then," Reynolds said. "I'm with you. Let's go prove it."

🌱 🌱 🌱

"You should really be talking to his immediate supervisor," he advised.

"I'm telling you, Joe," the young man asserted. "He's not just creepy anymore. He's a menace. He's downright dangerous!"

"Listen, Neil," Joe said. "From what I hear so far, you weren't even present during most of the incident. Why don't you let Angela tell me what happened?"

"Well, there isn't much to tell," she said. "I was doing some filing in the Archives Room. Dylan came in and started asking me why everyone is afraid of him. I kept telling him it wasn't true. But, he kept pushing the issue. He kept saying that everyone thinks he killed Karen."

"Well, to be honest," Joe said. "Most of the rumors that are floating around have singled him out as the killer. And, it's really not fair."

"Of all the people around," he said. "He's the most likely suspect. You can't tell me the thought hasn't crossed your mind, Joe."

"That may be true, Neil," Joe said. "But, I haven't indulged in any of the gossip. And, I try to treat Dylan the same as I always have."

"You treat him like a creep," he said. "Just like everyone else."

"That only makes his questions to Angela more understandable," Joe said. "You're right. I don't always treat Dylan as fairly as I should. But, that's *my* problem. Not his. And you can't blame him for being a bit defensive."

"He scared the hell out of Angela," he pushed. "You should've seen her when I ran into that room. She was almost in tears."

"Is that true, Angela?"

"Yes," she said. "He was really freaking me out."

"But, did he actually do anything?" Joe asked.

"He kept walking toward me," she said. "I asked him to stop. I told him he was scaring me. But, he kept walking toward me while asking why I was scared."

"But, did he threaten you?" Joe asked. "Did he try to touch you? Did he do anything to warrant your fear? Anything we can pin on him?"

"Not really, I guess," she admitted. "He's just always frightened me. And, the sound of his voice made my skin crawl. And, there's not enough light in the room. It was all dark and shadowy. And, he just kept walking toward me and questioning me, even though I begged him to stop."

"But, he didn't touch you?" Joe asked. "Or even try to touch you?"

"I guess not."

"Exactly how did you cut your arm?" Joe asked.

"I backed into the sharp edge of a filing cabinet," she explained. "While trying to get away from him."

"But, he wasn't actually pursuing you," Joe stated for clarity.

"No," she said. "But, he knew he was making me nervous. I told him I would scream if he didn't get away from me."

"And, what happened after you cut yourself?" Joe asked.

"I wanted to leave the room," she said. "I wanted to bandage my arm, but Dylan was in the way. I told him to get help, but he just stood there. He just stared at my arm! It was as if watching me bleed excited him or something."

"Really?" Joe asked. "Maybe he was just nervous, too. Did you ever think of that? You know how he gets around girls."

"That's part of the problem," she pointed out.

"Yes," Joe stammered. "Well, I..."

"So, I started to scream," she continued. "I didn't know what else to do. My arm hurt and I was scared."

"And, that's when you came in?" Joe asked Neil.

"Yes," he nodded. "I heard screams, so I came in to help. Zeblonsky was blocking her only exit. And, he was just staring at her."

"Was he literally trying to block her exit?" Joe asked.

"Maybe not intentionally," he admitted.

"What did you do?"

"I called him a weirdo or something," he said. "And, I told him to get lost."

"Did you threaten him?"

"I don't know," he shrugged. "I may have."

"If you did," Joe informed him. "You may be in more trouble than he is."

"But, he scared her half to death!" he defended. "You should have seen her!"

"I was really frightened," she concurred.

"But, he never actually did anything," Joe said.

"He kept approaching me!" she argued. "Even when I begged him to stop! Even when I threatened to scream!"

"We'll have to sort that out," Joe said.

"If I threatened him," he pointed out. "It's only because Angela was bleeding and on the verge of tears. He was watching her bleed, for God's sake! He's a psycho! Besides, we're all still freaked out over Karen. And, my girlfriend is still missing. He may be a killer *and* a kidnapper!"

"It's not likely that he kidnapped anyone," Joe said. "He lives with his mother. And, there's no proof he killed anyone either. We're all a little on edge. But, we can't take it out on Dylan. There's no justification for treating him badly."

"He just stood there and watched me bleed," she reminded.

"So you said."

"If he hurt my Cynthia, I'll…"

"Neil!" Joe scolded. "That's enough! I'll set up a meeting with Dylan's supervisor, Rick Nadler. And, I'll include Steve Callahan, Angela."

"That's fine," she said.

"We'll all sit down with Dylan," Joe said. "And we'll get to the bottom of this."

"We all know he's a dangerous little freak, Joe," he said. "He deserves to get fired before anyone else gets hurt!"

"We'll decide who deserves what at the meeting," Joe politely corrected. "Let's just hope you haven't given Dylan a legitimate axe to grind."

"Dylan doesn't use axes," he poked with a snide glare. "According to Karen's autopsy, he uses long, sharp knives."

"That's not funny, Neil!" Joe averred. "You'd better conduct yourself properly at the meeting. You could be in danger of losing your job if you threatened Dylan."

"We could *all* be in danger," he said. "No matter what!"

Chapter 5
Rage Potential

He stormed across the large room. He marched angrily down long rows between cubicles. He was still fuming as he approached the boss's office.

He took a deep breath for composure before knocking on the door.

"Come in," said the voice inside.

He stuck his head in the door. "Mr. Nadler?" he asked. "Can I talk with you please?"

"Ah, Dylan," Nadler smiled. "I'm glad you're here. Come in and sit down. I was going to call you. Just before lunch, I got a call from Joe McMahon. Apparently, there was an incident this morning."

"That's what I wanted to talk to you about, sir," he said as he took a seat.

"Joe was a little sketchy on the details," Nadler said. "Why don't you tell me exactly what happened?"

"I went into the Archives Room to do some filing," he explained. "Angela Pierce was in there. She had lots of filing to do. But as soon as I walked in, she made up some lame excuse about having to leave."

"How do you know it was just an excuse?" Nadler asked.

"It *was* a lame excuse!" he insisted. "She's just like everyone else in this dump! She can't stand to be alone in the same room with me! I scare her just like I scare everybody else in this place! I never did anything to these people! But, every day I have to watch people avoid me, walk the other way whenever I'm near or talk to me like I'm a homicidal maniac or something!"

"I'm sure you're exaggerating."

"Please don't lie to me, sir," he said. "I hear the rumors and snickering behind my back! I know what people think of me here!"

"Listen, Dylan…"

"All I did," he went on. "Was ask Angela why she was scared of me. I asked her why everyone treats me like I have The Plague! She wouldn't tell me! She wouldn't even talk to me! She just said if I didn't go away, she'd scream. How would you feel if people acted like that around you all the time?"

"It can't be as bad as all that," Nadler began.

"All the time!" he reiterated. "I work here, damn it! And, I do a good job!"

"Yes you do."

"I shouldn't have to put up with this shit from these people," he insisted. "I just wanted to know why she's scared of me. And, it's been worse since Karen got murdered. Everyone treats me like I killed her!"

"Well, Karen's death has been hard on all of us," Nadler said. "It's natural in these cases for people to start rumors and advance half-baked theories."

"But, why do they all have to be directed at me?" he asked. "I never did anything to any of these people! I don't deserve this!"

"Maybe some issues need to be addressed," Nadler allowed. "Tell me what happened to Angela's arm."

"She cut herself on a filing cabinet," he explained. "Trying to run away from me just because I was talking to her. Then, she started screaming at the top of her lungs as if it was my fault. That's a clear indication of how far out of hand this problem has progressed."

"And, that's when Neil came in?" Nadler asked.

"Yes," he said. "Worthington came busting in like he thought he was a knight in shining armor or something. The arrogant, slimy bastard!"

"Name-calling is unnecessary and counter-productive," Nadler said.

"Tell that to Worthington!" he averred. "He called me a warped little psychopath! He threatened to bash my brains in!"

"He did?"

"That's illegal, isn't it?" he asked. "He should be fired!"

"Let's not do anything hasty."

"Everybody knows Neil and Angela have a thing for each other," he said. "But, that's no reason for him to threaten my life! Not just because I was alone in the same room with some girl he's trying to impress! I won't stand for his macho mock heroics! I don't have to! I want him fired!"

"Alright, Dylan," Nadler said. "Calm down. Joe called me to set up a meeting for tomorrow. Is 10:30 good for you? You and I can sit down with Angela, Neil, Joe and Steve and we'll work everything out."

"Good!" he said. "Then, you can fire Worthington! Maybe we can get people to start treating me with the respect I deserve around here!"

"You should try to cool down in the meantime," Nadler advised. "You're seeing your psychiatrist today, aren't you?"

"Yes," he said. "I'll be leaving in about half an hour."

"See what he recommends," Nadler said. "You need to get a hold of yourself. I expect you to act in a professional manner tomorrow. If we need to take action against anyone, that will be decided at the meeting. Still, nothing can be gained by raving like a lunatic, Dylan. You'll only make Neil look better."

"I know," he muttered. "Thank you, sir."

He took his time stirring his coffee. He watched the light brown liquid swirl around in the cup. There were still a number of issues sitting like heavy weights in his stomach.

Finally, he looked up at the pretty girl sitting beside him on the sofa.

"You took another day off from work?" he asked.

"I thought I told you," she said. "I took the whole week off right in the beginning. Karen was my best friend."

"Then, what are you doing here?"

"I'm here for you," she said. "We're the two people who are going to miss her the most, Peter. We need to be there for each other."

"What about her parents?"

"They have each other for comfort and consolation," she said. "By the way, you never told me how your dinner went with them last night. You barely grunted when I asked you about it."

"What do you want me to say, Michelle?" he said. "Her parents were there. My parents were there. Everyone was still terribly upset. The wake is on Friday, by the way.

And, the funeral is on Saturday morning at 10:00 in The Cathedral of the Disciples of Christ. That's the same place where she married me less than a week before."

"Thank you," she said. "I meant to ask you about that."

"I'm not surprised you didn't bother to ask," he said.

"Why do you say that?"

"You seem to have other things on your mind lately," he said.

"What?" she asked. "Are you talking about that kiss? Don't you dare try to blame me for that, Peter! You're just as guilty as I am."

"I had to face my parents and hers last night," he said. "Everybody's crying over her death. She's not even buried yet, and I have to deal with this!"

"You have nothing to feel bad about, Peter," she said. "We both have a lot of pain to get through."

"Before you left," he reminded. "You said something about feelings that went back a long way. What was that all about?"

"Well, it's true," she stated while looking him in the eye. "There was always a little something between us, Peter. You know that."

"No there wasn't!"

"If you want to feel guilty because Karen's gone," she said. "That's fine. But, the fact remains. That kiss has been a long time coming."

"You're nuts!" he said. "We may have flirted a little. That's only natural. You are a beautiful girl, Michelle."

"Thank you."

"But, that doesn't mean…"

"Yes it does!"

"Michelle," he said. "You have to listen to me. I have a lot of things to feel guilty about. I haven't been the greatest person in the world lately. I certainly haven't been the best person I could've been to Karen."

"What do you mean?"

He took a moment for courage.

"About a month ago," he finally explained. "I slept with Cynthia Trott."

"What?"

"It happened twice," he continued. "She had an argument with her boyfriend. I was getting anxious about the wedding. I guess I was getting cold feet. It was a mistake, and I've regretted it ever since. I loved Karen. I really did."

"Cynthia?" she gasped. "You must be kidding!"

"I ended it as soon as I came to my senses," he expounded. "I wrote her a letter explaining how I felt and everything. I'm surprised she kept the letter. I'm even more surprised her boyfriend found it. Now, she's missing."

"I heard she was missing," she said. "But, I never caught any details. Do you think her boyfriend killed her?"

"It's the most likely scenario."

"Poor Cynthia!" she sighed. "I didn't know her that well. But, I liked her. Even though I heard she was a bit of a slut. I can't believe you slept with her."

"Like I said," he reiterated. "It was a moment of weakness for the both of us."

"I hope she's okay," she said. "She seemed like a nice girl."

"Do you see why I feel especially guilty?" he asked. "I've already done too much cheating on Karen. I can't do any more."

"You're not cheating now," she pointed out. "Karen's dead."

"That doesn't help."

She took his hand.

He tried to pull away for a moment. She held his hand firmly.

She looked him in the eye.

"She's gone," she whispered. "Torturing yourself won't bring her back."

He looked into her eyes. He felt a few tears well up.

"She was my wife."

"I know."

There was a long, brutal silence.

Then, there was a kiss.

Then, there was another. It was a longer kiss.

It was a kiss that really had been a long time in coming. And it was a kiss that would carry them to a venue where the dream outweighed the pain.

He watched the young man take a seat. He looked down at his notes. He surveyed his own chicken-scratch with a frown.

Finally, he said, "How are you today, Dylan?"

"I've had better days."

"What's wrong?"

"Everyone at work has been acting like they think I killed that girl at her wedding reception," Dylan said.

"In all honesty," he asked. "Did you do it?"

"No! Of course not!"

"Then, why does everyone think you did?" he asked.

"That's what I'd like to know."

"What makes you think they blame you?" he asked.

"They treat me like shit," Dylan said. "They always have. Everyone is always afraid of me. Women avoid me. Men just laugh at me behind my back. It's always been that way. I don't know why. I try to get along with everybody."

"Are you sure you're not just being paranoid?" he asked.

"Isn't that for you to diagnose, Doc?" Dylan shot back.

"If you say so," he allowed. "So, what specifically happened today?"

"I went to do some filing in a back room," Dylan explained. "There was a girl in there. As soon as I walked in, she acted like she had to escape. I asked her why she was afraid of me. And she cut her arm on a file cabinet."

"Oh dear," he said. "Was she hurt?"

"She'll be okay," Dylan said. "But, she was bleeding."

The doctor looked at his patient. "Bleeding?" he asked.

"Yes," he nodded. "And, you guessed it. I just stood there. She's such a pretty girl. She asked me for help. And, I just stood there and watched her bleed."

"You just watched?" he asked. "You did nothing to help her?"

"I couldn't help it," he said. "She wasn't bleeding all that much. She wasn't in any real danger. But, it was such a turn on!"

"You're still getting turned on by watching other people bleed?" he asked.

"Yeah," Dylan nodded with a grin. "It was almost sexy in a way. I swear girls bleed different than boys."

"That makes no sense, Dylan."

"The way her blood flowed out of that tiny gash in her arm," Dylan explained. And then ran down her flesh. It almost had a fluid, female motion to it. It was quite exciting."

"Are you saying," he spelled out for clarity. "That you are sexually aroused by watching girls bleed?"

"Not really," Dylan said. "I enjoy watching anyone, really. But, girls have their own certain way that's especially fascinating."

The doctor regarded him with renewed interest.

"Are you *sure* you didn't kill Karen?" he asked again. "I'm your doctor. You can trust me."

"I didn't kill anybody!"

"You know, the police came to see me today," he informed his patient. "They wanted to know if I thought you could've killed her. That Japanese detective looked especially intense. He really wants to pin this on you."

"What did you tell them?"

"I told them the truth," he said. "At least, to some extent. I don't think you killed her. I still don't think you're capable of such an act. I think you are angry, but not to the levels necessary to commit that crime. I think you are more confused and unsure of yourself. But, it's not because you hate women."

"Do you think the murderer hates women?" Dylan asked.

"From what I've seen of the case," he said. "The killer has a lot more issues than you do. And I think he just hides it better."

"What do you mean?"

"People fear you, Dylan," he said. "Because of your insecurity. It shows at skin level, because you are uncomfortable with your emotions. Your biggest problem is that you are not in touch with yourself. Even this thing you have for blood is a combination of your anger at the world brought about by your own inner knowledge that your lack of confidence, though reinforced by others, is purely self-induced. It is a conflict that must be dealt with. However, it does not make you an immediate threat to anyone."

"What about the killer?" Dylan asked.

"His problems are deeper and more complex," he explained. "He is more comfortable with the negative emotions that drive him to do what he does. You know you need some help. He does not! He doesn't fear women. He hates them!"

"Why?"

"I can't say," he shrugged. "I don't even know who it is. If I were to guess, I would say his feelings for Karen set off an inner conflict against his misogyny. When she rejected him, he didn't take it well. And her marriage set him over the edge."

"Do you really think so, Doc?"

"I'm just guessing," he said. "It's kind of like Psycho-Scrabble for us shrinks. It's a fun game to play with newspaper stories like this. Like I told the cops, maybe one of the bridesmaids didn't like her dress. Maybe the groom's cousin was pissed off that he had to pay for his own drinks. Who really knows?"

"So, why are you telling me this?" Dylan asked.

"It's the basis for what I told the cops," he said. "They wanted a psychological profile that would give them a reason to pin this on you. I just told them that if they're looking for a nut case, they're looking in the wrong direction."

"Thanks."

"It's okay," he said. "There was a grain of truth to it. But, it made me think."

"About what?"

"About how we can help you."

"What did you have in mind?" Dylan asked.

"If my theories about the killer are correct," he postulated. "He has the advantage over you in that he is comfortable with his negative emotions. He has allowed them to be a positive part of his psychological make-up."

"So?"

"We all have a certain capacity for all emotions," he explained. "Both positive and negative. You have the capacity for love, just like anyone else. You also have the potential for rage, just like everyone does. Your biggest problem is that you need to acquaint yourself with these emotions. You have to take them out, learn how to use them and become comfortable with them. In this way, you can become more comfortable with people. And once you do that, people won't fear you as much."

"What are you suggesting?" Dylan asked.

"I want to acquaint you with the capacity for love that lives inside you," he said. "I want you to get to know the rage potential that lives in each and every one of us. I want you to break free of the insecurities that keep you chained up in the prison you have devised for yourself."

"What do I have to do?"

"Only by exposure to the raw, bare, elemental emotions that most of us take for granted," he explained. "Will you ever become comfortable with yourself and everyone else around you."

"How do I do that?"

"Do you want people to stop treating you as if there's something wrong with you?" he asked.

"Yes."

"I mean, do you really want it?"

"Yes, Doctor!"

"Are you ready to explore your emotions, my boy?" he asked. "Even if my methods appear at first to be a little extreme? Even if it means getting in touch with your rage potential?"

"Yes, Doctor! Anything!"

"Then, I may be able to help you," he said slowly. "It might even be a bit of a turn-on for you, too."

❧   ❧   ❧

"So, are we all set, Angela?" he asked.

"Yes, Steve," she said. "Tomorrow at 10:30 will be fine. I'm only sorry I'm causing so much trouble after only working here for a week and a half."

"Think nothing of it," he said. "It's not your fault. If Dylan acted in an inappropriate manner, you have every right to speak out."

"And, I hope you're not mad that I talked to Joe McMahon before I came to you," she said. "It's just that he was closer at the time. And since Neil was involved, it seemed only fair that his boss should be included."

"It's no big deal," he said. "Everyone has been notified. It doesn't matter who heard what and when. The incident in the Archives Room is the only important issue. By the way, how is your arm?"

"It'll be okay," she said. "That bandage makes it look worse than it is. They didn't have to wrap my arm up like a mummy."

"Would you like the rest of the day off?" he offered. "It's the middle of the afternoon anyway. We can survive an hour or two without you."

"You wouldn't mind?" she asked. "It's not so much because of my cut. I'm just a little rattled from the confrontation. Dylan really scared the hell out of me."

"You can leave if you want," he said. "It's not a problem. But, are you sure you're not blowing this incident out of proportion? A lot of people react poorly to Dylan. And, Karen's death has made everyone a bit jittery. But, he really has never done anything to anyone. I'm sure he's harmless. He's just a little different."

"I told him he was making me nervous," she insisted. "I begged him to get away from me. But, he wouldn't leave me alone."

"You said he was just trying to talk to you," he reminded. "Are you sure we need to pursue this?"

"Well," she said pensively. "I'd like to think we can resolve this matter. But, Dylan needs to learn that when someone tells him to back off, he should respect that person's wishes. You can't just back someone into a corner without consequences."

"I understand how you feel," he said. "But, will you at least consider a peaceful resolution? You are both good employees. I'd like to see both of you stay and work things out. Dylan's really not so bad. He's just a bit misunderstood."

"I'll try, Steve," she allowed. "But as I said, he has to learn to respect people's wishes."

"Good girl," he smiled. "All right, Angela. Good night. See you tomorrow."

"Good night."

She was still mulling things over as she walked out of his office. She barely had the chance to close his door behind her when two girls anxiously approached.

"Hi, Angela," they chorused.

"Hello, Jennifer," she said impatiently. "Hi, Sarah."

"Oh my God!" Jennifer gasped. "Look at your arm! Are you okay?"

"Yes," she said. "It's not as bad as it looks."

"We heard about what happened," Jennifer said. "Did Dylan do that to you?"

"No," she said. "I backed into a filing cabinet."

"We heard about what Dylan did in the Archives Room," Sarah said. "We heard about the big meeting tomorrow. Are you going to get him fired?"

"I hope so," Jennifer added. "That little weirdo gives me the creeps!"

"Me too," Sarah agreed. "The sooner he's out of here, the better."

"I don't know," she said. "He didn't really do anything."

"That's not what I heard," Sarah said.

"You'd think that killing Karen would be enough to fire him," Jennifer said. "But, that little space cadet seems to live a charmed life."

"I'm going home for the day," she said. "Can we talk tomorrow?"

"Okay," Jennifer said. "But, you have to at least tell us about having Neil come to your rescue. I hear he threatened to beat Dylan to a pulp."

"I told you he likes you as much as you like him," Sarah grinned. "And now that his girlfriend is gone, you have a clear shot at him, sweetie!"

"I don't have a thing for Neil!" she insisted. "And, he doesn't have a thing for me!"

"If you say so."

"Hi, girls," said a male voice from behind.

Jennifer gasped with a giddy delight when they turned to see who it was.

They nearly giggled as they chorused, "Hi, Neil!"

"Look, Angela," Sarah said. "It's Neil!"

"I can see that."

"How are you girls today?" he asked.

"We're good," Sarah said.

"Hey, Neil," Jennifer said. "We heard about how you saved Angela from Dylan in the Archives Room. You're a real hero."

"It wasn't anything special," he said.

"I wouldn't have blamed you if you punched him," Jennifer said. "He deserved it."

"Let's not get carried away," he said. "There wasn't…"

"Excuse me," another male voice interrupted. "Mr. Worthington?"

He turned. "Hello, Detectives," he said. "What can I do for you?"

"Can you please come downtown with us, sir?" Sumaki asked. "We would like to ask you a few questions about the disappearance of Cynthia Trott."

"What?" he asked. "Are you kidding me? I'm the one who called the cops."

"That's true," Sumaki said. "You called two hours after you admitted noticing that she was missing."

"I explained that to you," he insisted.

"Our lab determined that letter with your fingerprints on it was genuine," Reynolds explained. "That makes you a prime suspect. Please come with us, sir."

"Am I going to need to call a lawyer?" he asked.

"That's not a bad idea," Sumaki said.

The three women watched the three men leave together.

"Wow, Angela," Sarah whispered. "That could put a real crimp in your plans with Neil."

"I don't have any plans with Neil," she insisted.

"Is she going to want to start something with the kind of guy who'd kill his girlfriend out of jealousy?" Jennifer asked.

"Neil didn't kill Cynthia," Sarah said. "Dylan did it to cover up Karen's murder."

"What about Karen's ghost with the bloody bridal veil?" Jennifer asked.

"Will you two please stop?" Angela protested.

There was an uneasy silence.

"Okay," Jennifer finally said. "You're right. You've had quite a day."

"That's true," Sarah agreed. "First, you were attacked by Dylan. Then, your boyfriend gets hauled off by the police."

"He's not my boyfriend!"

"Go home and get some rest," Jennifer said. "We'll talk tomorrow."

"I just hope your boyfriend gets out of jail in time for your big meeting tomorrow," Sarah added. "Good night, Angela."

She watched the two busybodies leave. She walked over to her desk. She packed up a few items.

Then, she slowly walked out of the building.

She thought about Neil... and Dylan... and the girls.

She wiped her eyes with the back of her hand. Then, she walked to her car.

It was another golden sunset. A few clouds splashed gray streaks against a canvas where orange and pink came together to form colors no artist could devise. The sun looked big, fat and proud of itself for providing another bright, clear day. Still, it was ready for a short vacation somewhere beyond the horizon of Thorn Ridge.

He drove his car down a long highway as the sky began to grow dark. Traffic was moderate. His route was laid out comfortably before him.

He was tired. He was a bit aggravated. It had been an exhausting day.

He needed to get into the right lane. He planned at getting off at the next exit.

He checked the traffic. He glanced in the rearview mirror.

His path was clear. He pulled his car into the desired lane.

Everything was fine. He yawned. His eyes were tired. He was sick of watching the road. He would be slowing soon. He needed to check the traffic behind him.

He looked in the rearview mirror again.

Unfortunately, his view was blocked by a shadow. The shadow appeared to be sitting in the back seat of his car. It looked as though it was wearing a bridal veil that had been doused in blood.

He gasped with shock. He involuntarily steered the car off the road while slamming on his brakes.

The car screeched as it spun off the road. It was out of control. The soft shoulder, grassy verge and trees rapidly approached the car as the tires skidded noisily beneath him.

Trees were approaching too quickly. The car began to turn sideways. His heart was racing. He put everything he had into standing on the brakes.

Finally, the car came to a halt.

He didn't think he hit anything. However, his vehicle was clearly off the road. His heart was still pounding. His breathing was heavy and labored.

He didn't want to look in the mirror. Still... he had no choice!

He nervously glanced up into the mirror.

Everything appeared normal. There was no shadow. There was no bloody veil.

He breathed a sigh of relief.

He sat for a minute while his breathing and heart rate returned to normal. He checked the mirror again, just to be safe.

Nothing seemed out of place. All he saw was a stream of cars passing by on the road beneath the deepening twilight.

He needed to get out for a minute. He needed to stretch his legs. He needed to feel clean, fresh air in his lungs.

He got out and walked around the car a few times. The nearest tree was only a few inches from the front of his vehicle. His front tires had dug deep grooves into the mud beneath the grass.

He kept checking the windows for signs of shadows and veils.

Everything seemed fine.

After a few minutes of watching the traffic, he walked over to the passenger's side. He opened the door. He leaned in. He wanted to find something on the cluttered seat. He moved a flashlight out of his way. He moved the wrapper from a fast food burger place aside. He brushed a blood-soaked bridal veil aside.

Then, he stopped. He jumped backwards with a scream.

Cautiously, he peered back into the vehicle. The front seat was still cluttered.

But, there was no sign of the veil.

Slowly, he raised his hands. Blood stained his fingertips and palms.

He screamed in terror.

He just stared. And, he kept screaming as the bloodstains that came from nowhere remained thickly caked on his hands.

He looked up into the sunset.

"Leave me alone!" he shouted. "Please! Just leave me alone! I'm sorry, Karen! I'm sorry! You know I didn't want things to turn out this way! But, how could you marry that asshole even after he cheated on you!"

He glanced around at the spreading field of stars above him.

"I never would have cheated on you, my darling!" he screamed. "I loved you! By God! You know how much I loved you!"

He began to weep openly.

"And, I killed that Trott slut, too!" he cried. "I did everything you asked! You know I did! I did it for you, sweetheart! I even put her where you told me to! Please leave me alone with my grief now! Just leave me alone!"

He sobbed into his bloody hands.

"I loved you, Karen," he blubbered. "My God! I loved you!"

He cried into his bloody hands for a minute or two. Then he wiped his eyes on a handkerchief. He wiped his hands as well.

However, none of the blood came off. His palms and fingers were as caked as they had been at the start.

He jumped back into his car. He started the engine. The wheels splattered mounds of mud on the grass as he pulled the car frantically back onto the road.

Then, he raced home as quickly as he could.

He was determined to wash the blood off his hands...

No matter what it took!

Chapter 6
Conquest

The days were growing noticeably shorter. Rotting leaves still lay around in damp, dingy piles in the streets. All the trees were tragically bare and gaunt. The sun had nearly disappeared behind a cold, urban skyline.

The darkness outside seemed unfeeling and stoic. It did not give a sense of danger. It left her more with a feeling of sadness; as if each of the dim stars above, though huddled together in groups, felt terribly alone.

A few leaves floated by the window. A breeze must have picked up.

She carelessly regarded the diner's menu as she sipped her coffee.

"Hi, Angela," said a voice.

She looked up with a smile. "Hi, Barbara," she said. "Thanks for coming."

"No problem," Barbara said. As she took her seat in the booth, the smile vanished from her face. "Oh, God! What did you do to your arm?"

"I had an argument with a file cabinet," she explained. "It's nothing serious. They overdid the bandage a little. It's not as bad as it looks."

"God, Angela!" Barbara said. "When you took an office job, I didn't think we had to worry if you were going to get home safely on a day-to-day basis."

"It's just a scratch," she reiterated.

"So, why did you call me?" Barbara asked. "You sounded unhappy on the phone. What's the matter?"

"I don't know," she sighed. "I'm starting to think I don't like this job very much."

"Why?" Barbara asked. "You've only been there a week and a half. It's an office job. How bad can it be?"

"The work's not that bad," she said. "I kind of like my boss, as far as bosses go. Over all, it's an okay way to make a living."

"So, what's the problem?"

"It's the people," she explained. "Too many people at the office get on my nerves."

"Like who?"

"Do you remember I told you someone got murdered over the weekend?" she asked.

"Yes."

"Everyone is guessing who did it," she said. "Rumors are flying around all over the place."

"That's only natural," Barbara said.

"A lot of people think it's this creepy little guy who everybody hates," she explained. "I'm still not sure if it was him. He is a scary little guy. He even scared the hell out of me today."

"What did he do?" Barbara asked.

"It doesn't matter right now," she said. "The two big office gossips are just as much of a pain. They're both in their twenties. Jennifer and Sarah are their names. They're not essentially evil. But, they get too tied up in hearing, starting and spreading rumors. And they don't just stick with rumors about the creepy little 'killer' guy. Now they're starting in on me too."

"What are they saying about you?" Barbara asked.

"They're trying to say I'm in love with this guy named Neil," she said.

"Well, are you?"

"No!" she declared. "I'll admit he's a nice looking guy. But, I'm not in love with him. Jennifer and Sarah are just spreading rumors because that's all they have in their lives. It's what they live for."

"So, you're depressed," Barbara summed up. "Because a couple of office busybodies are spreading rumors about you and some guy?"

"Kind of," she said. "It's not just that. It's a lot of things. I have a meeting tomorrow to clear up some stuff. That creepy guy that scared me. I might try to get him fired."

"Why?" Barbara asked. "You still didn't tell me what he did."

"He trapped me in a corner," she said. "So he could tell me he didn't kill anyone. He wouldn't let me leave. At first, it just made me think he *was* the killer."

"Did something change your mind?" Barbara asked.

"Yes," she nodded. "Just before I left today, the cops hauled Neil out of the office."

"They did?" Barbara gasped. "The guy you're supposed to be in love with? Did they arrest him?"

"Not really," she said. "They just asked him to go downtown for questioning. It's enough to make you wonder. How many suspected killers do I work with?"

"Do you think he did it?"

"I don't know," she shrugged. "I think they were actually talking to him about 'a matter that may be related' or something. He and his girlfriend were at the wedding where the bride was killed. Now his girlfriend has disappeared. It's enough to really make you wonder about everybody in the whole office."

"You're not thinking of quitting, are you?" Barbara inquired.

"I'm not sure," she muttered. "The thought has crossed my mind. I mean, what kind of place hires murderers? What kind of place hires creeps that trap you in corners in isolated rooms and won't let you leave? What kind of place hires guys who have to be hauled downtown by the cops because their girlfriends have disappeared?"

"Apparently," Barbara answered. "The same place that hired you."

"Thanks a lot!"

A waitress asked, "Can I take your order, ladies?"

"I'm not hungry," she said. "I'll just have another coffee."

"I'll have coffee and a green salad please," Barbara said. "With Italian dressing."

"Thanks," the waitress said. "I'll be right back with your coffee."

Barbara watched her leave.

"You know, Angela," she said. "No workplace is perfect."

"Yes," she agreed. "But, we're talking about killers here."

"I guess you have a point," Barbara admitted.

"I wonder if he did it," she said. "I heard his girlfriend was cheating on him. Is Neil the kind of guy who would kill a girl just for that?"

There was a pause.

"I wonder if Neil committed both murders," she continued. "There's been some speculation that whoever killed the bride is also responsible for both murders."

"I thought you said Neil's girlfriend only disappeared," Barbara observed. "Why have you referred to it as 'murder' twice so far?"

"Face facts, Barbara," she said. "The girl's been missing for two days. What are the chances that she's still alive?"

"Not good, I'm afraid."

"Exactly!" she said. "And given the theories most people have put forward, her chances become even less."

"So, who do you think is responsible?" Barbara asked.

"That's just it!" she said. "I don't know what to think. I really hope Neil didn't have anything to do with either crime. But, you should've seen how he looked when those detectives escorted him out of the building. He was talking about getting a lawyer. How can you believe in someone when you have to watch a scene like that?"

"Do you need to believe in Neil for some reason?" Barbara asked.

"No," she said. "I just hope he'll be around for our meeting tomorrow."

"Is he supposed to be there for the meeting?" Barbara asked.

"Yes," she said. "He sort of 'rescued' me from the weirdo who cornered me today."

"Oh."

There was another pause.

"You know, Angela," she said. "If I didn't know any better, I'd think you do have a little crush on Neil."

"Why does everybody say that?" Angela defended. "Can't somebody care about another person without having a crush?"

"Everyone thinks you have a crush?" Barbara asked.

"I told you about those girls at the office," she said. "They've been spreading rumors all over the place. You'll be seeing 'Angela Loves Neil' on the front page of The Times tomorrow, the way things are going."

"Well, I don't think it's front page news," Barbara said. "But, it just might be true."

"No it's not!"

"Fine, Angela," Barbara said. "You just dragged me over here to tell me you don't have a crush on a guy I don't even know. I never even heard of this guy. And, you dragged me over here to tell me this for absolutely no reason at all. I understand."

"Stop it, Barbara!"

"What's your problem?" Barbara asked. "I'm only agreeing with you."

"You wear sarcasm about as well as you wear that sweater," she snipped. "Honest to God! Who picked out that color?"

"Hey," Barbara defended. "There's no need to get nasty."

"I'm sorry," she said. "I guess this situation at work is really getting to me. And, where the hell is that waitress with our coffee?"

"Calm down, sweetie," Barbara said. "I'm sure she's coming."

There was another uneasy pause.

"I have to say, Angela," she finally added. "I'm not sure whether you have a crush on that guy or not. But if you don't, maybe you should get out of that office. Maybe you should get out either way."

"Do you really think so?"

"It might be a good idea," Barbara said. "It's only been a week and a half. And, that place has already damaged more than just your arm."

❦ ❦ ❦

"Are you staying home tonight, Madeline?" he asked.

"I hadn't planned on it," she said. "But, I guess we do need to talk."

"We certainly do," he said. "Are you still seeing your gigolo, or have you ended your little mid-life crisis fling?"

"Let's start this conversation in a positive manner, shall we?" she suggested. "You're the psychiatrist. You're supposed to know the proper way to conduct yourself in a marital disagreement."

"I'm sorry, dear," he said. "Do you find my anger over your infidelity inconvenient? Should I be more civil in the face of your thoughtless, selfish indulgence and deceit?"

"You can start," she said. "By dropping the word 'gigolo' from your vocabulary. You know his name. You certainly paid enough money to find out all about him."

"And, *you* certainly paid enough of my money," he said. "To keep him in his desired lifestyle."

"I'm not going to have this conversation with you," she declared. "If you can't behave like a mature adult. If you can't avoid terms like 'gigolo' and 'my money', then trying to even talk to you is a complete waste of my time."

"A complete waste of time?" he asked. "You mean like our marriage?"

"Maybe I should just leave," she said. "You're obviously not ready to have this conversation yet."

"Oh, I'm ready, Madeline," he said. "I'm ready, willing and able to hear how twenty years of marriage and devotion can be discarded as easily as an old, greasy banana peel."

"I didn't discard our marriage, Joshua," she said. "I was just looking for something different. I needed a break. I needed some excitement."

"Then, why hasn't your little joy-ride ended?" he asked. "Has getting caught added to the thrill of your little charade? Does tearing my heart out add to your elation?"

"No."

"When are you going to end it, Madeline?"

"It's not as easy as doing whatever you say, Joshua," she informed him. "There are his feelings to consider. And mine."

"And, my feelings aren't worth shit, I suppose?" he inquired.

"Of course they are," she said. "It's just..."

He didn't like the feel of the long pause that followed.

"It's just..." she struggled to continue. "I love him, Joshua."

"You love him?" he growled. "You love the gigolo who has you spend my money on him? How does that work, Madeline? Tell me! I'd love to know! Maybe we could work something out! Maybe you can come back to me if I let you spend someone else's money on *me* for a change! What do you think?"

"There you go again, Joshua!" she snipped. "I thought you were going to avoid saying things like, 'gigolo' and 'my money!'"

"No," he disagreed. "You asked me to avoid those terms. I never replied. However, if you prefer, I can stick to words like 'cradle-robbing' and 'heartless bitch.'"

"Very nice, Joshua," she argued. "Is that your Harvard education kicking in? Is this how they teach you to deal with interpersonal relationships in Psychology class? Or are you as inept in your job as you are in your marriage?"

"I'll give you 'inept!'" he fumed. "You're going to leave him, Madeline! As God is my witness, you are going to leave that little parasite!"

"That's not for you to decide," she insisted.

139

"The hell it's not!"

"You were the one to tell me," she reminded. "Women tend to look for commitment and security in a relationship. Men tend to look more for conquest and ownership. These are the main components to most people's attraction to the institution of marriage."

"Don't presume to throw my own words back up at me," he snarled. "Besides, those aren't *my* words. Any first year Psych student knows about that!"

"That's still what you said," she reminded. "Is that what you're doing now, Joshua? Is this your idea of conquest and ownership? Am I just a conquest to you, my dear husband?"

"You're my wife!" he insisted. "That's supposed to mean something to you!"

"It does," she said. "At least until the divorce papers come through."

"Divorce?" he asked. "Is that really what you want? Who will pay for your gigolo then, sweetheart? Do you think he will provide commitment and security when the gravy train comes to a crashing halt? Who will pay to keep that parasite from running away?"

"You, of course," she answered with a snide smile. "My 'gravy train' is going nowhere. You will always pay, my darling."

"You bitch!" he sneered.

"I think we're done here," she said. "I'll admit I wish this talk had been more mature and productive. But, my husband the psychiatrist is too busy disregarding his years and years of training and education."

She grabbed her coat.

"By the way, darling," she concluded while heading for the door. "When you're done wiping your ass with your Harvard diploma, don't forget to flush."

"This is your last warning, Madeline," he threatened. "If you don't end your pathetic, sordid little affair, I will! I swear to God I will!"

He stopped shouting when the door slammed shut.

"What the hell was I thinking?" he asked.

"Oh, Peter," she sighed. "You're not going to tear yourself up over this, are you?"

"How can you be so cold?" he asked. "Karen's not even in the ground yet!"

"She's dead, Peter," she declared. "That's the important thing. It's not like you're cheating on her."

She nuzzled her head up against his neck and shoulder. She pulled the covers up closer and tighter around her body.

"It's exactly like I'm cheating on her," he disagreed. "I cheated on her one month before the wedding. I still don't know how she found out. Cynthia swore she didn't say anything. But, who else could have left that anonymous note? Nobody else knew about us. It only happened twice, and I was very discreet."

"That's all in the past," she assured him.

"Do you know how much I had to beg Karen to go through with the wedding after that?" he asked. "And, do you believe Cynthia had the nerve to show up at the wedding with her boyfriend? I don't think that poor bastard ever found out. At least, not until the day Cynthia disappeared. I can't believe she kept that letter! Sure, it's flattering. But, it was a foolish thing for her to do."

She lifted her head and looked him in the eye. "Do you think that guy killed his girlfriend?" she asked with sudden alarm.

"It's very possible."

"I don't like that, Peter," she said. She snuggled up next to him beneath the covers. "What if he decides that you're next?"

"I'm not too worried about that," he said. "That little pencil-pushing pretty-boy is no threat to me. I'm more worried about this situation. My bride has only been dead for three days. I really loved her, Michelle. How did I end up in bed with her Maid of Honor already? What does that say about me?"

"It says you're human, honey," she said. "It says you're hurt, angry, confused and maybe a little scared. Nobody knows what happened. The future is uncertain. You needed comfort and reassurance just like anyone else. Just like me."

"But, I loved her, Michelle," he insisted. "What kind of tribute is this to the woman I married three days ago?"

"It doesn't matter when you married her," she said. "She's gone now. And no amount of whining about the past is going to bring her back. We have to move on. We both have to move forward with our lives. You forget: I loved her too. She was my best friend. We're both going to grieve over her death. But, I'm not going to feel guilty over living a life after she's gone. I have nothing to feel bad about here. And, neither do you."

He rolled over a little in the bed. He rolled out from under her.

"It's not that easy for me," he muttered. "And, if you really cared about her, it wouldn't be easy for you either."

She looked over at him. She opened her mouth to speak. Then, she gave up with a sigh.

She slowly rose from the bed. She walked to the bathroom. She had to feel her way down the hall through the intimidating darkness.

He stayed in bed under the covers. They offered warmth. They seemed to offer security. He looked up at the ceiling.

It hurt to remember Karen. It pained him to think of what he had just done.

Yet, he couldn't put it out of his mind.

When she finished in the bathroom, she went to the sink. She could barely see her reflection in the mirror. It was too dark. Her face reflected back at her as a series of lighted stripes and shapes among abstract patterns of shadows and shades of darkness.

She washed her hands in the sink. Then, she bent down and rinsed her face in cool water. She listened to the water gurgle out of the faucet.

She tried to imagine who could've sent Karen the anonymous note about the affair. If it wasn't Cynthia, it would've had to have been Peter.

That made no sense. It couldn't have been Peter! Could it?

Could Peter be behind some or even all of the terrible things that had happened?

No! It was impossible, she thought. It just didn't make any sense!

She watched her face in the mirror. Then, she reached over to dry herself on the towel that was draped over the towel rack to her left.

She glanced back in the mirror.

She gasped with fright.

There appeared to be a shadow standing a few feet behind her in the mirror. She couldn't make out who the person was. But, you couldn't mistake that bridal veil. It was covered in a thick coat of blood!

She spun around to face the shadow.

But, it was gone.

She shrieked in terror. She ran toward the bedroom. She was still screaming.

He hopped out of bed and met her at the bedroom door. She jumped into his arms.

"What's the matter, Michelle?" he asked.

"I saw her!" she sobbed into his shoulder. "Oh, my God! I saw her!"

"Who?" he asked as he held her. "Who did you see?"

"Karen!" she cried. "I saw Karen!"

"Karen?" he asked with surprise. "That's impossible! Karen's dead, Michelle!"

"It was her," she insisted amid a wave of tears. "It was just a shadow in the mirror! I couldn't really make out her face! But, I recognized that veil from her wedding! It was soaked in blood! Just like it was at the reception! It was Karen! Oh, my God! It was Karen!"

He was confused. He felt a chill up his spine.

The girl in his arms was trembling. Something had obviously frightened her.

"Even if it was her," he questioned. "How could she get in?"

"It was her!" she wept. "It was Karen!"

After a few moments, he reached over and turned on the lights. He looked around. Nothing seemed out of place.

He let go of the girl who clung to him.

"Okay," he said. "I don't know what's going on. But, I'll go and investigate. I'll check out the whole place to see if I find anything. Wait here."

"Don't you dare leave me alone!" she practically screamed. "I'm going with you!"

He turned on the light in the hall. Together, they made their way cautiously down toward the bathroom.

"Where did you see her?" he asked.

"In the bathroom mirror," she said. "I was standing at the sink. She was just outside the door. But when I turned around, she was gone."

"She's not there now," he said.

"Of course, not!" she said impatiently. "I just told you she disappeared! She could be anywhere in the apartment!"

"All right," he said. "Calm down. If anyone's here, we'll find her."

"I have to tell you," she said shakily. "That veil really freaked me out!"

"Don't worry," he said. "You're safe with me."

He turned on the bathroom light. He didn't expect to find anything. But he remained alert as he glanced around the small room. No one was there... not even in the tub.

He turned on the living room lights. He wanted to make sure each room was well lit before he entered.

"Do you see anything?" she asked.

"No," he said. "I think you must have been seeing things. Talking about Karen and Cynthia must have gotten you all worked up."

"I know what I saw, Peter!"

"Let me look around a little more," he said with an agitated sigh.

He searched the living room and kitchen. He checked cupboards and closets. He stayed tense and expectant as he opened every door.

However, he found nothing out of place.

"I'm sorry, Michelle," he finally said. "There are no ghosts here."

"She was there, Peter," she insisted. "I saw her in the mirror! I swear to God!"

"Listen, honey," he said in the most soothing tone he could muster. "Karen's death has taken a toll on all of us. Believe me. I know. And that ridiculous story Cynthia's boyfriend told about her disappearance was a childish, irresponsible way of covering up his own actions."

"I saw her, Peter!" she persisted. Tears welled up in her eyes. "I know it sounds crazy! I wouldn't believe it either, if someone else suggested it! But, I really saw her! That veil looked just like it did at the reception! I saw it as clear as day!"

"Sshhh," he said. He took her into his arms. She allowed him to hold her as he told her, "I know you think you saw her, sweetie. But, believe me. It was just your nerves. Everything's fine now."

She clung tightly to him. He could feel her still trembling as he held her.

"What if it was really her?" she asked. "What if Karen really is watching us?"

"Now you really are being crazy," he said.

"She could be watching us right now!" she gasped.

She pulled away from him. She started glancing nervously about the room.

"You're overreacting," he told her. He took her back into his arms. "You're letting your imagination run wild. Maybe you're finally feeling some guilt over what we just did. I wouldn't blame you."

"This isn't guilt, Peter!" she insisted. "I saw Karen! Why won't you believe me?"

"Because it's preposterous," he stated. "Karen is dead. And there are no such things as ghosts who go around taking revenge on people."

"You're right, I suppose," she sighed. "Maybe I am getting carried away. Maybe I'm even feeling a twinge of guilt. After all, Karen was my best friend. I didn't mean for this to be an act of disrespect towards her."

"Of course not," he agreed.

"We've always had a little something between us, Peter," she said. "You know that. I've always stayed away for Karen's sake. But, the attraction has always been there. Then when Karen died, I guess I got confused."

"I understand."

"I was distraught," she continued. "I was sad over Karen, but I still had feelings for you. And being with you was almost like having Karen near. Or maybe sharing a part of her with someone close."

"That's okay," he said. "So, what would you like to do now?"

"I don't know," she said. "I can't stay here! But, I don't want to go home, either. I don't want to be alone."

"I thought we covered that," he said. "Whatever you saw is gone. It's over."

"Peter!" she averred. "Whatever that was, it almost scared me to death!"

"So, what do you want to do?"

"I don't know," she said. "I need to calm down. Maybe if I had some tea it would help."

"Alright," he said. "I'll stay in the kitchen with you. We'll have some tea. Nobody can bother you if we stay together. You'll be safe with me. Okay?"

"Okay," she said with a fragile smile. "Thank you, Peter."

He kept his arm around her shoulder as he walked her to the kitchen.

It was a sharp, annoying darkness. It was almost beautiful in a way. Still, it had a rude countenance like a spoiled Hollywood starlet. Just being outside on a night like this could make a person feel oddly and inexplicably uncomfortable. The pale moon and stars did not want to bow to the will of such a darkness. Yet, they stayed still in their places as if under obligation to a contract.

His apartment was well furnished. Even now, she had to wonder how he had paid for such extravagances. And still, he lived in this neighborhood.

She wondered. And still, she stayed seated on the sofa.

"I thought you would've enjoyed dancing tonight," he said.

He handed her a glass of wine.

"I did," she said. "I enjoyed it very much."

She watched him sit beside her.

"Then, what's the problem?" he asked. "You didn't seem like you were having a good time. You've been distracted all evening."

"I told you," she reminded. "I had another big argument with my husband just before I left the house tonight."

"I know," he said. "That's why I took you dancing. To take your mind off your troubles."

"To be fair, Grant," she said. "You didn't take me as much as I took you."

"What do you mean?" he asked. "It was my idea to go. I drove. I chose the club. I did everything you could have wanted."

"Yes," she said. "But, who paid for everything?"

"What?" he asked with surprise. "I paid for dinner, didn't I?"

"But, who paid for everything else?" she asked.

"What is this all about?" he questioned. "Is this because of your husband? I thought you were happy with our little arrangement."

"I am," she said. "I guess. Sort of."

He leaned over. He put an arm around her for damage control. He looked into her eyes.

"You know how I feel about you, Madeline," he said. "Don't listen to your husband. He'll say anything just to break us up. He just doesn't want to lose you. I can't blame the little bugger. The thought of losing you would drive me crazy, too."

"But, some of the things he says," she explained.

As she looked into his eyes, it became difficult to remain firm.

"The first time he called you a gigolo," she said. "It just made me so angry. But now, every time I pay for something…"

"You've always paid because you wanted to," he interjected. "And, you only paid *when* you wanted to. I never forced you to pay for anything."

"But, I do pay for almost everything," she persisted.

"That was always our arrangement," he said. "But, that can change if you want. I make decent money in the insurance business. I can afford to pay a lot more than I do. You always offered to pay for things, because you have access to much greater resources than I do."

"Well…" she began.

She could already feel herself crumbling beneath the persuasive allure of his gaze.

"Joshua is a doctor," she continued sheepishly. "He makes a fortune."

"That's what you've always said, sweetheart," he gently reminded. "So, what's the problem? I was just going along with you."

"But, I only offer because…" she continued.

She managed to look away. She needed to glance down at her lap.

Then, she intentionally gazed off toward the kitchen.

"Because," she made herself press forward. "I don't want to lose you."

"You won't lose me," he assured her. "I'm not going anywhere. I told you, Madeline. I love you, sweetie. I'm here for the duration."

"You say that," she persisted. "But, how do I know for sure?"

He kissed her with all the persuasive allure of his gaze.

"I love you, Madeline," he coaxed. "You can believe that."

The next kiss was long and affirming.

When she finally pulled away, she glanced back down at the carpet.

"I hate the way things have turned between Joshua and me," she said. "He gets so angry. And, I've never seen him act so demanding."

"The thought of losing a woman like you," he said. "It's easy to understand how he must feel."

"The things he says," she continued. "He gets so mean and callous. And, the way he makes me feel when we argue. He brings out the worst in me. I say things to him that I can't even believe when the words come out of my mouth."

"Residual passion," he postulated. "You used to have a strong love for each other. There's bound to be some leftover crumbs of what you once had together.

But now, whatever is still there can only turn to animosity."

"He's supposed to be a psychiatrist," she said. "Acting the way he does should be so beneath him."

"He's still a man."

"I want out," she said. "I want to just leave him. But, I wish there was a way to do it without all this hostility."

"Sometimes," he said. "It's hard to avoid those feelings. That's why it's best to just make a clean break."

She looked back up at him. She searched for resolution.

"Grant?" she asked meekly. "Are we doing the right thing?"

"Of course we are, sweetheart."

"Are you sure you really want…"

He interrupted her with a kiss. It was the kiss he knew she was hoping for.

"I'm sure I really want," he whispered. "The same thing you want. We both want it, and we can have it if you just believe. Stay strong, Madeline. All you have to do is go through with the divorce, just like you planned. Once you take him for everything he's got, we can get out of Thorn Ridge and never look back."

"But, what if I don't get his money?" she asked.

"You will."

"But, what if I don't?" she questioned. "What if it wasn't even an option? Would you still love me? I want to hear you say it, Grant."

He looked into her eyes again.

"Of course I would," he said. "I keep telling you. I'd love you no matter what. But when we have Joshua's money, we can do anything and go anywhere we want. We can both reach the dreams we've worked so long and hard to attain. Together! You want us both to reach our dreams together, don't you?"

"Yes, but..."

"Then, stop doubting yourself," he advised. "Stop doubting me! Stop doubting *us*! Stay with me, honey! And, we'll both achieve our dreams."

The next kiss transported her to the dream she sought. Once again they found a way to find comfort and certainty. Once again he found a way to erase all doubt from her mind...

...At least for the evening.

Chapter 7
Warped Little Psychopath

Dense clouds clogged the sky like cholesterol hardening against the wall of an artery. A cool, October rain drizzled down upon the streets of Thorn Ridge. The rain was just an annoyance. It made the roads slippery and dampened people's spirits. It did nothing to cleanse or freshen.

It just was!

She busied herself with a few mindless tasks around the office. She kept her eye on the clock. She couldn't help feeling a little jittery. However, she kept her focus on the files spread out before her.

"Good morning, Angela," he said.

She looked up and smiled. "Hi, Neil," she said.

She leapt out of her chair and threw her arms around him. With a degree of pleasant surprise, he returned the hug.

"How are you?" she asked. "I was worried about you when you left with the cops yesterday. Are you all right? What happened?"

As she realized what she had done, she pulled away from him. Her face turned bright red with embarrassment.

"Oh, I'm sorry," she stammered nervously. "I shouldn't have done that."

"That's okay," he said. "I'm fine. I have a good lawyer. And, those cops had no reason to hold me. They were just blowing smoke because they still have no solid leads. I'll explain everything at the meeting."

"You are innocent, aren't you?" she asked.

"Of course," he smiled. "I keep telling the cops they should go after Zeblonsky, but I guess that would be as obvious as looking for their nose in the middle of their face. They seem to hate easy answers."

"I wonder why."

"Who knows?" he said. "So, are you looking forward to our upcoming meeting?"

"Not really," she admitted. "I haven't even been working here for two weeks. It can't look good for me to be caught in the middle of this kind of controversy already."

"Why?" he asked. "It's not your fault. Zeblonsky is the only one who caused any problems. Frankly, I'm looking forward to getting all this out in the open. With any luck, maybe we can fire the little creep."

"Well, I'd hate to be responsible for anyone losing their jobs," she said.

"You're not responsible," he said. "He did it to himself with his own actions. You're the victim here, Angela."

"Even so," she said. "I'm not going to enjoy this."

"We'd better get going," he said. "It's just about 10:30."

They walked to the meeting room. It had a few pictures on the wall. There was a computer in the corner. Most of the room was taken up by a long wooden table which was surrounded by sixteen comfortable chairs.

When everyone involved took a seat, a familiar older man closed the door and sat at the head of the table.

"Hello, everyone," he addressed. "I believe we all know each other. And, I believe we all know why we're here. As Angela's supervisor, I have been asked to head this meeting. Dylan and Neil were both involved in this incident. So, they are accompanied by their supervisors, Rick Nadler and Joe McMahon. Would you like to start, Angela?"

"Thank you, Steve," she said. "I was in the Archives Room doing some filing when Dylan walked in. I remembered some more pressing work that I needed to attend to as he entered, so I said 'hi' and politely excused myself. But, he wouldn't let me leave."

"I knew what kind of filing you were doing," Dylan piped in. "You were nowhere near being done. You just wanted to leave because it was me."

"Dylan..." Rick began.

"It's the truth," Dylan continued. "You wouldn't have had anything more pressing if anyone else had entered the room."

"Yes I would have," she argued.

"You wouldn't have had something more important to do if *Neil* had entered," Dylan insisted.

"That's enough, Dylan!" Rick ordered.

"Everyone here does this to me all the time," Dylan said. "Any time I enter a room, everybody has something more important to do than talk to me. They can talk *about* me! Behind my back! They can laugh, and make up stories!"

"I'm sure you're exaggerating," Steve said.

"No I'm not!" Dylan went on. "Don't patronize me! All I was doing was asking Angela why she's so scared of me. I only wanted her to answer one simple question. But she was too busy trying to run away from me to give me the simple, common courtesy that any human being deserves!"

"You wouldn't let me leave!" Angela argued. "I told you that you were scaring me! I begged you to let me leave, and you wouldn't!"

"What did I do that was so terrible, Angela?" he asked. "I said 'hello.' I asked why you needed to leave so quickly. I asked you to talk to me for a few seconds. Is that so horrible? Is the simple act of treating me like a human being too much to ask?"

"You wouldn't let me leave," she persisted. "Even when I threatened to scream. You scared the hell out of me, Dylan!"

"But, why?" he asked. "Why did you threaten to scream? Don't you see where I'm coming from? How would you feel if people refused to even talk to you? How would you feel if everyone treated you like you were some sort of disease that needs to be avoided? How would you feel if you could constantly hear people laughing at you behind your back? How would you feel if people threatened to scream just because you asked them a simple question?"

There was a heavy pause. She couldn't answer.

"I've done nothing to you people," Dylan averred. "And, everybody in this room is guilty of treating me like crap! You've all talked about me! You've all given me those looks! And, it's gotten worse since Karen got killed. Everybody just naturally assumes that I'm a logical suspect to her murder!"

"Well, Karen's death has taken a toll on all of us, Dylan," Steve said. "It was a brutal surprise that has put everyone on edge. There are bound to be certain rumors."

"And, they're all pointed at me!"

"There may be some people…" Steve began.

"It's everybody!" Dylan spouted. "All the time! And, I'm sick of it! I've done nothing to deserve this! I'm a damned good worker, aren't I?"

"Yes you are," Rick said. "You've always done a fine job."

"So, why must I be subjected to this treatment?" Dylan said. "That's all I was trying to do. I asked Angela because she's still new here. She hasn't had as much time to be corrupted by the likes of Worthington and his pals."

"But you do understand," Rick said. "That you can only impose yourself on someone to a limited extent. Once Angela told you she was scared, you had an obligation to back off. You won't win any friends by cornering girls in dark, secluded rooms."

"I didn't mean to corner her," Dylan said. "And, I didn't mean to scare her. I don't mind apologizing to her if I went too far. I do owe her that much. I'm sorry, Angela. I didn't mean to cause you any distress.

And, I'm sorry about your arm. I hope you can forgive me. And, I hope you can understand why I was so persistent."

"Well... maybe... I don't know."

"Let's move on to the subject of your arm, Angela," Steve directed. "How are you feeling today?"

"Not bad, I guess."

"You told me," Steve reminded. "That you backed into a file cabinet because Dylan scared you. But, you said it was not a result of his trying to make actual contact."

"I suppose," she reluctantly agreed. "But when I found I was bleeding, I asked Dylan to help me. And, all he did was stand there staring at me like some sort of maniac."

"Let's try to avoid name-calling," Steve advised. "Okay, Angela?"

"But, he looked really spooky," she insisted. "It was like he enjoyed watching me bleed. It looked like he was getting some sort of sick thrill from it."

"It just caught me by surprise," Dylan defended. "It confused me. I didn't expect it. Maybe I felt a little guilty."

"And, that's when you began to scream?" Steve asked.

"Of course," Angela said. "Dylan was already freaking me out. Then I was in pain, I was bleeding and he was just gawking at me."

"I wasn't gawking," Dylan argued. "I told you I was confused."

"And, that's where you came in, Mr. Worthington?" Steve asked.

"Yes," Neil said. "I heard Angela screaming, so I went in to see what was wrong."

"And, what did you see?" Steve asked.

"Angela was on the verge of tears," Neil said. "She was scared to pieces, she was bleeding and Dylan had her cornered and wouldn't let her leave."

"I didn't have her cornered!" Dylan insisted.

"That's how it looked," Neil said.

"Why don't you tell them what really happened?" Dylan averred. "You came charging in there like you were some super hero, so you could impress your little girlfriend here! You ordered me to leave and threatened to bash my 'F'ing' brains in!"

"Angela was terrified and bleeding!" Neil argued. "You were obviously not trying to help! You looked like you were threatening her!"

"I did not!" Dylan spat back. "I was just standing there! You were the only one who was threatening anybody! And, you called me a warped little psychopath!"

"Did I?" Neil asked. "Oh well. That's okay. You *are* a warped little psychopath!"

"Neil," Joe warned. "We discussed your behavior before the meeting."

"You should have seen him, Joe," Neil defended. "You should have seen how petrified Angela looked."

"Oh, you are so full of it!" Dylan demanded. "You were just trying to impress your little girlfriend because you want her! I wish you two would get a room and get it over with already!"

"Dylan!" Rick warned.

"Angela's not my girlfriend!" Neil argued. "I have a girlfriend! Or should I say I *had* one! But, she disappeared! And I think we all know who's responsible!"

"What the hell does that mean?" Dylan growled.

"You know exactly what it means!" Neil spat back.

"Do you see, Mr. Callahan?" Dylan inquired. "This is precisely why I was trying to talk to Angela in the first place."

"Well, you did corner Angela in a dark back room," Steve reasoned.

"I didn't mean to," Dylan said.

"That's the kind of behavior that scares people," Neil pointed out. "Do you want to know why people don't like you? There's your answer. You do things like that. And you're always lurking about in places where you don't belong. You just suddenly appear out of nowhere."

"At least I didn't have the cops haul me out of here in handcuffs," Dylan shot back.

"I was never in handcuffs," Neil corrected impatiently. "They just wanted me to go downtown to answer some questions."

"They asked me questions too," Dylan said. "But, they didn't have to haul me down to the police station."

"That's enough, Dylan," Rick said. "What happened with the police, Neil?"

"There's not much to tell," Neil said. "They found it suspicious that I didn't report my girlfriend's disappearance right away. But when I found out she had cheated on me, it hit me kind of hard. And between Karen's death and the weird phone call about bloody veils, everything caught up to me. I needed a moment to sort things out."

"And, the fact that your girlfriend was either missing or dead meant nothing?" Dylan poked.

"I'm not going to warn you again, Dylan," Rick averred. "Your job is hanging by a thread right now. Keep quiet."

"Go on, Neil," Joe invited. "What did you tell the police?"

"What can I say?" Neil shrugged. "I told them what I just told you. I told them where I went. The cops bullied and yelled. My expensive lawyer told them to leave me alone. They had nothing, and I'm innocent. So, they let me go."

"Well, we're all glad to see you back, son," Joe said.

"Thanks."

There was a pause that grew very uncomfortable.

"Well, Dylan and Neil," Steve finally said. "It seems you both have sufficient grounds for dismissal. Dylan cornered Angela, refused to back off and scared her half to death. Neil threatened Dylan with serious bodily harm. I guess the only fair thing to do is fire the both of you. Will that make everyone happy?"

No one spoke.

"Well, what do you say?" Steve pressed. "Should we fire both of you or neither of you? Which would you prefer?"

Still, no one replied.

"The way I see it," Steve said. "You are both basically good employees. I'd hate to lose either one of you. Rick and Joe? Don't you agree?"

The supervisors nodded in agreement.

"So, Angela," Steve said. "I realize Dylan scared you, but he apologized. And, I'm sure he sees that he should never make anyone feel scared or trapped ever again. And, if anyone asks you to let them leave, you won't stand in their way. Isn't that right, Dylan?"

"Yes."

"So, can we put this behind us, Angela?" Steve asked. "We all feel bad about what happened to you. But if you choose to have us fire Dylan, I'm sure he'll press his option to have us fire Neil as well. And we'll have to agree. It's only fair. Let's face it. Dylan has a strong case against him. What will it be, Angela? Should we fire both of them or none of them?"

After a few moments of consideration, Angela reluctantly said, "None of them."

"You're telling me," Dylan said. "That Neil is not going to get fired for threatening to bash my brains in?"

"Angela is willing to forgive you," Steve said. "And you have learned your lesson, Neil? You realize you were wrong?"

"He was threatening her!" Neil insisted.

"I was not!"

"Neil!" Joe commanded. "You know the rules! You can not threaten any employees at any time! You can either apologize to Dylan for your deplorable behavior, or I can exercise my right to fire you for your unsuitable actions. Then, we can keep Dylan, and everyone's conscience will be clear. Is that understood?"

"Yes," Neil muttered. "I'm sorry, Dylan. I shouldn't have threatened you."

"It's easy to understand why tempers are running a little high," Steve said. "Karen's murder affected us all very deeply. And of course, Neil has the added burden of his girlfriend's disappearance. I think everyone overreacted a bit."

There was a contemplative pause.

"And, Mr. Zeblonsky raised a valid point," Steve continued. "There is an issue with the way certain people are treated in the workplace. These issues need to be addressed. But, we should all reassess the way we behave toward our coworkers. There are no clear winners or losers in this incident. I just hope we can all learn from our mistakes and try to create more pleasant conditions for everyone around us."

There was another pause. No one could feel truly victorious.

"Well then," Steve said. "If there is no further business, I believe we're finished. Thank you for your time and cooperation, everyone. I hope that we can all put this little incident behind us and resume our duties as mature professionals in a harmonious work environment. I hope there will be no hard feelings. Thanks again, and have a good day."

Everyone stood and filed out of the room.

Neil allowed Joe to get back to his office before addressing him.

He followed his supervisor into his private office. He closed the door behind him.

"I still can't believe it," he said. "That little scum bucket is going to get away with what he did to Angela. He should've been fired!"

"You too," Joe said. "Weren't you listening to Steve Callahan? Neither one of you behaved in an appropriate manner. I guarantee Dylan is having this same conversation with Rick Nadler even as we speak. I don't think either one of you learned your lesson."

"You weren't there, Joe!" he insisted. "Angela was terrified!"

"I'm sure Dylan didn't mean to harm her," Joe said. "Although, I can picture Angela freaking out a little."

"Zeblonsky is a creepy little guy," Neil said.

"But, he's basically a decent worker," Joe said. "And, he had a point when he complained about how some people treat him. And, that includes you. You have a responsibility to act in a professional manner at all times to all people. Is that understood?"

"Yes sir."

"We all have to face things we find disagreeable," Joe said. "I've been interviewing candidates for Karen's replacement all week. Despite the constant nauseating reminder that she's dead, the applicants have all been unsuitable."

"Really?" Neil asked. "What's wrong with them?"

"To start with," Joe said. "All the applicants have been women. We already have too many girls in this office. They tend to be catty, unpredictable and undependable. Women can't work with other girls. The constant bickering drives me up a wall."

"I know what you mean," Neil snickered. "Still, girls have their uses. And this is 2005. You have to keep up with the times."

"I know," Joe admitted. "I guess I'm still a little old-fashioned. I'm sure a decent candidate will come along. And if I have to hire a girl, so be it. But, I hope I see someone with acceptable qualifications soon. I hate this part of the job."

"If you don't like hiring women," Neil asked. "How did you end up having so many of them working under you?"

"I was promoted to this position," Joe said. "Most of these girls were hired before I got this job. Including Karen."

"Well, you better get used to working with girls," Neil said. "It's part of the territory. You'll just have to cope."

"Don't I know it," Joe laughed.

Neil needed to take a little walk when he left his boss's office. After crossing a few large rooms packed with cubicles, he found himself in a more amicable setting.

"Hi, Angela," he said.

She looked up from the work on her desk. "Hi, Neil," she smiled. "How did you like the outcome of our meeting this morning?"

"It could've been worse, I suppose," he said. "But, I was more worried about you. Are you okay with how things turned out?"

"Well," she began cautiously. "Part of me would have been happier if Dylan had gotten fired. But, I don't enjoy seeing anyone get canned on my account. Mostly,

I didn't press the issue because of you. I didn't want to see you get fired just for trying to protect me."

"You could still push this, if you wanted," he advised.

"I don't think so," she said. "I'll let it go. Dylan apologized. He was told not to do it again. Maybe I did overreact. Maybe we all did. I'm still new here. I don't want to make too many waves."

"It's your decision," he said. "But, I think you're a nut if you let him get away with what he did."

"Like I said," she reminded. "I'm still new here. I need this job. Please just drop it."

"Okay."

He glanced down at the floor. After a pause, he added, "It's pretty funny what Dylan said about us, isn't it? You know, about you and I having a thing for each other?"

"Uh, yes," she said nervously. "It was pretty funny."

"I have to admit," he said. "I was thinking about asking you to have dinner with me tonight, though. Just as friends, of course. I was just worried about how you are after the results of the meeting."

"Dinner?" she asked cautiously. "I don't know. This is kind of sudden. Besides, aren't you concerned about your girlfriend? She's still missing, isn't she?"

"Of course I'm concerned," he stated. "Every minute she's missing decreases the chance that we'll find her alive. It's tearing me up inside. But as I said, this is just a friendly dinner. I could use some sympathetic female company."

"I'm the only girl you could ask?"

"No," he said. "But, you're the girl I most want to ask."

"I'm still not sure it's a good idea," she said.

"Listen," he confided. "Obviously, Cynthia and I were having our problems. She wouldn't have cheated on me otherwise. We were heading for a breakup anyway. But, I'm still frantic about what happened to her. I can't take it anymore. I just want some company for dinner. I was hoping it could be you."

"Well..." she said as she thought. "I'll mull it over and give you an answer later. Is that okay?"

"Thank you, Angela," he smiled. "That's all I ask."

As soon as he was gone, a coworker ran up behind her.

"I just saw Neil ask you out to dinner," she practically giggled. "You're going to take him up on it, aren't you?"

"I don't know, Sarah," she said impatiently. "Why?"

"Just curious," Sarah said. "That's all. You should go, Angela. It's about time you two love birds got together."

"We're not love birds," she insisted. "It's just a friendly dinner."

"Of course it is," Sarah nodded with mock sincerity. "I can't wait to tell Jennifer. She'll be so happy for you."

"Please don't tell Jennifer," she begged. "All sorts of rumors will be flying around from here to China."

"Don't be ridiculous," Sarah scoffed. "I'll tell her in confidence. Jennifer can keep a secret. She won't tell a soul."

"Right!" She rolled her eyes sarcastically. "Jennifer can keep a secret! When it comes to rumors, she's as harmless as a hurricane."

"Don't worry," Sarah reassured her. "We'll keep everything under wraps. Gotta go. Keep me updated. See ya."

Angela just shook her head as Sarah hurried out of the room.

❦ ❦ ❦

He picked up the phone and dialed the number. He waited for a response.

Then he said, "Hello, Mr. Polopous. This is Joshua Freitag. How are you?"

"Not bad," Polopous said. "I must say I'm surprised to hear from you, Doctor. I thought our business was concluded. What can I do for you?"

"How would you like to do one more little project for me?" he asked. "It would just be for tonight. You'll be well paid, of course."

"I'm intrigued," Polopous said. "I'm in the middle of another case right now. But, I might be able to tear myself away. What do you need?"

"All I need you to do," he explained. "Is follow Langley and my wife tonight. Call me when they're headed to his place for the night. Give me a few minutes warning before they get there. Just call when they're headed home. I'll give you one night's fee and I'll throw in an extra $2,500.00 for your trouble."

169

"From the sound of it," Polopous said. "I think I deserve an extra $5,000.00 for my trouble, Doctor."

"Why, Mr. Polopous," he commented. "If I didn't know better, I'd swear you were trying to take advantage of my generosity and good nature."

"Not at all," Polopous said. "But, it sounds like you're planning something unscrupulous, despite my warning. If you get caught, my livelihood as well as my good reputation could be in danger."

"You will never be in danger," he assured. "Everything is covered. Nobody knows of your involvement. You are totally in the clear."

"My fee stands."

"As you wish," he sighed. "I will call you shortly to confirm. As soon as you call to say Langley is headed home, your job is done. You can let me know about payment arrangements at your discretion."

"I'll be waiting for your call, Doctor."

He hung up.

❧ ❧ ❧

It was just before lunch when he knocked on the office door. When he was invited to enter, he opened the door and went inside. He closed the door behind him for privacy.

"Hello, Mr. McMahon," he said.

"Oh... hello, Dylan," Joe said. "What can I do for you?"

"I know this probably isn't the best time," he said. "But, I was wondering when we could discuss the raise you promised to look into for me."

"A raise?" Joe asked. "Are you kidding me? You want to discuss a raise?"

"You promised to talk to Rick Nadler for me," he reminded.

"Are you insane?" Joe asked. "Do you realize what just happened here today, Dylan? It's an absolute miracle you didn't lose your job!"

"Nevertheless," he said. "You promised you would pull some strings for me if I did certain favors for you."

"That was before all this nasty business with you and Angela Pierce," Joe said. "By the way, what were you thinking? How do you think you deserve to keep your job after scaring that poor girl half to death?"

"We went through all this at the meeting," he reiterated. "All I did was try to talk to her. You don't know what it's like. People are always treating me like shit. And, it's been worse since Karen was killed. Everybody thinks I killed her."

"That will all blow over in time," Joe said.

"But the fact remains," he said. "I have to deal with it now."

"I'm sorry to hear that, Dylan," Joe said. "But, there's nothing I can do."

"You owe me, Mr. McMahon!"

"I know," Joe said. "And, I will take care of it when I can. But, you have to give the agency time to cool off after the Angela incident."

"It wasn't an incident!"

"Are you blind?" Joe argued. "Were you even at that meeting today? People wanted to fire you! Angela wanted to fire you! And, no one can blame her! You say

171

I owe you? I've been covering for you since yesterday! I worked my ass off both in and out of the meeting to keep you employed here!"

"And, what about me?" he persisted. "Do you know what I've done for you? It's not just the people here who think I killed Karen! The cops have been bothering me too!"

"Well, I'm sorry," Joe muttered. "But, I don't have time for this. I have to leave. I have some things to take care of this afternoon."

"I got paint on my tires from the parking lot of that hotel last week," he informed him. "Remember? When I went to the hotel to check the company that ran their security cameras?"

"Keep your voice down!"

"I did that for you, Mr. McMahon!" he reminded. "You promised me if I could hack into their system and blank out their cameras for you, you'd fix a raise for me with Rick Nadler!"

"Not so loud!" Joe ordered. "I had every intention of keeping my promise."

"I only went to the hotel so I could find out what company ran their cameras," he went on. "It's a good thing I knew about the hotel's lunch buffet. If I hadn't eaten there, the cops would have nailed me for having paint on my tires!"

"You screwed yourself," Joe pointed out. "When you cornered Angela. Now you'll have to wait for your raise. I can't go to Rick now. He'd laugh in my face!"

"The cops questioned me in front of my mother," he said. "My mother! Do you know what that's like? And believe me. My mother's the living bitch queen from Hell! But, I kept my mouth shut. I covered for you, because you promised me a raise. Not to mention a transfer out of that office."

"You obviously don't understand..."

"Oh, I understand a lot of things," he interrupted. "I understand that you lead a charmed life. No one seems to remember that incident with you and Karen two years ago when she spurned your advances. She almost brought you up on charges, but Steve Callahan swept everything under the rug and the whole incident was hushed up,"

"Watch your mouth, Dylan!"

"Have you been stalking Karen all this time, Mr. McMahon?" he asked.

"No!"

"Neil's girlfriend was a friend of the bride," he reminded. "Is that what she remembered when she called him Monday? You were there when Neil got that phone call. Is that why his girlfriend disappeared?"

"I have no idea what happened to that girl!" Joe insisted.

"Where did you hide the body, Mr. McMahon?"

"Nowhere!" Joe bellowed. "I had nothing to do with that!"

"The Maid of Honor was Karen's best friend, wasn't she?" he pressed. "I wonder how much she knows. She must know something. I wonder how long it will take her to remember."

"Get out of my office!"

"Will she be the next person to disappear, Mr. McMahon?" he continued with a smug grin. "You can't keep everyone from remembering. Your good luck can't hold out forever. Some day, too many people will remember."

"I could crush you like the parasite that you are!" Joe warned. "If you try to cross me, you will pay, Zeblonsky!"

"Oh, don't worry about me," he said. "I'll keep quiet. After all, I guess I'm an accomplice. Your secret is safe with me as long as I keep my job and get my raise."

"You'll have to wait at least a few months before a raise is even a possibility," Joe said. "And that's even if I still feel like getting one for you."

"Oh, you *will* get me my raise," he averred. "And a transfer. And, don't even try to threaten me, Mr. McMahon. Believe me when I tell you I have a dark side. And, my dark side is very... very dark!"

There was a look in his eyes that Joe found unsettling.

Then, he turned and left the office.

He quickly made his way to a place where he could have some privacy. Then, he took out his cell phone and dialed.

"Hello?" said a voice on the other end.

"Hi, Dr. Freitag," he said. "This is Dylan. I would be glad to have a late lunch with you, as long as I'm not being charged for the time. I would love to hear what you have planned."

"Excellent, Dylan," said the doctor. "How would you like to meet me at The Belmont on Saxon St. at 2:00?"

"Can we make it 2:30?" he asked. "I have a few things to take care of first."

"2:30 it is," the doctor said. "See you then."

Meanwhile, Joe walked casually out of his office.

"Hi, Joe," Neil smiled. "What did Zeblonsky want?"

"Oh, nothing," Joe said. "He's still griping about the meeting. I told you I don't think either one of you has learned your lesson. If you two don't learn to get along, one of you is going to get fired. I hope it isn't you."

"Don't worry," Neil said. "I'll be good. Where are you going?"

"I'm leaving for the day," Joe said. "I have some personal business this afternoon."

"Well, have a good day."

"That's what I'm hoping for."

She was feeling much better. Whatever she'd seen the previous night was just a figment of her imagination. Perhaps the story of Cynthia's disappearance had gotten to her. Maybe she felt guilty for sleeping with Peter.

Who knows?

She still felt a twinge of guilt. After all, Karen had been her best friend. But, Karen was gone now. Nothing could bring her back.

She and Peter were both absolutely heartbroken over their loss. If they were able to find consolation and comfort in each other's arms, who was it really hurting?

Certainly not Karen!

She was happy to be back in her own apartment. Last night's vision was fading into distant memory like a bad dream.

That's all it was...

... Just a bad dream.

The wake was scheduled for the next day. The funeral would be the following day. She knew she would be going through a box or two of tissues.

But, that was still 24 hours away. She still had tonight with Peter. She was supposed to meet him back at his place in just a few hours. They would console each other all night long.

Still, she hoped no one would suspect anything at the wake or funeral. They would have to stay distant and aloof.

It was only a matter of respect for the families. It was a matter of being tasteful and discrete.

However, it was not her immediate concern. At the moment, she wanted to relax with a nice, long, hot shower. She turned the water on in her tub. She listened to the water spraying out of the shower head.

Then, she went to her bedroom. She gathered up the clothes she had chosen. She laid them out carefully on the bed. She wanted to give the water in the shower plenty of time to heat up.

She really was feeling much better. She looked at her face in the mirror.

Then, it suddenly struck her!

How could she have forgotten? How could she have been so stupid? The answer had been right in front of her the whole time!

Karen had told her about that guy from work. What was his name?

He had scared her once or twice. She hadn't mentioned him recently, though. As Karen's friend, she should have remembered. Perhaps grief or the sudden shock of Karen's death had driven the thought from her mind.

Maybe she had been too concerned about Peter.

One way or the other, she should probably call the police. That detective left her his card, didn't he? Where had she put it?

Oh well. She had plenty of time to think about it after her shower.

She opened the shower curtain. Immediately, she was confronted by a soft, soothing cloud of steam rolling out from the hot spray of water.

That vision from the previous night had just been a bad dream. There was no such thing as ghosts!

Shadows wearing bloody bridal veils?

Ha! What a ridiculous notion! There was nothing to fear.

Without a care in the world, she stepped into the shower.

🌿 🌿 🌿

After ordering their lunch, they leaned back in the comfortable booth.

"Thanks for buying me lunch, Dr. Freitag," he said. "This is a pleasant surprise."

"Think nothing of it, Dylan," he said. "You've been a patient of mine for quite a while. You've put a lot of

177

money in my pocket. There's no reason why I can't spring for lunch once or twice."

"This is a beautiful restaurant, too," Dylan observed. "The Belmont, huh? I've driven by here thousands of times. But, I've never been inside. It's gorgeous in here."

"I'm glad you like it."

"So, what's going on, Doctor?" Dylan quizzed. "Why are you doing this? I'm sure you have a plan to help me with my, shall we say, 'abnormalities'?"

"I hate to use words like 'abnormalities'," he said. "You have unique ways of dealing with your insecurities, but I would hardly call you abnormal."

"Well, semantics aside," Dylan said. "What are you suggesting for me?"

The doctor took a moment to compose his thoughts.

"I'd like to propose a new technique of my own design," he said. "Whereby you delve into your weaknesses by indulging them."

"What do you mean?"

"Let's begin here," he began. "Why did you call me today? You seemed very anxious to start something radical. I'm guessing there have been developments at work. Didn't you tell me you got in trouble for confronting a woman at work? As I recall, you even enjoyed watching her bleed. What has happened since then?"

Dylan told him everything that had happened that day. He included the entire contents of the meeting as well as his discussions with Rick Nadler and Joe McMahon afterward.

Freitag listened intently without saying a word.

When his patient had finished, the doctor said, "Let me get this straight. You're telling me that you hacked into the security system of the motel? In exchange for which Joe McMahon promised to pull some strings to get you a raise, promotion and transfer as well as a certain cash payment of a thousand dollars?"

"Yes."

"You didn't know what he was planning?"

"Didn't know. Didn't care."

"Didn't it bother you when you heard about Karen's murder?" he asked.

"Why would it?" Dylan asked. "She meant nothing to me. She wouldn't even give me the time of day when she was alive."

"Do you have no regard for the sanctity of human life?" he asked.

"Sure," Dylan shrugged. "I would never actually hurt anybody. But, I'm not above doing a big favor for a big boss at work if it'll get me more money."

"But, you're an accomplice to murder!"

"Not intentionally," Dylan reasoned. "Who's going to know? Besides, it's not like I'm ever going to hurt anyone ever again."

"But, you're extremely angry at a number of people at work," he summed up. "You're mad at this Angela Pierce. But, the real targets of your animosity are that Neil Worthington fellow, and especially Joe McMahon."

"Joe made promises," Dylan said. "And, he ought to deliver. Sure, I got my thousand bucks, but I want the rest of my payment!"

"Surely, you see Joe's point," the doctor reasoned. "With all that has happened, you have to give the office time to simmer down."

"Why does everybody act like I did something wrong?" Dylan insisted. "All I did was try to talk to a girl. Why is that such a crime? I asked her what her problem was! And, everyone acts like I attacked her with a Samurai sword! I'm sorry she got scared! I apologized already! Get over it!"

"Well, let's move on to the problem at hand," he suggested. "There may be a way for you to channel your anger and use it to your benefit."

"How?"

"There are some interesting misconceptions and shortcomings in the field of psychiatry," he explained. "One of these is in the area of hypnosis. They say a person can't be hypnotized to do something he wouldn't ordinarily do. Such as, a person can't be conditioned to commit murder even under hypnosis."

"I've heard that."

"The problem with that theory," he continued. "Is that it only deals with the immediate conscious and subconscious parts of the mind. The ego, superego and id are all involved. But, it doesn't reach beyond the parts of the mind that are reasonably accessed through our limited capacity for memory."

"Okay," Dylan said. "I'm with you so far."

"Additionally, people only use about 15% of their brain," he went on. "The fact that some people are good with science or math while other people have a talent for art or even auto mechanics is just a matter of the slightest shift in which part of the brain that we use.

And much of the responsibility for these slight shifts lies in our conditioning."

"Really?"

"Well, other natural factors play a role, of course," he admitted. "Like genetic predisposition. But, my point is that much of the human brain's natural capacity has gone completely unexplored. And when we try to stretch beyond our self-imposed boundaries, our instinctive ties to violence is one of the first tendencies we run across."

"Instinctive ties to violence?"

"Man is a violent animal by nature," he expounded. "We were born to hunt. We may have developed the façade of a civilized society, but suits and ties and governments and machines and computers don't even begin to mask the true essence of our being. We haven't even begun to outgrow dreaming up reasons for violence and wars. Just look around you. Even politics, which is supposed to be the cornerstone of our civilized behavior, is a festering example of how we have not evolved in the slightest since the days when we first discovered fire."

"Assuming you're right," Dylan asked. "What are you proposing?"

"You cut yourself because you internalize your outward anger," he deduced. "Watching people bleed is a measured way of externalizing the rage that you naturally want to turn outward where you know it belongs. The problem is you were trained to suppress your anger."

"Suppressing my anger is a problem?" Dylan asked.

"Of course you can't unleash your rage at will," he allowed. "But, everyone needs a release."

"Like a hobby?"

"Sort of," he said. "That's recommended for most people. But, for you I was going to take a more radical approach. If you want to end your fears, you must confront the exaggerated limitations your environment has confined you to. Remember when I told you we were going to isolate and draw out your rage potential?"

"Yes."

"Take a look at this picture," he said. "What do you see?"

Dylan took the photo that Freitag handed him. "It's a man and a woman," he said.

"For you," the doctor said. "That man will be Joe McMahon."

"That's not Joe," Dylan corrected. "It doesn't look anything like him. He's much too young to be Joe."

"When you explore your rage potential," he said. "This man will become Joe for you."

Dylan looked at the doctor suspiciously. "Are you asking me to commit violence upon this man?" he asked.

"It won't be an issue of consciousness or conscience," he said. "I assure you. You won't be hypnotized per se. You will be 'reconditioned.'"

"Are you insane?" Dylan argued. "I've had the cops crawling all over me because of Karen's murder! Now you want me to actually kill someone?"

"You don't have to kill anyone," he explained. "It's all been planned and orchestrated. No one will know it's you. You can wear a mask and pretend it's a random robbery."

"You've got to be yanking me!" Dylan exclaimed. "For one thing, this seems highly illegal. Besides, I'm not a violent person."

"As I told you," he reminded. "You will be reconditioned."

"But, what about the woman?" Dylan questioned. "I don't even know who these people are!"

"That is inconsequential," he said. "You will be able to release the rage you feel against McMahon and the other people in your office. You will begin to confront the demon that limits your personal wellbeing and growth. You won't have to kill this man. But, I'm sure you will enjoy watching him bleed."

"But, this seems…"

"Trust me," he interrupted. "I'm a doctor. It's my job to make you better. I want to see you move toward a well-adjusted, normal life."

"But, are you sure…"

"Trust me, Dylan!"

He opened the front door with his key. He carried the plastic bags filled with groceries to the kitchen table. He didn't have to get much. But, there are a few things a person always seems to run out of.

He felt good… or at least as good as he could under the circumstances.

Of course, he was still utterly stricken with grief. Still, the previous night had been a gift from Heaven.

Michelle should be coming over soon. He could take her out for a quick dinner.

They shouldn't really go public. Frankly, he wasn't sure if they would continue seeing each other at all.

Still, he had something to look forward to this evening.

He put away the grocery items he had just purchased. It didn't take long. Then, it was time to get ready for his company.

He walked over to the bathroom. It was dark in the hallway. He turned on the light.

He looked in the mirror.

He opened the mirror and took out some toothpaste. He closed the mirror.

He turned on the water in the faucet.

He looked down while he squeezed some paste on his toothbrush. He picked up the toothbrush as he looked back into the mirror.

He gasped as he dropped the toothbrush into the sink.

The image in the mirror showed a shadow standing behind him. The image was about the basic size and shape of a person. However, he could not make out the face. And even though it was dripping with a thick coat of blood, he recognized the veil that his bride had worn at their wedding.

He froze. He just stared at the shadow with disbelief and fright.

Finally, he managed to spin around to face the apparition.

But, the shadow was gone!

His breathing was heavy. His heart was beating like synchronized thunder!

As he glanced around, it seemed as though everything was in order. He even looked back into the mirror to no avail.

The shadow had disappeared.

He even rubbed his eyes and looked again. It was no use. Whatever he'd seen had vanished.

He wanted to believe he had just imagined it. His mind was playing tricks on him. But, he had stared at it for over five seconds! It hadn't moved!

It was just there!

Even without a face, it seemed to resemble Karen a little.

A deep chill ran up his spine. Suddenly, he grew nervous. He needed to make a call. He needed to check on Michelle to see if she was alright.

The water was still running in the faucet. He turned it off.

Cautiously, he stepped out into the hall. He kept glancing around. He didn't want to run into any shadows with bloody veils.

Fortunately, there were none to be found.

When he reached the nearest phone, he made a quick call.

It rang once… twice… three times.

"Come on!" he said anxiously. "Answer the phone!"

After five rings, he got a voice mail message.

A strong sense of dread slowly filled his whole body.

He hung up the phone and ran out of the house. He jumped into his car and began racing toward her house as quickly as possible.

Along the way, he tried calling her on his cell phone again. He listened to it ring again and again.

"Please!" he begged desperately. "For the love of God, answer the phone!"

When the voice mail message came on, he hung up. He swore under his breath.

He sped past intersections and maneuvered through reckless lane changes. His mind tried to calm itself.

Shadows? Bloody bridal veils?

It couldn't be!

It was just an illusion. All the stories he had heard must have gotten to him. She would be alright.

She had to be!

What could possibly happen?

But as he drew nearer to his house, his sense of disaster grew stronger. His muscles grew tense. He could feel that something was wrong!

He parked his car by the curb. He ran up to her front door. He knocked loudly.

And as he knocked, the front door squeaked eerily as it opened just a crack.

A large knot tightened in his stomach. This couldn't be a good sign!

He burst into the apartment. He glanced around. Everything was alarmingly still.

"Michelle?" he called out.

There was no reply.

He called out her name again.

Still, there was no answer. The entire apartment was deathly quiet.

Cautiously, he ventured into the living room. His eyes constantly darted around in the intimidating stillness. He searched for signs of life. He scanned for anything out of place... or any clues that something may have happened.

Nothing moved. No one made a sound.

The knot in his stomach grew tighter. His heartbeat quickened.

Somehow, he just knew something was wrong!

He glanced over to the short hallway leading to the bath and bedrooms. Something caught his eye. With a consuming sense of disaster, he rushed over to investigate.

"Blood!" he gasped.

It was spattered against the walls. There were puddles on the floor.

But what scared him the most was the sickening sight he remembered from his own wedding reception. It was the trail of blood that indicated someone had been dragged to another location.

The bloody trail led into the bathroom.

Wasting no time, he ran into the bathroom. The grizzly trail ran over to the tub.

Of course, the curtain was closed.

There was a lump in his throat. He almost thought his heart had stopped beating. With terror in his eyes, he reluctantly approached.

He reached up to the curtain with shaky hands.

"Please!" he muttered. "Not again!"

He took a deep breath for courage. Then in one quick yank, he pulled the curtain open.

He fell backwards against the sink in shock. His eyes struggled to take in the gruesome sight of the girl seated in the back corner of the tub.

She was only wearing a blood-soaked bath towel. Her head rested back against tiles that were drizzled with dripping red stains. There was no sign of life in her pallid, expressionless face.

"Oh, God!" he screamed. "Michelle! *No!*"

Chapter 8
Morbid Experiment

A steady rain still pelted the streets. The sky was a dusky, dismal gray. He drove home. It wasn't even 4:00 yet. His mother would still be at work.

He didn't feel a thing.

The doctor had said it was nothing like hypnosis. He said it was over and everything went fine. There was no reason to worry. There was nothing to fear.

He didn't remember anything happening. He couldn't recall any procedure or anything out of the ordinary.

In fact, he felt great.

The last thing he could remember was having lunch with Dr. Freitag at The Belmont. The chicken and pasta was excellent! At this moment, he was driving home to get that black wool ski mask his mother had knitted for him.

He wasn't even sure why he needed it. It certainly wasn't cold enough outside yet. The winter chill was still a few months away.

All he knew was that he needed to have his ski mask.

And, a big knife.

What had the doctor said? It was a new technique. He was going to face some of his inner demons. He was going to confront one of his deepest fears. He was going to release some of the pent up anger he harbored against some of those people at work, like Joe McMahon and Neil Worthington.

He would get some help from that man in the photograph.

It would be safe and harmless.

Still, he might get the beautiful rush of watching someone bleed!

He parked his car in the driveway. He let himself in the house with the key. He quickly retrieved the ski mask from the closet in his room.

Then, he went to the kitchen. He opened the drawer. He specifically chose a long, sharp knife. He took it out and held it in his hand.

He looked at the shiny blade with a smile.

He always liked this knife. He wasn't sure why.

It always looked pretty to him, for some reason.

Then, he took the knife and his ski mask out to his SUV. He got in and started the engine.

Why was he doing this again?

He wondered. Did it have something to do with Dr. Freitag?

He shrugged. He couldn't really recall. It didn't seem to be worth worrying about. He shifted his vehicle into gear.

Then, he went for a nice, leisurely drive.

Police officers were crawling all over the apartment. They were tending to the body. They were taking prints and photographs. Some were checking evidence. Some had a difficult time handling the brutality of the murder scene.

Still, they all persevered. They had work to do.

One man was seated on the living room sofa. He was slumped over a little with his face in his hands.

"So, let me get this straight," Sumaki said. "Around 3:00 this afternoon, you came over to see Miss Dorsett. You knocked on her door and it fell open. So, you came in to investigate."

"That's right," he muttered.

"I thought you told us that she was going to come to your place," Reynolds said. "I thought you mentioned something about taking her to dinner."

"Yes."

"Then, why did you come over here?" Reynolds asked. "Did you have some reason to worry about her?"

"Well, sort of," he muttered. "Last night, she mentioned something about seeing a shadow in the mirror."

"A shadow?" Sumaki asked.

"Yeah," he nodded. "She said it was wearing a bloody bridal veil."

"Bloody bridal veil?" Reynolds asked.

The detectives shared a glance.

"I know it sounds ridiculous," he explained. "I thought it was stupid too, at the time. She heard the story about Cynthia Trott's disappearance. And of course, we're all still a bit shaken over Karen's death. But, that shadow last night scared Michelle to pieces!"

"So, you think," Sumaki summed up. "That Miss Dorsett saw a ghost last night because she was freaked out over what happened to your wife and Cynthia Trott."

"Why else would she be seeing ghosts?" he questioned.

"You still haven't answered the question of why you came to check on her today," Sumaki pressed.

"Well, I…"

The detectives noted his hesitation. But, they allowed him time to collect his thoughts.

"Well, I don't really…" he stammered. "I hate to say it."

"Give it a try anyway," Reynolds said.

""I saw it myself," he finally admitted.

"You saw what?" Reynolds asked curiously.

"Karen," he stammered. "Or at least I saw that shadow with the bloody veil."

The detectives shared another doubtful glance.

"I know it sounds crazy," he added. "I wouldn't believe it either, if someone else told me this story. I'm sure it's just a reaction to everything that's been going on all around me. But, I could've sworn I saw Karen's ghost in my mirror at home! And she was wearing her bridal veil! I swear I saw it!"

"And, that's when you decided to come over here and check on Miss Dorsett?" Sumaki asked.

"Yes."

"And, you found her already dead in the bathtub?" Sumaki continued.

"I left everything just as I found it," he said. "I immediately called the cops."

"How late last night was it when Miss Dorsett saw whatever she thought she saw?" Reynolds asked.

"I don't know," he shrugged. "10:00 or so. Maybe later."

"So, you were with her 10:00 or later last night," Reynolds said. "And, you were going to take her to dinner tonight. And, don't forget we've seen you together a few times. I have to ask, Mr. Broderick. Were you sleeping with Michelle Dorsett?"

He hesitated. He fumbled to respond.

"I have a better question," Sumaki added. "Were you sleeping with her before you were married?"

"No!" he declared. "Last night was absolutely the first time!"

"Are you sure?" Sumaki persisted.

"Yes!"

"How did you end up in bed with the Maid of Honor at your wedding three days after your bride was killed at her reception, Mr. Broderick?" Sumaki asked.

"I don't know," he said anxiously. "It just happened. Why is my private life a matter of concern to you people? Shouldn't you be trying to find a killer?"

"We are, Mr. Broderick," Sumaki answered. "First, your bride is killed on her wedding day. Then, the woman you were having an affair with one month earlier turns up missing the next day. Then, you sleep with your wife's best friend. And, we have to walk into a murder scene like this one."

"What's your point?"

"It seems that every girl who sleeps with you," Sumaki surmised. "Ends up in the morgue."

"Don't tell that to any of your next prospects," Reynolds poked. "That sort of thing can really turn a girl off."

"Wait a minute," he grumbled. "You're not trying to pin this on me, are you?"

"You are the one solid common link between all the victims," Sumaki pointed out.

"Why would I possibly want to kill any of those girls?" he asked.

"Who knows?" Reynolds shrugged. "Maybe something better came along."

"I don't like your tone!"

"I don't like a lot of things, Mr. Broderick!" Sumaki averred. "I don't like to see two girls dead and one girl still missing in less than a week! Especially when they all share one thing in common: they all had the poor taste to wind up with a dirt bag like you!"

"Wait a second!"

"Where is Cynthia Trott, Mr. Broderick?" Sumaki demanded.

"I don't know!"

"Can I see you for a moment, Detectives?" a uniformed officer interrupted.

"Sure," Sumaki said. "Don't move, Mr. Broderick."

When they were far enough away to have some privacy, the officer said, "There are no fresh prints in the whole place other than the victim's. Whoever did this was wearing gloves."

"What about footprints?" Reynolds asked.

"I'm checking that now," Sumaki said. He had already squatted near the dragged smears of blood on the floor.

"Here's one or two partial sneaker prints," Sumaki pointed out. "How much do you want to bet they match our friend, Mr. Broderick? But, wait a minute! They seem to be facing the bathroom. If he were dragging the body behind him, shouldn't the prints be facing the other way?"

"Check this out!" Reynolds said. "Here's a shoe print. It's a shoe, not a sneaker. It's facing away from the bathroom. And there's another one very close to it. They're just about right on top of each other."

"Yes," Sumaki said. "It looks like the person who actually dragged the body was wearing shoes instead of sneakers. And the shoe foot is a few sizes larger."

"And, those shoe prints have been there longer," Reynolds added. "I guess it's lucky for us that our murderer got that much blood on the floor before he even started dragging anybody anywhere."

"Well, that's just wonderful!" Sumaki commented. "Maybe Mr. Broderick didn't do this, after all. But, he still seems to be the main link in these crimes."

"They're all linked to Karen, anyway," Reynolds observed. "And, nobody would have a closer tie to Karen than her newlywed husband."

"Still," Sumaki said. "It seems like anytime Peter fools around on his wife, that woman turns up either dead or missing. But, who else would've had such an interest in his sex life?"

"Well, it couldn't have been Karen's ghost," Reynolds joked. "She wouldn't have been wearing men's shoes."

"Yes," Sumaki grunted. "We have partial footprints at this murder scene, but none at the hotel. I still think Karen's murder was a crime of passion. This one was probably done more quickly. The killer is now just trying to cover his ass. He's getting desperate. He's making mistakes."

"That's good for us," Reynolds said. "But, if this murder was committed just to cover the killer's ass, how does Broderick fit in?"

"I don't know," Sumaki muttered. "But then again, I don't know why the killer likes dragging bodies around, either. What's the significance of the dumpster and the bathtub? There are still a lot of questions to answer. Let's go answer them before the killer needs to cover his ass again."

"Or before Broderick gets another girlfriend," Reynolds added. "Either way, we'd better hurry."

🌾 🌾 🌾

"This is an awfully nice place," she commented. "What's it called? Taylor's Restaurant?"

"Yes."

"It looks expensive," she said. "I thought we were just going out as friends."

"We are," he said. "But, what's the point of going out at all, if you're not going to go to a nice place? I guess we could have gone to some burger joint, if you wanted. But as long as we're going out, I thought we'd both enjoy this more."

"I suppose you have a point," she admitted. "I'm not a big fan of greasy burgers."

"They don't have much in the way of greasy food here," he said. "Most of the dishes in this establishment are fantastic."

"Do you come here often?"

"Often enough."

"And, why did you want to bring me here?" she asked.

"It's familiar territory," he said. "It gives me the 'home turf' advantage."

"Which brings me back to my original question," she said. "If we just came here as friends, why do you need to have any advantage at all?"

"I don't know," he shrugged. "Force of habit, I suppose. Any time I'm out in public with a beautiful woman, I feel like I need to have an edge."

"I'm starting to think this may have been a mistake," she said. "You're resorting to flattery already. I know what it means when a guy starts that at this stage."

"Why are you so quick to label every word that comes out of my mouth?" he inquired. "Are you always this suspicious?"

"Only when I need to be," she answered. "And with you, I have a feeling I should remain ready for anything."

"Why do you say that?"

"Face it, Neil," she said. "It seems very suspicious that you would ask me out to dinner only three nights after your girlfriend disappeared. Aren't you concerned about her?"

"Of course I am," he said. "I'm worried sick about her. As I mentioned before, each moment that passes seriously decreases the chances that we'll find her alive. That's why I suggested this dinner. I just needed some female company. I just needed to spend some time with someone to take my mind off my troubles."

"I was afraid…" she began.

She glanced down at the table. She hoped she wasn't blushing.

"What?" he asked. "Go on. Continue."

"Oh… nothing."

"What?" he pressed. "Don't tell me. Let me guess. You were afraid I've been listening to the office gossip. Sure, I've heard the rumors, Angela. Jennifer Cibello. Sarah Krause. Lorraine Bishop. I've heard their stories and the tone in their voices. They love dropping rather obvious hints. Believe me. I hear it on my end, too. And, I have to admit. In my case, it might be a little bit true."

"What do you mean?"

"Well…" he ventured cautiously. "Maybe I do light up a little whenever I see you."

"Neil!" she gasped. "Is that why you took me to some fancy, romantic restaurant?"

"Don't get me wrong," he quickly defended. "This is just a friendly dinner, just like I told you. I really am torn up about Cynthia. But, I must be honest, Angela. I noticed what a beautiful girl you were the first day you walked into The Blue Arrow Agency not even two weeks ago."

"Thank you," she said. She knew she was blushing now. "I guess. So, what are you saying?"

"Nothing, really," he said. "Just telling the truth."

"Come on, Neil," she said suspiciously. "Guys don't 'just tell the truth' about something like that unless they want something."

"I just wanted to get things out in the open," he said. "There's a certain mutual attraction here. And, I just didn't want to hide it anymore. Jennifer, Sarah and Lorraine are never going to leave us alone until we at least admit how we both feel."

"And, you needed to take me to Taylor's Restaurant to admit it?" she asked.

"It's more private," he said. "More intimate."

"'More intimate' is what I'm afraid of," she said.

"You never struck me as the kind of girl who was afraid of intimacy," he said.

"I never struck you at all," she said. "I hardly know you. I'm only afraid of intimacy with you, because you already have a girlfriend."

"She's missing," he reminded.

"And if this is how you show your concern," she said. "I'd rather not get too close. If we were dating and I disappeared, I suppose you'd be sitting at this table with Jennifer Cibello right now."

"Not at all," he said. "She may be a reasonably attractive girl. But, we've worked together for three years, and I've never had any interest in her."

"Why not?"

"You know what she's like," he said. "She's shallow. She's a scatter-brain. There's absolutely no substance there. Office gossip is her life. Can you imagine what she must be like at home?"

She giggled just a little.

"I'd hate to even think about it," she smiled.

"So, you see?" he said. "I wouldn't be sitting here now with just any girl. And, the rumors had nothing to do with it. The rumors are only circulating because there's at least a little truth to them."

"Is there really?" she asked in a tone of disbelief.

"I think so," he said. "Don't you?"

"I never put much stock in anything Jennifer, Sarah or Lorraine has to say," she stated.

"Then, why are you here?"

"Curiosity," she said. "Plain, simple curiosity."

"Is that so?" he asked. "Do you often let guys take you to a place like this out of 'plain, simple curiosity'?"

"Not often," she admitted. "But, you're not the first."

"Listen," he said seriously. "Of course I'm worried about Cynthia. But, it's no secret that we were having problems. Things weren't working out between us."

"Really?"

"I'm sure you heard," he reminded. "She slept with Karen's fiancé a month before the wedding. That's why I didn't call the cops right away when she disappeared. Do you think she would have done that if we weren't on the verge of breaking up?"

"I guess not," she allowed. "So, what was the problem?"

"I don't know," he sighed. "I guess we wanted different things in life. Actually, I don't think either one of us knew what we wanted. But somehow, whatever we wanted just wasn't coming together the way it should."

"So, what do you think you want?"

"If I knew," he said. "I probably wouldn't be wasting time working in The Payroll Unit of a useless little company like The Blue Arrow Agency. Honestly! Does anybody even really know what that place does? What vital services do we render? Why do we exist? Frankly, I think it's just a front for the mob."

"Are you kidding me?" she giggled.

"Think about it," he pressed. "Money comes in and goes out. Paperwork runs rampant. People come and go. And, what impact do we really have on anybody? It's all complete nonsense."

She was still laughing.

"You have a great outlook," she teased.

"I'm a realist," he said. "It's one of my shortcomings."

"And, how many shortcomings do you have?" she asked.

"Not many," he said. "I do have a weakness for beautiful girls with substance, though."

"That's right," she said. "I forgot. I have 'substance'. That's nice to know. I'll have to use it to watch you carefully. You like throwing the word 'beautiful' around too much. I have a feeling that's another one of your shortcomings."

"Not at all," he said. "I usually try to avoid that word. You're a rare exception to the rule."

"Is that because I have substance?"

"Partially," he said. "But mostly, I say it because it's true."

"Put it back in the holster, boy," she ordered with a smile. "This is still supposed to be just a friendly dinner. Remember?"

"Sure… on paper," he agreed. "But, you also have to remember that I'm a realist."

"So am I," she said. "And, you still have a missing girlfriend to contend with."

His smile disappeared.

"Believe me," he said. "I know. That's why we're here. So I can forget about it."

"Well, don't forget for too long."

"You're certainly not making it easy," he admitted.

"That must be one of *my* shortcomings."

"Maybe we can work on that."

"What makes you think I want to work on that?" she asked.

"If you didn't," he said confidently. "You wouldn't be here."

The mood settled naturally into a more subtle, captivating conversation. Despite her best efforts, a few layers of her defenses were peeled away. In the atmosphere of this charming restaurant, it became more difficult to cling to her strong sense of denial.

When the meal was over, he asked, "Would you like to go out somewhere? Maybe we could catch a movie or something."

"No," she said. "I don't think it's a good idea. I'm tired. I think I'll turn in."

"Are you sure?"

"Yes," she said as she stood. "Thanks for the offer. And, thanks for dinner, Neil. I had a wonderful time.

But, I'm going to take it slow. I'm still not sure why I even came here with you."

"You came out because you wanted to," he informed her.

He rose to his feet.

"I still haven't convinced myself that this wasn't a big mistake," she said. "I mean, I enjoyed your company and everything, but I still haven't defined what we're doing here."

He helped her with her coat. He walked her to her car.

The rain had stopped. The darkness possessed a solemn quality. It was silent, cool and moist. It was not a cordial darkness.

Yet, it was not unappealing.

"I don't think you need to convince yourself of anything," he said. "And, I don't think you need to define anything, either. You're here because of one thing I know we both have in common."

"And, what's that?"

"We're both realists."

There was a kiss. She didn't know where it came from. She wasn't expecting it.

It didn't stop soon enough to keep her from feeling uncomfortable.

Yet, she never actually felt uncomfortable.

"Good night, Angela," he said. "I'll see you tomorrow."

"Good night, Neil."

She got in her car. She felt a bit uneasy. There was a definite twinge in her stomach. Somehow, things didn't seem as clear as they should.

She wished that kiss hadn't happened.

But, it had! There was no taking it back!

Still, she refused to smile. Yet somehow, she was forced to consider the question she had tried so hard to avoid:

Had Jennifer and Sarah been right all along?

She decided not to think about it. She cleared her throat as she started the car. Then, she shifted into gear and pulled out of the parking lot.

And, she made a point of focusing on the traffic as she drove home through the dark, solemn streets of Thorn Ridge.

❦ ❦ ❦

He was sitting in a bar when the phone rang. It was a quiet, classy place. He was talking to the bartender. He made a point of being out in public.

He needed an alibi.

He politely excused himself and stepped away from the bar.

By the third ring, he answered, "Hello. Joshua Freitag here."

"Hello, Doctor," said the caller. "This is Polopous."

"Good evening, Mr. Polopous," he said with a smile. "I assume you have some good news for me."

"Yes sir," Polopous said. "The subjects are headed to Langley's home right now. They should be there in approximately ten minutes."

"Excellent," he said. "How would you like your payment?"

"Meet me tomorrow at The Extra Point Sports Bar on Tivoli St. around 1:30," the caller instructed. "Do you know the place?"

"Yes," he said. "I know where it is. Tomorrow afternoon at 1:30? That should be fine. I take it you would prefer your payment in cash, as per usual?"

"It's strictly for accounting purposes, you understand."

"Of course," he said. "Thank you, Mr. Polopous. See you then."

He hung up the phone.

✯ ✯ ✯

He sat quietly in his SUV. He wasn't really sure why he was there. The radio was playing. His window was rolled down.

The rain had stopped. The soothing darkness was filled with the pungent aroma of wet, rotting leaves. Somehow, he found it relaxing.

There was a knitted ski mask in his lap. There was a large knife resting in the seat beside him. He wasn't too familiar with this neighborhood.

Why was he parked in this spot? Why did he feel compelled to stay here?

It didn't really bother him. He felt great. He didn't really remember anything after sitting down for lunch with Dr. Freitag. Perhaps this had something to do with the technique the good doctor was recommending to help cure him of his social insecurities.

He sat and listened to the radio. It didn't matter. He wasn't being charged for this session. There was no reason to avoid trying whatever little morbid experiment the doctor had in mind.

Who knows? It might help. It might even be fun!

Then, his cell phone rang. He answered, "Hello?"

"Hello, Dylan," said the caller. "This is Dr. Freitag. Now listen to the sound of my voice. Joe McMahon is on his way. Joe McMahon is approaching your location. Your chance to confront him is minutes away. Do you hear me, Dylan? Joe McMahon!"

"Yes, Doctor," he muttered.

He hung up the phone. He was staring straight ahead. It looked as if he was in a daze. He picked up the ski mask. He put the knife in his coat. Then, he stepped out of his vehicle.

His gaze remained steady. He did not blink.

He walked calmly up the block. The streetlamps did little to illuminate his path through this unfamiliar territory. He still found the darkness quite soothing.

Three unsavory-looking characters approached him. It didn't phase him in the least. He never felt more relaxed.

His gaze remained steady. He did not blink.

The three men walked past him. They laughed as they shared a joke. They didn't seem to notice him, the ski mask in his hand or the knife in his coat.

His destination seemed to be about two blocks away. He didn't know why he had parked that far away from where he was meant to be. It didn't really matter, though.

His gaze remained steady. He did not blink.

There was a Laundromat on the corner and a small park across the road. It almost seemed like a nice place to be. He still wasn't sure how he decided to come here.

But, this was the place!

He had never seen this stone building before. But, this was where he was supposed to be. Somehow, it felt right to be here.

He was wearing a coat. Still, he shivered against the cold.

His gaze remained steady. He did not blink.

For some reason, he decided to try the door handle. He figured the outside door would be locked. Still, it didn't hurt to try.

The handle slipped in his gloved hand. He didn't remember putting gloves on. But, it didn't really matter. The door seemed locked. But, the lock was loose. It wouldn't take too much effort to gain entry.

He wasn't sure why, but he felt compelled to give the door one quick, hard shove. He heard the loud snap. The latch broke.

The door opened. He was pleased. But, he did not smile.

His gaze remained steady. He did not blink.

A light was on inside the building. There was an apartment door on the ground floor. And, there was a narrow, dingy stairwell leading to the second floor.

The lighting was less than adequate. A single bulb cast long, eerie shadows against every surface possible. Combined with a slight musty odor, it made for a disconcerting atmosphere.

He didn't mind. Inexplicably, he still felt a need to come inside.

The last thing he could really remember was having lunch at The Belmont. It was a gorgeous restaurant.

He entered the building. He closed the door as best he could. The odor seemed a little worse inside with the door closed. The lighting seemed a bit more scant. The shadows appeared to taunt.

It was okay, though.

He just went over to the narrow stairwell. For some reason, he slowly started to climb the stairs. There was no apparent explanation. He just felt the need to climb the stairs.

The first step creaked beneath his foot. So did the second.

Still, he didn't care.

His gaze remained steady. He did not blink.

He heard one stair creak beneath his stride, then the next. He just walked up to the second floor. He didn't know why. It was just what he wanted to do.

He felt relaxed. Everything was fine.

His gaze remained steady. He did not blink.

When he reached the second floor, he stopped. There was a landing with an apartment door. Beside him, a stairwell went up to the third floor.

He stood on the landing. This was where he wanted to be. He didn't know why. But for some reason, he really wanted to stay on the second floor landing. The lighting was still inadequate. Everything looked dirty. Shadows were long, deep and menacing.

Yet, he felt perfectly at home.

He just pulled the ski mask over his head and adjusted it so he could see properly.

Then, he reached in his coat and wrapped his fingers around the hilt of the knife.

It felt cold and hard in his hand. It was comforting. It felt reassuring.

At this point, all he had to do was wait. He still didn't know why. And it didn't matter. He just wanted to wait.

A few minutes passed. He didn't really notice. He didn't care. He didn't even know why he was there. He just wanted to wait.

And, he felt good.

Finally, the downstairs door burst open. He heard a man and woman laughing in the doorway. They didn't even seem to notice the street-level door was unlocked.

The voices were happy. They were enjoying each other's company.

Suddenly, he didn't like their voices. He could guess who they were. And, he could guess who they were laughing at!

They were still laughing as they walked up the stairs. They made too much noise. They were still laughing as he silently pulled the long knife out of his coat.

They were still laughing... even though he didn't like it!

He crouched down into one of the long shadows. He didn't want to be seen until it was too late.

Their shadows moved on the wall as their voices grew louder. He gripped the knife tightly. He braced himself for their arrival.

Suddenly, they were standing before the apartment door. They didn't see him. They only cared about themselves.

It was them! He recognized them. Their very presence infuriated him.

Finally, he leapt up out of the shadows with an angry shout. He stood between them with the knife in his hand. He glared at the startled man with a rage he had never experienced before.

"McMahon!" he growled. "I've been looking forward to this! You owe me, McMahon! After all I've done for you, you're going to pay!"

"What?" the man stammered. "Who's McMahon? How did you get in here?"

"Don't fuck with me, McMahon!" he snarled. "I've taken all I can take!"

With one furious thrust, he buried the long knife in the man's stomach up to the hilt. The man howled out in pain as he fell back against the wall.

The woman was screaming in terror.

As much as the masked intruder enjoyed watching the wave of blood washing over his victim's belly, sheer rage drove him to plunge the blade into the man's chest.

His victim cried out again. Then he slid down the wall until he was slumped over on the landing. He grunted once or twice. But, he seemed unable to move.

The masked intruder smirked as he relished the vision of blood running over his victim like a babbling red brook.

The woman was still screaming.

The intruder turned to face her. She stood frozen in her panic with her back against the wall. He didn't seem to notice that she was a bleach-blonde in her middle forties. He only recognized the look of horror on her face. He'd seen it before.

And, she wouldn't stop screaming.

"Angela!" he bellowed. "I was only trying to talk to you, Angela! Why won't you talk to me, you bitch!"

She shrieked with pain and terror as he sank the blade deep into her shoulder.

The blood spilled out over her coat. The masked intruder welcomed the appealing sight. And when he extracted the blade, the blood seemed to flow more freely.

He stared at the woman's coat. He was mesmerized. He was transfixed.

She was frozen. She was screaming and crying hysterically.

She was bleeding so sweetly! And, she was bleeding just for him!

He reveled in the sight of the blood running over her coat.

The man on the landing tried to get up. But, the pain was unbearable. The simplest movement was excruciating. He fell back against the wall.

Still, he had to protect his woman!

With great difficulty, he got out the knife he always kept strapped beneath his pant leg. And with one desperate, agonizing lunge, he sliced a deep gash into the thigh of his assailant.

The masked man screeched in anguish. When he fell, he tumbled headlong down the stairs to the ground floor.

When he stopped rolling, he was laying still on the torn linoleum. He didn't move.

The man on the landing tried to get up off his back. He grunted with pain. He knew it would be nearly impossible to move. Quickly, he reached into his pocket and fumbled around for his keys. He pulled them out and handed them up to his companion.

The masked intruder downstairs was beginning to stir.

"Madeline!" Grant instructed. "Take my keys, go inside and lock the door immediately! Then, call the cops! Hurry!"

She was afraid to move. She was still crying in a painful hysteria.

The masked intruder began to crawl awkwardly up the stairs.

"Take the keys, Madeline!" Grant ordered. "Now! Go in the apartment! Lock the door and call the cops! Do it!"

"I can't!" she cried. "I can't!"

She stood frozen. She shrieked in terror as she saw the intruder crawling up the stairs.

"McMahon!" the assailant hollered with vengeful rage. "I'm not done with you, McMahon! I'll get you for screwing me over, you fucker! I'll get you!"

Madeline screamed.

"Madeline!" Grant demanded. "Take the keys! Don't worry about me! Go! Lock the door and call the cops! Do it, Madeline! Now!"

"He's coming, Grant!" she screamed. "Help me!"

"Take the keys, Madeline!" Grant shouted. "Now!"

The intruder was halfway up the stairs. "You're going to pay, McMahon!" he growled. "You're going to pay!"

"Take the keys, Madeline!"

She saw the long blade covered in blood. The intruder was still making his way up the stairs.

Madeline screamed with fright.

"Take the keys, sweetheart! You can do it!"

"I only wanted to talk to you, Angela!"

Out of sheer panic, she grabbed the keys from Grant's hand. She turned toward the apartment door. With a trembling hand, she struggled to fit the key in the lock.

"You can do it, honey!"

"Don't run from me, Angela! Talk to me, you worthless whore!"

She cried out in a fear that wouldn't fade. Her hand wouldn't stop shaking. She couldn't see through the fresh wave of tears in her eyes. Her shoulder hurt like hell.

She felt around with her fingers.

"Hurry, Madeline!"

With pure desperation, she finally managed to slip the key into the lock. She opened the door. She took the key, ran inside and slammed the door closed.

Grant breathed a sigh of relief as he heard the lock click into place.

Then he turned to his assailant. He knew his capabilities were limited. He knew he couldn't get up to his feet. Still, his very life depended on his courage. As best he could, he brandished his own bloody knife.

It was smaller than his attacker's weapon, but it was all he had.

"Listen, pal!" he threatened. "I don't know what your problem is, but my girlfriend is inside calling the police! You're done, pal! It's over! Don't come any closer, or I swear I'll slice you to ribbons!"

The masked man stared at the man lying on his side on the landing above him. The man on the landing had his own knife. But, the guy was bleeding. He took a few moments to enjoy watching the blood flow over the man's clothes.

It felt like medicine for his soul. He felt better already.

Then, he looked at the man. He looked at the knife. He glanced down at the large weapon in his own hand. Then, he glanced up at the apartment door.

Suddenly, he didn't know where he was.

"I mean it, pal!" Grant warned. "My girlfriend is calling the cops! It's over! If you don't leave, I'll cut out your spleen and feed it to you through a straw!"

The intruder watched the man bleed. It was such a pleasing sight! But, it scared the hell out of him!

Had he done this?

He looked down at his bloody weapon. Then, he glanced up at the apartment door. He could feel the horrific pain in his leg.

The cops? The thought made him grimace.

The man was still bleeding on the landing.

Still, he knew he couldn't stay and watch. He couldn't face the police.

Finally, he turned and started back down the stairs. It was difficult to move with the agonizing gash in his leg. However, he managed to hobble down the stairs and out of the building.

Upon slamming the door behind him, he rushed toward his vehicle as quickly as possible. He was favoring his wounded leg. He was aware of his bleeding. Each step brought another wave of pain.

The two blocks to his SUV was a torturous distance to travel. As he stumbled, he wondered once again why he had parked so far away.

It must have been for his protection. It must have been so his vehicle would not be recognized at the scene of the crime.

He had to admit The Space Eagle stood out in a crowd.

He wanted to strangle that stupid shrink! This was all his doing! Why had he planned this rather extreme, dangerous and illegal stunt?

Luckily, there were almost no people in the street. The darkness seemed more intimidating than it had earlier. It was a judgmental darkness.

It was a darkness of condemnation.

He grunted as he approached The Space Eagle. His movement was slower and more labored. The bruises and abrasions from his fall down the stairs were getting harder to ignore as well.

He hobbled up to his vehicle. He leaned up against its finely painted side. He took a moment to catch his breath.

However, he knew he couldn't take too long.

As soon as he was able, he made his way over to the driver's side. He unlocked the door and climbed with great difficulty up into the seat. There were some old dirty clothes in the back. He grabbed a few old shirts to use as bandages.

He tied them quickly. He'd lost too much blood already. And, he knew he had to get away from the area.

A siren could be heard in the distance.

He started the engine and drove.

He heard the screeching of his tires as he raced away from the curb. He didn't know where he was going.

He just drove. He drove away from the encroaching sirens.

After tearing off his ski mask, he reached for his cell phone.

When someone answered his call, he shouted into the phone, "Dr. Freitag? What the hell did you do to me? What did you send me into?"

"Dylan?" Freitag asked. "Is that you? Where are you?"

"I don't know," he said. "I'm driving. I don't know this area."

He looked for a street sign.

"I'm on Nelson Blvd.," he said. "I think I'm heading north."

"What happened?"

"I'm not entirely sure," he said. "Everything's still kind of blurred. I stabbed some guy at least twice. I thought he was Joe McMahon. I was yelling at McMahon. He wasn't Joe! Why did I think he was Joe?"

"You were releasing your rage," Freitag told him. "That's good. That's what we wanted. Remember?"

"But, I stabbed somebody I don't even know!" he shouted. "I could go to jail!"

"You were wearing your ski mask, weren't you?" Freitag pointed out.

"Yes," he replied. "But, how did you make me do that? I thought people couldn't be hypnotized to hurt somebody!"

"You weren't hypnotized," Freitag corrected. "I explained this to you. My technique does not deal with hypnosis. I only allowed you to explore the outer fringes beyond your subconscious. I allowed you to stop fearing the emotions that you have always suppressed. I just helped you to stop being afraid."

"But, I committed a violent crime!"

"Who's going to know?"

"But, the bastard cut my leg!" he declared angrily. "It's a deep gash, too!"

"Your leg got cut?" Freitag asked. "How did that happen?"

"Angela wouldn't stop screaming," he explained. "Or the woman I thought was Angela. That wasn't Angela, was it? I was so angry at her! I told Angela I only wanted to talk to her. After I stabbed her, I was watching her bleed."

"You stabbed the woman?" Freitag asked. "I didn't tell you to stab her! I never told you to see her as Angela!"

"She bled so sweetly, too," he continued. "The way the blood ran down over her coat! It was mesmerizing!"

"I never told you to confront that woman!" Freitag demanded. "Is she okay?"

"I bandaged my leg," he said. "But, it's a real nasty cut. I should probably go to the hospital."

"No!" Freitag ordered. "Don't go to the hospital under any circumstances! You can be identified by the wound! You don't want to get caught! You probably shouldn't go home tonight, either."

"But, what am I going to tell my mother?"

"I don't know," Freitag sighed with aggravation. "Damn! You weren't supposed to get hurt! You weren't supposed to leave any way to be identified!"

"But, Angela was bleeding," he reasoned. "It was so beautiful! I couldn't help myself!"

"Is the woman alright?"

"I guess so," he shrugged. "She locked herself in the apartment."

"Alright," Freitag grumbled. "Do you know where Robbins Rd. crosses the highway just north of the city?"

"Yes."

"Stay on Robbins Rd.," Freitag instructed. "Go about a mile past the highway. You'll find a little farmhouse off to the right. Pull off the road and wait for me there. I'll get some medical supplies and meet you there. Then, we'll decide what to do next."

"But, what about…"

"Just go!" Freitag insisted. "I'll see you there in about an hour!"

The young man hung up the phone. Then, he dialed another number.

"Hello," said the voice on the other end. "Eunice Zeblonsky."

"Mom?"

"Dylan?" she asked. "Where are you? You're dinner's gone stone cold."

"I won't be home tonight, Mom," he explained. "I've had some trouble. I have to take care of a few things."

"Trouble?" she asked. "What kind of trouble?"

"I can't go into it now," he said impatiently. "I have to go. I'll call you as soon as I can. 'Bye, Mom."

"Dylan?" she asked. "What's going on? Dylan?"

He hung up. He turned the ringer off, so he wouldn't have to listen to it. Then, he steered his vehicle in the direction of Robbins Rd.

And, he stepped heavily on the gas pedal.

Chapter 9
Keep Your Balloons Tied Down

They walked down the long corridor. They were tired, but determined. A medical team rushed past them with a patient on a gurney. They watched the hurried spectacle as it disappeared through the swinging doors down the hall.

A nurse pushed an old man in a wheelchair. A kid with his arm in a cast was crying in his mother's lap. People in scrubs ran quickly by them. A young woman on crutches gave them a curious glance.

They ignored it all. They just took the first elevator they encountered. The older of the two hit the button for Floor 3.

They stepped out onto the third floor. After asking directions, they walked to the room they wanted.

Both beds inside were occupied. The woman was closer to the door.

They flashed their badges as they approached.

"Mrs. Madeline Freitag?" he asked.

"Yes."

"I'm Detective Sumaki," he said. "This is my partner, Detective Reynolds."

"I've already talked to the cops," she said. "More than once, in fact."

"I know, ma'am," he said. "They just checked your home. Your husband's not there. We came to talk to you because he's involved in another case."

"He is?" she asked. "My God! How many people is he trying to kill?"

"It's nothing like that, ma'am," he said. "Our chief heard your name when it came in. He knew we were talking to your husband because one of his patients could be connected to another incident."

"We hear you suspect your husband may have sent someone to attack you," Reynolds questioned. "Because he threatened to step in if you didn't end an extramarital affair?"

"Yes," she said. "He told me I'd regret it if I didn't stop seeing Grant."

"Grant is your lover, ma'am?"

"That's right," she said. "Grant Langley. We were entering his residence when we were attacked. He's in another room now, because his injuries are a lot worse than mine. Last I heard, the doctors were very concerned about his condition."

"What exactly happened, Mrs. Freitag?" Reynolds asked.

"It's so hard to remember," she said. "Everything happened so fast. It's just like I told the officers that talked to me before. We were coming back to Grant's apartment after our date. We got up to his door on the second floor, and some guy jumped out of the shadows in a ski mask."

"He was wearing a ski mask?" he asked. "So, you can't make a positive ID?"

"That's right," she said. "At first, I thought it was a robbery. The man must've broken in. The door on the ground floor is usually locked."

"He broke into the building?" Reynolds asked. "So, what makes you think it wasn't a burglar?"

"He never asked for money," she said. "He just started calling Grant some weird name. I think he called him McNabb or McMahon or something."

"McMahon?"

"Yes. I think so."

The detectives shared a glance.

"He kept calling Grant 'McMahon' or something," she explained. "The guy said he was going to get even with him for screwing him over. Then, he stabbed him! At least twice! It nearly scared me to death!"

"I can see why."

"Then, he turned to me," she continued. "He was calling me Angela!"

The detectives shared another glance.

"He was yelling at me," she went on. "I was so frightened! He was saying, 'I only wanted to talk to you, Angela!' Then, he stabbed me in the shoulder. It hurt like hell! But, then the strangest thing happened."

"And, what's that?"

"He just stopped," she explained. "He just stopped ranting like a lunatic and just stared at me."

"He stared at you, Mrs. Freitag?" Reynolds asked.

"Yes," she nodded. "It was the oddest thing. I couldn't see his face because of the ski mask. But, I could have sworn he was staring at me. If I didn't know better, I'd swear he was watching me bleed. It almost seemed like he was mesmerized by it. Almost like he got some sick thrill from watching me bleed!"

"Is that right?"

"That's when Grant cut him in the leg," she said. "Grant always carries a knife for protection. He tells me it's easy to make enemies in the insurance business."

"Langley is in the insurance business?"

"Yes," she said. "He works for T.F.I. Their main offices are on Essex Blvd."

"So, what happened after Langley cut the intruder in the leg?" he asked.

"The guy fell down the stairs," she answered. "Grant couldn't get up. He handed me his keys and told me to go inside and call the cops. The intruder was coming up the stairs. He was still yelling at McMahon and Angela. But, Grant said that when I went inside, the little weirdo left."

"Can you give us any kind of description of the intruder, ma'am?" he asked.

"Like I said," she reminded. "Everything happened so fast. And, he was wearing a ski mask. But, he was taller than I am. But, not as tall as Grant, though. I'd guess he was 5' 8", maybe 5' 9". He was a bit on the pudgy side and wearing a brown winter coat. And now he has a big gash in his left shin, about halfway up."

"Langley cut him about halfway up his left shin?" Reynolds asked.

"I think it was his left shin."

"And, you think there's a good chance this attack was initiated by your husband?" he asked.

"Didn't you hear me?" she replied. "The man never robbed us. He was calling Grant by some other name. He was calling me Angela. This was not a rational human being. And, my husband was furious when he found out about Grant! First, he had some guy follow me around for a few weeks."

"You're husband hired a private investigator?"

"I guess," she said. "And, I've never seen him as angry as he got during our conversation."

"Was he always a jealous man?" Reynolds asked.

"No," she said. "That's why all this caught me off guard. He's always been such a gentle, caring man. I didn't think he was even capable of the anger he's displayed this past few days."

"How long have you been cheating on him?" Reynolds asked.

"Oh... I'd say about four months or so," she guessed after consideration.

"Was this the first time?"

"Absolutely," she declared. "I never wanted to cheat on Joshua. He was always a wonderful man. I don't even know why I ever started seeing Grant. I guess he was so young, vibrant and exciting. I was in a rut. I was bored. I needed a change. Grant was just what I needed. Of course, I'd never leave him now. We're in love!"

"Yeah," Reynolds said with a straight face. "I'm glad to hear it. Can you think of anywhere your husband might go besides your house?"

"Not really," she said. "We have a little summer place we use up in The Catskills. But, that's so far away. Then, there's that place down in Florida."

"Anywhere closer, ma'am?"

"Wait a minute," she gasped. "The Steins are on vacation for two weeks. Sometimes, they let him use their farmhouse. It's a white building just north of the city. It's on Robbins Rd. about a mile past the highway. You don't think he'd go there, do you?"

"You'd know better than we would," he said.

"I'll bet that's where he is," she said. "The Steins' farmhouse!"

"Thank you, Mrs. Freitag," he said. "You've been a big help. We'll look into this situation and keep you apprised."

"I hope you catch that little creep who attacked us," she said. "There's something not right about that guy! And, you can tell my husband that I'll see him in court!"

"Yes, ma'am," he nodded. "Why don't you get some rest now? We'll talk later. About a mile north of the highway, you say?"

"Yes," she said. "It's a big white house on the right."

"Thanks again, Mrs. Freitag," he said. "Good night."

The detectives made a hasty exit.

As they waited for the elevator, Reynolds said. "McMahon? We talked to a Joe McMahon at Zeblonsky's workplace, didn't we?"

"And, we ran into an Angela, too," he reminded. "She was a pretty little thing."

"That's quite a coincidence," Reynolds said. "And, we've seen Zeblonsky at his house in a brown coat. How much do you want to bet he has a big gash in his left shin?"

"Let's go pick him up."

"Do you think Freitag's been manipulating him this whole time?" Reynolds asked. "What are the chances the good doctor is behind our entire case?"

"Not good," he said. "We'd have to make a connection between him and Karen. It's more likely that he just went after his wife as a crime of passion. I'm sure he knows more about what Zeblonsky is capable of than he lets on."

"I think Freitag knows more about this case than he's telling," Reynolds surmised.

"That's very possible," he said. "We'll check the Stein house after we pick up Dylan Zeblonsky. Then, maybe I can go home and get some sleep."

"Sounds good to me," Reynolds commented. "Maybe we can bring a squad car with us, just in case. There's no telling what that slimy shrink did to Dylan. Maybe we can send a car up to that farmhouse ahead of time."

"That's not a bad idea."

He was lying down in the back seat of The Space Eagle. He needed some rest. His leg was still throbbing with a strong, dull pain.

At least, it had stopped bleeding.

It was growing colder outside. The darkness was growing deeper and more ominous.

He didn't want to be here. He was confused, unsure and very angry.

Why had he let Freitag talk him into this? The man was supposed to be a well-educated professional! He was supposed to be a doctor!

He looked up at the ceiling of his SUV. He rubbed his temples against the looming headache that was taking hold.

The front window was open just a crack. He wanted to be able to hear if someone pulled into the long driveway.

It seemed to be taking forever for the doctor to get here! He wouldn't be able to stand waiting much longer!

Finally, he heard the gravelly sound of a car driving up beside his vehicle. He propped himself up on his elbows and looked outside. He breathed a sigh of relief when he saw Freitag getting out of a Cadillac.

With an agonized effort, he got up. He concealed the knife in his coat, just in case. Then, he stepped out of his SUV.

"Hi, Dylan," Freitag said. He took in a quick overview of his patient. "I see you found the place okay."

"Yes."

"Oh, God!" Freitag exclaimed. "You're a mess! How bad is your leg?"

"He only cut me once," he grunted. "But, it's a pretty deep cut."

"Let's get you inside," Freitag said. "I brought lots of bandages, disinfectant and things. We'll fix you up as best we can."

"Thanks."

The doctor put his arm around his patient and helped him walk over to the house. He carried a bag of medical supplies as well.

He opened the door with a key. Then he helped the wounded young man through the door and turned on the lights.

"Make yourself comfortable on the sofa, Dylan."

"This is a nice place, Doctor," he said as he looked around. "In fact, it's incredible! How long have you had it?"

"It's not mine," Freitag said. "It belongs to some friends of mine. Mike and Vicky Stein. He's a foot doctor. She does pediatrics. They're on a two week vacation. They sometimes let me use their place when they're away."

"They must be doing quite well for themselves," he commented.

He plopped himself down on the sofa.

"Yes," Freitag said. "They're doing fine. I had no intention of using their place this week, but this is an emergency. Take your coat off. Make yourself at home."

"No, thanks," he said. "I'm fine."

"Would you like a drink?"

"A beer would be great," he said. "Thanks. I'm really thirsty. It's been a bad night."

"Given your condition," Freitag recommended. "How about some juice instead? You've lost a lot of blood. And we haven't figured out what to do with you tonight. Staying here is not really an option."

"Juice is fine," he said. "But, why can't I stay here?"

Freitag handed his guest a glass. He sat on the sofa.

"Why don't you tell me what happened first?" he suggested. "It'll keep your mind occupied while I look at that leg. It looks kind of nasty. But, you'll be okay. I think I can fix you up here without having to take you to a hospital."

"You're a *medical* doctor too?"

"I know enough to take care of this," Freitag said. "So, tell me what happened."

His memory was a bit foggy. Still, he did his best to recount the story as the doctor tended to his wound.

When he was finished, Freitag asked, "How does that feel?"

"Not bad," he grunted. "Thanks, Doc."

"Tell me again," Freitag inquired. "Why did you break into the building? That wasn't part of the plan?"

"I keep telling you," he reminded impatiently. "I don't know why I did any of that stuff. Everything seemed to go on pure instinct. I know it wasn't hypnosis, but I still want to know how you managed to talk me into doing those things! Why did I see those people as McMahon and Angela?"

"You weren't supposed to see the woman as Angela," Freitag explained. "You must have done that on your own. Your own anger at that girl carried over. Your anger at both of those people for similar reasons and over a concurrent incident must have driven the rage potential I was trying to bring out into greater proportions than I expected. As I explained to you, this technique is still largely experimental. Frankly, I'm tempted to believe you're in love with Angela. Is she the girl you mentioned before? The girl you 'kind of have a thing for'?"

"Uh…" he fumbled awkwardly. "Maybe."

"Is that why you confronted her in that file room?"

"Well… Possibly."

"Perhaps I should have taken that into account," Freitag theorized. "But, I didn't know. This technique is a legitimate way of digging out emotional insecurities, but I may have needed to study your condition a bit more before throwing you out into something so drastic. You needed to release your anger, but I didn't have proper control over your environment."

"You still haven't told me who those people were, Doctor," he pointed out.

Freitag glanced nervously down in his lap. He took a breath before answering.

Then, he replied, "The woman is my wife, Madeline. The man is her lover. His name is Grant Langley."

"What?" he gasped.

"Before you say anything…"

"Is that what this is about?" he interrupted angrily. "You sent me into that dangerous situation to take care of your marital problems?"

"No," Freitag defended. "It wasn't like that! As I explained, this is a legitimate procedure. I was trying to help you."

"Help me?" he jeered. "By making me guilty of attempted murder?"

"Listen," Freitag began. "The complexities of your emotional disturbance..."

"Don't!" he snapped. "Don't you dare try to rationalize what you've done!"

"Give me a chance to explain."

"You're supposed to be a psychiatrist!" he averred. "You're supposed to be taking care of the people who come to you for help! Have you ever listened to a word I said?"

"Of course I..."

"In all the sessions I've paid for," he pressed on. "Have you ever given a damn about what I go through on a daily basis? Do you know what I have to do just to keep my balloons tied down?"

"Keep your what?"

"Keep my balloons tied down," he explained. "I've always seen the fragile human psyche and emotional well-being as a bunch of balloons filled with helium. Everybody needs a way to keep their balloons grounded so they don't fly away. If your balloons fly away out of reach, a person goes nuts! And, everyone has things in their life that keeps their balloons grounded: family, friends, hobbies, their career or whatever they occupy their minds with to stay sane."

"That's almost poetic," Freitag stammered. "In a sick sort of way."

"So, do you know?" he angrily persisted. "Do you care? Do you know what I have to do in life to keep my balloons tied down?"

"I do care, Dylan."

"No you don't!" he argued. He jumped up to his feet. "You're just like all the rest! You're just like

McMahon! Sitting there in his big house on Park Place! All smiles when talking to your face! But as soon as you get what you want, it's every man for himself!"

"It's not like that."

"You knew the cops were talking to me about that murder last Sunday!" he reminded. "And, you deliberately sent me to kill your wife!"

"You weren't supposed to kill her," Freitag corrected. "You weren't even supposed to harm her. You were only supposed to stab the man and scare her."

"Now I'm going to jail!"

"You weren't supposed to get caught," Freitag pointed out. "That's why you wore a mask. It was supposed to look like a robbery. If you hadn't gotten cut, nobody could identify you and we'd both be home free."

"You see?" he growled. "You just admitted you were only thinking of yourself!"

"No, Dylan!" Freitag disagreed. "This is a legitimate procedure!"

"Legitimate?" he scoffed. "What you did to me is legitimate? You really want me to explore my rage potential? Is that what you want, Doctor? Well, how's this?"

He almost didn't realize he had pulled the knife from his coat.

Freitag gasped as he felt the blade sink quickly into his body just below the sternum up to the hilt.

"Is this rage potential, Doctor?" he shouted. "Is this what you want?"

He buried the knife deeply into his victim's upper chest. Then, he took a step backwards while clutching the bloody weapon in his fist.

"Dylan!" wheezed Freitag. "What are you doing?"

"No one talks to me," he seethed. "Unless they're using me! And you're as bad as everyone else! But now, you're finally doing something for me, Doctor! You are finally of some use to me! You're bleeding! And, it's a spectacular sight!"

"Don't, Dylan!" Freitag begged. "Please! Help me!"

The doctor tried to get up. He cried out in pain as he fell back to the sofa.

"So much blood, Doctor," he smiled with a glazed stare. "It flows so freely from your wounds! Thank you, Doctor! Thank you for finally serving a purpose."

"Dylan! Please!"

"It's a beautiful sight, Doctor," he teased. The look in his eyes grew progressively more frightening. "But, not as beautiful as your wife! She had a distinctly much more beautiful way of bleeding for me!"

"You son of a…" the doctor began as he tried to rise. But he cried out in pain as he fell back to the sofa.

"She bled so sweetly, Doctor," he taunted. "And, she bled just for me!"

"Don't you talk about my wife!" Freitag grunted with pain.

"Good-bye, Doctor," he said. "I have to save a life that no one else cares about. Mine!"

He turned and stormed off toward the front door. It was a labored effort. However, he was able to favor his wounded leg while getting his point across.

"Don't go, Dylan!" Freitag begged. "For God's sake! Please help me! We can work things out! You need my help!"

He gave up when he heard the door slam. Then, he tried again to get off the sofa. He cried out in agony as he failed.

Dylan drove The Space Eagle back toward town. He drove quickly while reaching for his cell phone. He dialed and waited for a response.

"Hello, Mr. McMahon," he finally said. "It's Dylan."

"What can I do for you, Dylan?" Joe asked. "It's kind of late."

"It's kind of late for all of us," he said.

"What does that mean?"

"I've had a busy night," he explained. "My psychiatrist sabotaged my progress for his own personal gain. He sent me on an angry rampage. So far, I've stabbed three people this evening, Mr. McMahon."

"What?"

"I'm in trouble," he said. "I need your help."

"Why did you stab three people?"

"My shrink said he wanted to help me get in touch with my feelings," he answered sarcastically. "It was supposed to be therapy."

"That's his idea of therapy?"

"Evidently."

"So, what do you want from me?"

"You have to give me a place to hide," he explained.

"Are you kidding me?"

"You owe me, McMahon!" he averred. "I've done plenty for you!"

"I'm not harboring a fugitive!" Joe declared.

"You're a murderer!" he reminded. "You can't possibly try to pretend you're squeaky clean in any of this!"

"Don't blame me for whatever mess you dug yourself into," Joe argued.

"I can blame you for whatever I want!" he insisted. "You're the reason I stabbed that man in the first place!"

"What are you talking about?"

"I thought he was you when I stabbed him!" he snarled.

"What? Why?"

"And, I left my shrink at some farmhouse just outside of town," he continued. "I stabbed him and left him to die! I told him everything, McMahon! I told him everything I've done for you! I told him how you repaid me!"

"Are you insane?"

"That's what they tell me," he snickered. "That's why I'm seeing a shrink! Let's just hope he's a good one! Let's hope he's the kind of shrink who won't spill your secret!"

"Why would he?"

"Hey," he informed him. "He's the kind of shrink who sent me to kill his unfaithful wife! If that's indicative of his sense of ethics, I doubt he would risk further jail time just to keep your secret! He's never even met you!"

Joe frowned as he listened to the caller laugh over the phone.

"So, what makes you think I'll help you, Dylan?" he asked.

"'Cause you owe me!"

"Screw you, pal!" Joe barked. "Thanks to you, I have my own problems!"

He slammed the phone down as he hung up.

"I'm absolutely exhausted," he muttered.

"I know, Dave," he said. "Just be thankful there's only 24 hours in a day."

"Why?" Dave asked. "If there was 48 hours, I might have a chance of getting some sleep tonight."

"Don't get melodramatic," he teased. "It's not even 11:30 yet. And, it looks like we might be able to nail Zeblonsky on all these murders after all."

"I hope so," Dave muttered. "I'm sick of this entire case. And, I hate hospitals! They are always so depressing."

They were silent for a moment. They listened to the loudspeaker announcing an emergency for a Dr. Austin.

"How long are we going to have to wait?" Dave snipped impatiently.

"Who knows?" he shrugged. "Freitag was in bad shape when they got him in here. It's a good thing we sent a squad car up to that farmhouse before we got there. If he had to wait any longer for medical attention, we probably would have lost him. There's a good chance we won't even get to talk to him tonight."

"That's just marvelous!"

Finally, the tall, thin doctor stepped out to greet them. "Detective Sumaki? Detective Reynolds?" he addressed.

"How is he, Dr. Tamrakian?" he asked.

"He'll probably pull through," the doctor informed them. "He's lost a lot of blood, but we have him stabilized. Was this done by the same guy who stabbed those other two? The wounds looked very similar."

"That's what we're guessing," he said. "Can we talk to him?"

"You probably shouldn't," the doctor said. "He really needs to rest. I'm not sure if you'll get much out of him, anyway. I just gave him a sedative."

"Can we try?" he insisted politely. "It could be a matter of life and death."

"Okay," the doctor acquiesced with a sigh. "But, keep it short."

"Thank you, Doctor."

They rushed over to his room.

As soon as they entered, Sumaki gently asked, "Dr. Freitag? Can we speak with you, please?"

He looked up at them without a word. It was easy to tell he would soon be asleep.

"Did Dylan Zeblonsky do this to you, Doctor?" Sumaki asked.

"Can't tell you."

"Come on, Doctor," he pressed. "This is no time to stand on convention. We have an attempted murderer on the loose."

"Doctor/patient privilege."

"Face it, Doctor," he continued. "Those days are over for you. Sending Dylan out after your wife and her lover killed your medical career."

"You can't prove anything."

"When we find Dylan," he pushed. "We're going to find a big gash in his shin, aren't we? I don't know how you did it. But, he thought his victims were people he worked with. It'll be over as soon as we catch him. And now, we're going to get him for a few murders that he completed a bit more successfully."

"He didn't kill anyone."

"Karen Broderick?" he reminded. "Cynthia Trott is still missing. And, he just killed Michelle Dorsett earlier today. She was the Maid of Honor."

"It wasn't Dylan."

"How do you know, Doctor?"

Freitag closed his eyes.

"Stay with me, Doctor," he insisted. "What do you know?"

"Dylan was supposed to get paid…"

Freitag's voice was drifting.

"Paid for what, Doctor?" he asked. "Who was supposed to pay him, and for what?"

"Computer glitch," Freitag muttered. "Paid to hack into the hotel security system. The killer didn't pay."

"Who didn't pay, Doctor?" he pressed. "Who's the killer?"

"Can't say! My career!"

"Your career's over anyway, Doctor," he reminded. "You sent your patient out to kill your wife. You're going to lose your license no matter what. You had to know that."

"Doesn't matter," Freitag muttered. "She would've taken everything in the divorce. No Madeline! Nothing! Life was over! I was finished!"

"Who's the killer, Doctor?"

"I can still go out with some dignity... some class," Freitag muttered.

"We have two girls who are dead, Doctor," he reminded. "And one girl's still missing. The classiest thing you can do right now is tell me who's responsible."

The doctor muttered something under his breath.

"Don't fade out on me, Doctor," he ordered. "Stay with me! Who's the killer?"

"Dylan thought Grant was Joe McMahon," Freitag muttered. "That's why he stabbed him. Dylan was mad at Joe. Joe wouldn't pay."

The detectives shared an optimistic glance.

"Are you saying Joe McMahon killed Karen Broderick?" he asked.

"Dylan was mad at Joe," Freitag repeated groggily. "McMahon wouldn't pay."

"Do you have McMahon's address?" he asked.

"Park Place... I think..."

"Let's go!" he told Reynolds. "Thanks, Doctor. Get some rest."

The detectives ran out of the building.

After calling in to the station to get his address, they rushed over to McMahon's Park Place home. A few uniformed officers stayed with them in the front of the building. A few more officers circled around to the back.

They knocked a number of times. They announced that they were the police.

There was no reply. All the lights were out inside.

"Do you believe it?" Reynolds said. "McMahon's not even here! Somebody must have tipped him off."

"Zeblonsky must have called him," Sumaki surmised. "It's not surprising. I kind of half expected to find him here with McMahon. Remember? That's why we brought some officers with us. And now, we're not going to be able to get a warrant until tomorrow morning. Damn it!"

They walked around to the side of the building.

"What do you want to do now, then?" Reynolds asked.

"Let's take a look around the property," he recommended.

"What are you hoping to find?" Reynolds asked.

"We won't know 'til we look."

They searched around for a few minutes. It was difficult to see in this debilitating darkness. Besides, they were both fatigued.

"Detectives!" an officer called out.

As the officer approached, Reynolds asked, "What is it, Collins?"

"There's a big patch dug out back," Collins explained. "It looks like they were going to start some construction work. We found a body. A young woman."

"Let's see what you got," Sumaki said.

They followed Collins to the back of the house.

"We were scouting around," Collins said. "Checking out the site. Wexler tripped over something buried in a shallow spot in the dirt."

They stepped out into the dirt. Reynolds aimed his flashlight at the spot where two officers were uncovering the body.

"Oh, God!" Reynolds winced. "That's a nasty sight! She's pretty torn up, too. And, take a whiff. Smells like she's been here a few days."

"It looks like we found what's left of Cynthia Trott," Sumaki deduced.

"That was our guess," Collins agreed.

"Well," Reynolds smiled. "It looks like this evening wasn't a total waste after all."

"Okay," Sumaki nodded. "Let's put out an All Points Bulletin on Joseph McMahon. It appears we found ourselves a murderer."

Chapter 10
Whispers

The following morning was sunny, but cold. A brisk breeze had kicked up. People were forced to bundle up outside against the blatant reminder that winter was on its way.

However, life resumed its cumbersome duties once a person got back inside.

She was busy cross-checking files at her desk. She hated this part of the job. Still, she knew it was a task that needed doing.

The intrusion of a friendly voice came as a relief.

"Good morning, Angela," she said.

Angela kept a smile on her face as she looked up from her desk. "Hi, Lorraine," she said. "How are you today?"

"A little freaked out, actually," Lorraine said. "Did you hear about what happened last night?"

"No," she said. "What happened?"

"First of all," Lorraine began. "Another girl from the wedding last weekend was killed. They found her body yesterday afternoon."

"Oh no!" she gasped. "Who do you think keeps killing these girls?"

"Don't you watch the news?" Lorraine asked. "They think it might be Joe McMahon."

"Joe? Really?" she asked with wide eyes. She felt a knot in her stomach.

"They found the body of that Cynthia Trott woman," Lorraine explained. "She was buried in a shallow grave at a small construction site behind Joe's house. The police have already been here this morning looking for him."

"Joe McMahon?" she gasped. "That's so hard to believe. He seems like such a nice man."

"That's because you don't work directly for him," Lorraine informed. "He's never nice to the girls who work for him. I tend to think he doesn't like women very much."

"Really?"

"You wouldn't remember this," Lorraine added. "But a few years ago, Joe had a bit of a crush on Karen. He asked her out a few times, but she turned him down. I think she was going to file charges against him, but the assistant managers hushed it up and glossed everything over. This company is a bit of a Good Old Boy Network that takes care of its own. That's probably why nothing happened to Dylan the other day. I hear Joe was over talking to Steve, Rick and the assistant managers. He said you were blowing everything out of proportion."

"I was not!" she argued. "Dylan really frightened me!"

"You don't have to convince me, honey," Lorraine said. "I know what a slimy little weasel he is. He scares a lot of people. You did the right thing by letting it drop. I don't think you would have gotten too far. Even though nobody likes Dylan, this place would have had a bad reaction to a new girl making waves."

"Come to think of it," she recalled. "Neil said something last night about Joe complaining that all the applicants to fill Karen's position were women."

"So, you did go out with Neil last night?" another interested party chimed in.

"Oh… hi, Jennifer," she said. "I didn't see you."

"I just got here," Jennifer explained. "I just came over to find out if you went out with Neil last night."

"We were just discussing the news," Lorraine said. "Michelle Dorsett was killed. And the police found the body of Cynthia Trott behind Joe's house."

"Yes, I heard," Jennifer said. "Can you believe it? I knew Joe was a dirt bag, but I never thought he'd go this far. I bet the agency won't be able to cover his ass this time."

"Have they done that in the past?" she asked.

"They have with Karen," Jennifer nodded. "Something should have been done about that a few years ago. I heard rumors he's been bothering her the whole time. Of course, Karen's always denied it for fear of reprisal."

"If everybody suspected Joe," Angela asked. "Why didn't anyone tell the police?"

"I don't think anyone really suspected Joe," Lorraine said. "He hasn't really done anything in the past two years. At least, not anything you could prove. Karen wasn't saying anything. He had the whole agency behind him. And he's usually so well-mannered, you just wouldn't think he was capable of such a heinous crime."

"It was just a lot easier to believe Dylan was a murderer," Jennifer added. "And now, both Joe and Dylan are out today. And, so is Neil. At first, I thought Neil was out because of your date last night. But, then I heard about Cynthia. And since you're here, I guess maybe you didn't sleep with him."

"Of course I didn't sleep with him!" Angela averred. "It was just a friendly dinner."

"You're not capable of having a friendly dinner with Neil," Jennifer teased. "You two are too hot for each other."

"Nobody's too hot for anybody!"

"Then, why did you kiss him?" Jennifer quizzed.

"Who told you I kissed him?"

"What's going on?" Sarah asked as she approached.

"Angela kissed Neil on their date last night," Jennifer informed her. "She was just going to tell us all about it."

"I knew it!" Sarah grinned. "I knew you two were going to hit it off! How was it?"

"Nobody 'hit it off' with anybody last night," Angela insisted. "It was just a friendly dinner."

"How was the kiss?" Sarah pressed.

"It wasn't really a kiss," Angela defended. "It was just an accident."

"Yup!" Sarah teased with a smile. "You're blushing, sweetie. I'd know that shade of red anywhere. Angela's in love!"

"That must've been some kiss," Lorraine poked.

"Don't kid yourself," Jennifer added. "Angela's been in love with him since the first time those two met."

"I have not!"

"When are you going to see him again?" Jennifer asked.

"I don't know," Angela said. "We didn't discuss it."

"You have a clear shot at him," Lorraine informed her. "Now that Cynthia's out of the way, Neil is yours for the taking!"

The girls shared a laugh.

"Cut it out!" Angela argued. "I'm not taking anybody!"

"You could go to Karen's wake today," Sarah suggested. "I'm sure he'll be there."

The reminder of Karen's wake brought a sullen mood back to the group.

After a pause, Lorraine asked, "Is anybody going to the wake today?"

"I am," Jennifer said. "Karen was kind of a friend. I think almost everyone from Blue Arrow is going to be there. This place will practically be empty this afternoon."

"Are you going, Angela?" Sarah asked.

"I doubt it," she said. "I hardly knew her."

"Is there anything you'd like us to tell Neil for you?" Sarah asked.

"No."

"Okay," Sarah grinned. "We'll just tell him you're waiting for his call, because you can't wait to kiss him again."

The girls laughed.

"That's enough, Sarah!"

"That's right," Jennifer nodded with false sincerity. "I'm sure they won't kiss again unless Angela has another 'accident.' Isn't that right, sweetie?"

"Jennifer!" Angela snipped.

"Alright," Lorraine said. "We'll leave you alone. Today is a solemn occasion. We're saying good-bye to our good friend Karen today."

"And, Angela has to go all day without seeing Neil," Sarah added.

Three girls laughed.

"By the way," Sarah asked. "Did you hear about Joe? They found that Trott girl in some construction site behind his house. Can you believe it?"

"I know," Lorraine said. "We were just talking about it before you got here. And Michelle Dorsett was killed in her apartment yesterday!"

"Yes," Sarah gasped. "I heard about that! Do you think Joe is the murderer?"

"Who else could it be?" Jennifer asked.

"I heard Michelle saw a shadow wearing a bloody bridal veil," Sarah imparted. "Just like Cynthia Trott."

"What are you suggesting?" Angela asked. "You don't think it was Karen, do you?"

"Cynthia slept with the groom," Sarah said. "And, I hear Michelle did, too."

"Are you saying you believe in ghosts?" Angela asked.

"It's easy for *you* to be brave," Jennifer pointed out. "You didn't know Karen. And, you never beat her out for a promotion."

"Oh! I forgot about that!" Lorraine gasped. "Karen was up for that promotion you got last year!"

"If you see any bloody veils, Jennifer," Sarah offered. "Call me!"

"Will you girls please stop?" Angela asked impatiently. "You're being ridiculous! The cops found that girl's body near Joe's house. He's the only murderer!"

"Even if he killed Karen," Lorraine reasoned. "Why would he kill those other two girls?"

"I can't even imagine," Sarah whispered with wide eyes.

"Maybe Karen killed Trott," Jennifer theorized. "Then, she put the body behind Joe's house as a way to tell the cops who the original murderer is."

"Stop it, Jennifer," Sarah declared. "You're starting to scare me."

"How did the cops even know to look behind Joe's house?" Lorraine asked.

"I don't know," Jennifer said. "I haven't heard."

"Neither have I," Lorraine said.

"Do you think Karen could have sent them a sign?" Jennifer suggested.

"You guys are really freaking me out!" Sarah gasped.

"Will all of you just stop?" Angela insisted. "This is childish! We don't know all the details. All we know for sure is that there's no ghost running around in a bloody bridal veil killing everyone who screwed Karen over!"

There was an awkward pause.

"Maybe you have a point," Lorraine sighed finally. "Karen couldn't possibly be behind any of this."

"Of course she couldn't!"

"Fine, Angela," Jennifer said. "But, stay away from Karen's husband, just to be safe. Stick with Neil, and you'll have nothing to fear."

"Right," Sarah agreed. "As long as you don't 'accidentally' kiss Peter Broderick, I'm sure Karen will leave you alone. Have a good weekend."

The girls said their good-byes. They continued to discuss the topic of Karen's ghost as they walked away from Angela's desk.

Angela rolled her eyes. Then, she went back to work.

❧ ❧ ❧

She leaned against the door with a certain amount of pain. She looked in at him. He was lying in bed. His eyes were closed. A tear came to her eye.

She listened to an emergency call on the intercom.

She watched him for a minute. Then, she walked slowly into the room.

"Joshua?" she asked quietly.

He opened his eyes.

"Hello, Madeline."

"May I sit down?"

"Please do."

She groaned as she took a seat near the bed.

"How do you feel?" he asked. "The doctor said your wound isn't that serious."

"It definitely hurts," she said. "But, I got off lucky compared to you and Grant."

"How is Grant doing?"

"He's still in very serious condition," she explained. "They say it's probably not critical, but he's not out of the woods yet. The second stab wound was dangerously close to the heart."

"That's a shame."

"What's a shame?" she asked. "That he's in bad shape? Or that he's probably going to live?"

"I don't know," he grunted. "Let me sleep on it, and I'll get back to you."

She allowed a moment of silence.

Then, she asked, "Why did you do it, Joshua?"

"Why did I do what?"

"Don't, Joshua," she averred. "I'm not an idiot. You sent one of your patients to attack me and Grant. He even went after you. Thanks to you, all three of us are in the hospital. Are you that opposed to the concept of my being happy?"

"You won't be happy with that gigolo, Madeline," he muttered. "He'll only spend my money and make a fool out of both of us."

"You're not going to goad me into raising my voice," she said. "Neither one of us can stand the stress right now. If you can't discuss this rationally, I'll leave."

"Don't go, Madeline."

"Then, tell me why."

He took a moment to compose his thoughts. He sighed heavily.

"I can't lose you, Madeline," he said. "You're my life. Everything I am is because of you. I've done everything for you. I've built my whole life around you."

"Surely, you knew that your career would be over when you pulled this stunt," she pointed out. "What were you thinking?"

"This wasn't a stunt," he explained. "It was a valid psychiatric procedure."

"You sent an unbalanced mental patient to kill me and my lover!" she argued. "How can you justify that? How can you call it a 'valid psychiatric procedure'?"

"I'm not well enough to go into the specifics with you now," he muttered. "And, you don't have the training to understand."

"Don't condescend to me, Joshua," she insisted. "You sent a sick man to kill me!"

"He's not a sick man," he corrected. "And, he's not a mental patient. He's a reasonable, intelligent young man who has a few social and emotional development problems that he needs to iron out."

"So, why did you have him attack me?" she questioned. "Honestly! I was so furious with you last night! I still am! Not to mention frightened! I'd still like to strangle you with your own IV hose! It took a long time for me to cool off to the point where I could talk to you."

"He wasn't supposed to attack you," he said. "He wasn't supposed to hurt you in any way. He was only supposed to go after the gigolo."

"If you can't call him by name," she said. "I'll go. I came here to talk this out like two human beings. If you are incapable of acting civilized, I'm wasting my time."

"I'm sorry," he said. "But what I told you is true. My patient was never supposed to hurt you. I never meant for you to be in any physical danger."

"Then, what went wrong?"

"I misjudged the scope of his anger at the world," he explained. "He's withdrawn and repressive. The idea was to teach him to release his anger through expression. I was trying to teach him that it is okay to show his emotions to others. But, I didn't properly calculate the depths of his rage. It went much deeper than I allowed for."

"Still," she said. "You must have known this would blow up in your face."

"It was just supposed to look like a simple robbery," he muttered. "I figured my patient would release some of his anger, maybe hurt Grant a little. But, nothing serious. I thought it would be just enough to scare you. You'd suspect I might be behind it, but nothing could be proven. My patient could not be identified. I'd never admit anything, but you would know I meant business. You'd know I would not stand for your infidelity. Looking back on it, I should've been more prepared for difficulties."

"Your career is over, Joshua," she politely informed him. "You're finished now. You do realize that, don't you?"

"What does it matter?" he muttered. "You were leaving. You would have taken everything in the divorce. My life was over anyway. It was worth the gamble. I threw the dice. I knew it would be a long shot, but it was my only chance."

She looked at him with a mixture of emotions that included both anger and pity.

"The doctors tell me Grant will probably live," she said calmly. "But, he has a long recovery ahead of him, if he makes it. He's in much worse shape than you are. Either way, I'll never forgive you for what you've done."

"I'm very sorry, Madeline," he said. "This is obviously not how I wanted things to turn out."

"It's too late for that now," she said. "The damage is done. You've shown your true colors. Still, I guess I'm sorry, too."

She looked at her convalescing husband for a few seconds.

"I love him, Joshua."

He muttered something under his breath. Perhaps it was more of a whisper.

It was not a happy statement, in any case.

"It wasn't intentional, Joshua," she continued. "I never meant to hurt you. These things just happen. I really did love you once. I guess I still do, in a way. But, I meant what I said. I'll never forgive you. I won't threaten you with what I plan to do to you in court. I won't take my anger out by strangling you with your IV hose, either."

He watched her with dreary eyes.

"You look so sad and vulnerable lying in your hospital bed," she commented softly. "It's almost pathetic, really. But, there's no need to threaten you.

The law and the courtroom are all in front of you now. What you have done to yourself is punishment enough. It's over for you, darling. And, you have no one to blame but yourself."

He watched her struggle to rise to her feet.

"Grant may have been more physically damaged than you last night," she admitted. "And, I'm sorry things didn't work out between us, Joshua. But, I know now why I made the right choice in choosing him over you. You've seen to that."

"How so?"

"Grant is a better man for me," she gently imparted. "Because he's not absolutely insane."

"You'll see how right he is for you after he gets his hands on your money," he said.

"Ssshhh," she whispered. "Get some rest, dear."

She turned to leave. She turned back with a delicate smile.

"Good-bye, darling," she said quietly. "I'll see you in court."

He opened his mouth to speak as she left.

But, he stopped himself without a word. He knew there was no use.

He just closed his eyes when she was gone. He acquiesced with a dejected sigh.

He sat in the back of his vehicle. He took a sip of bitter, cold coffee. He looked out of the window. There were a few high clouds floating through a pale blue sky. They looked rigid, stoic and unfeeling.

He thought it looked chilly outside.

He ran his fingers through his knotted hair. There was a nervous twitch in his leg.

He needed to calm down. He needed a plan.

He took out his cell phone and dialed. When he got a response, he said, "Hello, Joe. This is Dylan."

"What do you want, Zeblonsky?" Joe sighed with aggravation.

"Where are you?"

"Why is it any of your business?"

"Did you go to work today?" he asked.

"Of course not," Joe said. "And, it's a good thing, too. I watched the news this morning. The cops found Cynthia Trott's body buried in the dirt in a small property behind my house. They want to see me for questioning."

"So, you did kill Cynthia Trott?"

There was no reply.

"Where exactly did you bury her?" he asked. "Why did you bury her so close to your house?"

"My neighbors on the next street over are building a small shed," Joe explained. "It's not supposed to be anything fancy. Just a tool shed. But, they were going to wire it for lights and electricity. The ground was already dug up, but they haven't poured the foundation yet."

"But, why did you bury her there?" he repeated. "You must've known someone would find her eventually during construction."

"I know the family," Joe explained. "He told me they decided at the last minute to wait 'til spring to finish the job. I figured by the time they found the body, it would be there so long that the cops would figure anybody could've dumped it there. In hindsight, I probably should have buried it deeper. But, I had to worry about getting caught."

"That doesn't make any sense," he said. "You deliberately planted that body there to set up the family that owns that property. Didn't you?"

"Bullshit!" Joe barked. "You don't know what you're talking about! Those people didn't know Cynthia! Or anything about this whole mess! The cops would've disregarded them and turned to me immediately after she was found! They would've come to me within minutes of starting their investigation!"

"Then, why did you bury her there?"

"Because she told me to!"

"She told you to?" he asked with surprise. "Who told you to?"

"Never mind!" Joe snapped. "Why am I even talking to you? I still want to know why the cops even came looking for me last night! You must have spilled our secret! How do I know you're not recording this conversation?"

"I told you I wouldn't say anything," he reminded. "I'm on the run, too."

"That's right," Joe recalled. "You told me something about stabbing some people, and something about your shrink and his unfaithful wife. What happened?"

"I'm still not sure," he said. "The doctor told me it wasn't hypnosis, but it seemed like a similar procedure. I was never unconscious, though. It just seemed to open up my mind. Everything seemed brighter and fresher. I could see and breathe and feel everything so much clearer. And the next thing I knew, I was stabbing some man and a woman in some stairwell. I was furious at them! I thought they were the root of all the problems I'd ever had in my life."

"That's incredible!"

"I could've sworn that guy was you," he continued. "And all the anger I held toward you and Angela about the events over the last few days... actually, everything in my life just poured out of me as I stabbed them!"

"Why are you mad at me?" Joe asked. "Are you still mad about that raise? I told you we needed to give that situation time to cool down. I would've taken care of you at the proper time."

"You were just the focal point of all the rage I felt towards my whole life," he explained. "Don't harp on it now. I talked to my shrink, and when he told me he'd just made me attack his cheating wife, I unleashed on him too. That rage came back. And suddenly, *he* was the focal point of my anger. I told him about you, though. He must've survived after I stabbed him. *He* must have told the cops about you."

"Why should I believe you?"

"I'm calling from my SUV," he said. "I'm not going to the cops. I'll be wanted for three counts of attempted murder. That's assuming any of the victims survived. I don't even know if I've gotten over what that slimy shrink did to me. I don't even know if I'll be prone to fly into a rage with little or no provocation."

"That's all the more reason why I should stay away from you," Joe said. "You just admitted I'm one of your favorite targets."

"So, you're not going to help me?"

"Sorry, Dylan," Joe said. "You're on your own."

"I assume you have someplace safe to hide out," he said.

"Yes," Joe said. "Don't worry about me. I'm fine. What are you going to do?"

"I don't have the slightest idea," he said. "I slept in my SUV last night. I guess that will hold me over for the time being. But, I need to come up with something more stable. The cops will be after both of us. And, they won't stop 'til they find us."

"Well… good luck, Dylan," Joe said. "Sorry. I wish I could help. But at this point, I don't feel comfortable sticking my neck out for you."

There was a brief silence.

"Was it worth it, Joe?"

"What do you mean?"

"All of this," he said. "Killing Karen. Cynthia. All of it."

"Good-bye, Dylan."

He hung up. He glanced around the room. It was a nice place. He'd always liked it. However, he knew he couldn't stay here too long.

The cops would eventually be able to tie this place to him.

There was a rumbling in his stomach.

He stood. He walked into the kitchen. It was a beautiful kitchen. All the modern conveniences were presented tastefully at his fingertips.

He thought about Dylan for a moment. He almost cared about the little freak's plight.

Oh well.

He opened the refrigerator and perused its contents. There seemed to be the makings for a sandwich. He took out some bread and put it on the table.

Then, he took out some ham and put it next to the bread.

Then, he took out some Swiss cheese and put it beside the ham.

Next, he took out some mustard and set it beside the bloody bridal veil.

Next, he reached into the refrigerator. Then, he froze.

He spun around with wide eyes. He stared at the table. Everything was where it was supposed to be. There was no bridal veil.

Had it really been there? Had he imagined it?

He walked over to the table. There was nothing on the spot where he thought he'd seen the veil. All the items seemed to have been placed around that spot...

...As if it had been there all along.

He touched that area of the tabletop. It was smooth, hard and dry. It felt just as it ought to feel.

Then, he lifted his hand.

His palm and his fingertips were covered in blood.

He screamed in terror.

He froze. He just stared at the blood on his hand.

Then, he heard a voice.

It softly whispered, "Next, you will kill Peter Broderick."

"No!" he shouted. "No more killing!"

"You *will* kill Peter Broderick," she whispered. "You will do it just for me."

"No!" he insisted in a shaky voice. "I'm not going to kill anyone else! I'm already in enough trouble! You can't make me!"

There was no reply.

He glanced all around the room. He frantically searched for the source of the voice.

However, there was no one else in the room.

There was no sign that anyone had been there...

...Except for the bloody bridal veil that seemed to be back on the kitchen table.

He shrieked in absolute horror.

He took a deep breath before entering the building. He straightened his tie. Then, he opened the door and walked in.

A sign in the lobby pointed him in the direction of the wake for Karen Delia Ryland-Broderick. Apparently, there was more than one person being buried the next day.

People were milling in the hall as he approached the room. He didn't recognize any of them. He stepped into the room. It was filled with mourners talking together in groups.

Someone laughed.

Most of the conversations were hard to make out.

He felt out of place. He felt uncomfortable. He could see the casket at the far end of the room. It was a solemn reminder of why he had come here.

The casket was closed.

He looked around for a familiar face.

Finally, someone called to him. "Neil?" she said.

He smiled at her as he walked over. "Hi, Sarah," he said.

"I'm glad you came," she said. "I've been wanting to talk to you."

"It's always nice to see you, Sarah," he said. "I'm just sorry it has to be at an occasion like this."

"I know," she said. "Poor Karen. I don't think anybody's really gotten over it yet. And now we have to deal with the fact that the murderer may have been Joe McMahon."

"I heard about that," he sighed. "I still can't get over it. Even though he was my boss, he always seemed like a great guy. I can't believe he killed Karen. And now they found my Cynthia's body practically in his back yard! I don't even know what to say. If I get my hands on him, I can promise you I'll find a more inventive place to put the body when I'm done!"

"That's right," she gasped. "I didn't even think of how this would impact on you. How are you holding up, honey?"

"Okay, I guess," he muttered. "I figured she was dead. But, finding her body has put some finality to the matter. I have to start the grieving process all over again. Not to mention, I feel completely betrayed by Joe. I always regarded him as a friend."

"You don't think he'd have the nerve to show up here today, do you?" she asked.

"I should hope not," said another voice. "He's a fugitive now. He's on the lam."

"Hi, Lorraine," Sarah said. "I see you made it here okay."

"Yes," she said. "I got here a few minutes ago. So did Jennifer. She's over talking to the family."

They looked in the direction where Lorraine was pointing.

"Those people are her parents?" Sarah asked. "I should go over and pay my respects."

"And, that's Peter with them," pointed out another voice. "He was the groom."

They turned to face the older woman who was speaking.

"Oh, I'm sorry," she said. "I'm Rachel Carver. I'm a friend of the Ryland family."

"I'm Neil Worthington," he introduced. "This is Sarah Krause and Lorraine Bishop. We were friends of Karen's from work."

"Neil?" she smiled. "Yes! I remember you from the wedding last week."

"That's right," he said. "It's nice to see you again, Mrs. Carver. I just wish it was under better circumstances."

"So do I," she said. "But, please. Call me Rachel. It's nice to meet you, Sarah and Lorraine."

The girls greeted her warmly.

"I recognize Peter," Neil muttered. His eyes narrowed as he glanced over at the gathered family.

"Don't start, Neil," Lorraine advised. "Not here."

"I understand how you feel," Rachel said. "I'm not sure how I feel about him being here, either."

"Why?" he asked.

"It took me a long time to forgive Peter for cheating on Karen a month before the wedding," Rachel explained. "For Karen's sake, I eventually learned to overlook his indiscretions. I loved that girl. And, I wanted her to be happy. But then when I heard what he'd done this past week, I don't think I can ever forgive him."

"What did he do?" Sarah asked.

"I hear he slept with Michelle Dorsett," Rachel said.

"He did?" Sarah gasped.

"I'm not surprised," Neil said.

"Everybody's talking about it," Rachel continued. "Everyone's appalled. You can still hear the whispers going all through the wake of people wondering how he has the nerve to be here. I'm not sure if John and Yvonne Ryland know. I can't imagine they would be so civil to him, if they knew how he's disrespected their daughter's memory."

"Evidently," he grumbled. "The man has no respect for anybody."

"Seriously, Neil," Lorraine reiterated. "Don't start anything at Karen's wake."

"A lot of people have been wondering if that's how Michelle got killed yesterday," Rachel continued. "There's been a lot of speculation that Karen went after Michelle for sleeping with Peter."

"You can't possibly think Karen is responsible," Neil said.

"Who else could it be?" Rachel asked. "That McMahon person may have killed Karen, and maybe Cynthia. But, why would he go after Michelle?"

"I know why he killed Cynthia," Neil said. "He overheard a phone conversation where she told me she remembered something about the murderer. He was covering his tracks. But, I can't think of any reason for him to hunt down Michelle."

"Michelle was Karen's best friend," Lorraine reasoned. "Maybe he figured she would remember something Karen told her."

"That doesn't make any sense," Sarah argued. "There's a good chance that any one of a hundred people could have remembered what happened. I'm sure a number of people who already remembered chose to keep their mouths shut. But still in all, Joe wouldn't possibly try to kill everybody who knew about what he did in the past."

"Maybe if he had been stalking her all along," Neil theorized. "He may have guessed that Karen would have been telling Michelle about it."

"That's ridiculous," Sarah disagreed. "It's too much idle speculation. Nobody would kill anybody over so much wild guessing and hypothesizing."

"You're probably right," Neil said. "I'm just trying to make sense of all this."

"So, who killed Michelle?" Rachel asked.

They all looked at each other in wonder.

"Could it be...?" Sarah finally ventured.

She couldn't finish what she had started to say.

"... Karen?" Lorraine concluded.

There was an eerie pause.

"Hi," said a new voice. "What are you all talking about over here."

"Hi, Jennifer," Neil said. "The girls were just trying to convince me that Karen's ghost killed Michelle yesterday."

"Well," Jennifer reminded. "Michelle did see Karen's shadow wearing the bloody bridal veil one day before she was killed."

"Cynthia mentioned seeing something like that, too," Neil muttered.

"You have to admit," Jennifer said. "That's one spooky coincidence."

"I'm not even going to talk about this anymore," he declared. "This is childish. We're here to pay our respects to Karen's family. I'm going over to speak to her parents."

"Before you go, Neil," Jennifer added. "I've just got to know. When are you going to call Angela? She was wondering when she could see you again."

"Was she really?" he asked. He tried to hide his enthusiasm.

"She said she really enjoyed your hot date last night," Sarah added with a grin.

"I can't picture her describing our dinner as a 'hot date'," he said doubtfully.

"That may be true," Jennifer had to admit. "But, I know she wants you to call her. She's dying to see you again."

"Did she really say that?" he asked. That enthusiasm was getting harder to hide.

"Not in so many words exactly," Jennifer allowed. "But, believe me. She does. I know about these things. Trust me."

"I was hoping to see her today," he said. "Of course, I didn't go to work because of Cynthia. Why didn't she come to the wake?"

"She didn't really know Karen," Lorraine said.

"Oh," Jennifer said. "I meant to tell you, Neil. I'm sorry to hear about Cynthia."

"Thank you."

"Me too," Sarah said. "Perhaps a nice dinner out with Angela would help make you feel better."

"I did have a nice time with her last night," he said.

"So we heard," Sarah replied with a sly grin.

"I'd love to call her," he said. "But, I don't have her cell phone number."

"I'll give it to you," Sarah volunteered.

"Thanks."

"We should probably go over and talk to Mr. and Mrs. Ryland first," Lorraine suggested. "Peter wandered off, and they look like they could use some cheering up."

"Yes," Jennifer nodded. "We'll give you Angela's number later. Let's go talk to the Rylands first."

"Okay," he agreed. "Thanks, girls."

As they approached the Rylands, Peter was over at the far side of the room. He was talking to a friend.

"I'm sure some of these people know I slept with Michelle," he said. "I can't imagine how they found out. I didn't say anything to anyone. But, I've seen the looks people have given me. I've overheard some of the comments and judgmental whispers. I feel guilty enough already. I don't need their sanctimonious crap to add to my guilt. I already feel bad enough."

"Do you think Michelle might have mentioned it to somebody?" he asked.

"I doubt it," Peter said. "She wouldn't have wanted anyone to find out yet. She knew it was best to keep quiet at this stage. Besides, I think she felt a bit guilty herself."

"She would have to," he said. "If she cared at all about Karen."

"Can I confide in you, Scott?"

"Sure."

"Michelle saw Karen," he informed. "Right after we had sex. Just one day before she was killed."

"What are you saying?" Scott asked. "She saw Karen's ghost?"

"Yup," he nodded nervously. "Do you believe it? She was so scared. At first, I figured it was just her guilt playing on her. Then, she got murdered the next day! I found her body! It was a gruesome sight! I'll never forget it as long as I live!"

"Didn't you say the cops found some evidence?" Scott asked.

"Some inconclusive footprints," he explained. "They cleared me as a suspect. They didn't prove much else."

"But, aren't the cops looking at Karen's boss as the murderer?" Scott asked.

"Maybe for Karen and Cynthia," he said. "But, that doesn't explain Michelle's death. Why would that guy want to kill Michelle?"

"Beats me," Scott shrugged. "So, what are you trying to tell me?"

"Can you keep a secret?" he asked as he leaned in.

"You know I can."

"I saw Karen, too," he whispered.

"You're kidding!"

"No," he whispered. "It was just before I went to check on Michelle. In fact, that's the reason why I decided to check on Michelle to see if she was okay. And of course, that's when I found…"

He couldn't bring himself to complete his sentence.

"Michelle's body?" Scott concluded. "But, you don't really believe you saw Karen, do you?"

"She was wearing that bloody bridal veil," he continued. "Just like Michelle said. It really freaked me out! At first, I thought it might be my guilt. But then when I saw Michelle dead in her bath tub, I practically had a coronary! I tell you, I don't believe in ghosts. But after what I've seen, I have to admit I'm scared as hell!"

"Why are you telling me this?" Scott asked.

"Well, I have to tell *somebody*," he explained. "I can only see Michelle's sighting of Karen as a foreshadowing. It was a warning that Karen wanted her to die. When I saw Karen, it must have been an omen. It told me to check on Michelle. And, she was dead! Maybe it was also a sign that I'm next!"

"You can't be serious!"

"What else am I supposed to think?" he surmised. "There was no reason for Michelle to die. Karen's boss had no reason to kill her. Michelle's murder could only serve one possible function. Karen wanted revenge because of me!"

"Ghosts going after revenge?" Scott scoffed. "This whole mess is really getting to you, Peter. God knows, nobody can blame you. You've been through a lot this past week. But, you can't let yourself get carried away with this crap."

"You should've seen it, Scott," he insisted. "It was her! It was really her! And, that veil! I'll never forget that bridal veil as long as I live! I know it sounds preposterous! I wouldn't have believed it either! But, it was her, Scott! I swear to God I saw her!"

"Alright," Scott said. "Calm down. Everything's fine now."

"What if it was a sign, Scott?" he asked. "What if Karen's really coming after me next? What am I going to do?"

"Pull yourself together, Peter," Scott said. "Would you feel better if I let you stay with me and Terri for a couple of days?"

"You wouldn't mind?"

"Well, I'd have to discuss it with Terri, of course."

Peter saw the look of pity on Scott's face.

"Wait," he said. "No! I'm not going to do this. You're right. I'm acting like a fool. I'm letting all this shit get to me."

"You've had a rough week."

"No," he insisted. "I don't believe in ghosts. I'm not going to be a coward! I'm a man! And, I'm not going to go running off like a scared little schoolgirl because my mind is playing tricks on me. You're right. I've had a rough week!"

"I'm glad you're thinking straight again," Scott said.

"Right," he nodded. "I'll be fine. Thanks, Scott. You're a good friend. Sorry for that little display right then. But, I'm okay now."

"Don't mention it," Scott said. "Anytime."

"One more thing," he said quietly. "Don't tell anybody about this."

"Hey. It never happened."

❧ ❧ ❧

He smiled when he saw the number of the caller on his cell phone.

"Hello, Dr. Freitag," he answered. "How are you feeling?"

"Dylan? Where are you?"

"I think it's better to ask, 'Where are *you*, Doctor?'" he said. "I half expected to hear you were dead."

"I'm in the hospital," Freitag explained. "I'm still very weak. I'll probably be here for a week or so. Luckily for me, the police were on their way over to the Stein house by the time you left me there."

"How nice for you."

"My wife should be getting out tomorrow," Freitag continued. "Her lover got the worse of it. But, he'll probably pull through. It looks like everyone will live."

"So, I guess I'm not a murderer," he said. "Perhaps my rage has yet to live up to its full potential."

"The point is, Dylan," Freitag said. "You're not beyond all hope. You haven't killed anyone, and it's best to keep it that way. I will assume all responsibility for what happened, of course. If you turn yourself in, your legal liability will be minimal. You won't spend much time in jail, if any. They'll have me to throw the book at. I'll bear the brunt of the criminal proceedings. Plus, I'm sure my career is over. I'll pay the heaviest price. Turn yourself in, Dylan. Don't make things worse for yourself."

"I'm sorry, Doctor," he said. "I happen to like experiencing my emotions. I like expressing myself. It's liberating! It's exhilarating! I'm looking forward to expressing myself more often from now on."

"Don't, Dylan," Freitag advised. "This was supposed to be temporary. This was all a terrible mistake. Come back. Let me help you."

"Do you realize," Dylan asked. "That I've spent the day painting my SUV a thick coat of black? I'm almost done. I hate to do it. It took forever to paint that Space Eagle design on the sides. Now it's just a hindrance. It makes my vehicle too easy to identify."

"Please come back, Dylan," Freitag begged. "Turn yourself in. It's not too late for you. You can still get out of this without ruining your life."

"Don't worry, Doctor," he said. "I'll spare your life as a gift for opening my eyes. But, Joe McMahon, Angela Pierce and Neil Worthington still have to pay!"

"Don't do it, Dylan!" Freitag averred. "Something's wrong! The procedure wasn't supposed to last this long! You need help!"

"You have helped me enough, Doctor," he said. "Thank you. And, give my regards to your lovely wife. The one who bleeds so divinely."

"Dylan! Listen to me!"

"Good-bye, Doctor."

He hung up as he smiled. He dunked his paint brush into the can. Then, he slapped the black paint over the face of his beloved Space Eagle.

He watched its angry eyes disappear under a thick coat of black.

Chapter 11
Dearly Departed

"I see you found another expensive, romantic restaurant," she observed.

"You make it sound like you think I have a hidden agenda," he replied.

"It's not all that hidden."

"Listen, Angela," he said. "I just want to have a nice, quiet dinner where we can get to know each other a little better. I know it seems like the girls at the office are pushing us together, but I really do want this. I really want us to get a little closer."

"I could kill Jennifer," she said. "I don't believe she gave you my cell phone number. And at a wake, no less! It's nice to see she has her priorities in order."

"Is it really a problem?" he asked. "My having your number?"

"I don't know," she shrugged as she turned her eyes to the table. "I guess not. I just wish I was in on their little plan."

"Jennifer and Sarah both intimated that you were hoping I'd call," he said.

"Did they?" she asked. "I'm not surprised. I can just picture them giving you some embellished account of how I was mooning over you in the office or something."

"Were you mooning over me?"

"I'm sure they saw it that way," she said. "I just told them we had a nice friendly dinner. Then, they started going through the phone book so they could help me pick out wedding invitations."

They shared a chuckle.

"That's our girls," he smiled. "Always digging around to find something to gossip about. They're basically harmless, though. I suppose."

"Yeah. I suppose."

"To tell the truth," he said. "I wish they'd let the subject drop too. I get the impression you still think they had something to do with why I've asked you out."

"Well, it's only natural to wonder," she said. "I have a lot to wonder about, actually. After all, you just lost your girlfriend."

"Yes," he said. "And, thanks for bringing that up."

"I'm sorry," she said. "But under the circumstances, I still have to worry about your motives."

"I don't blame you," he said. "I know it must seem a bit strange. I'm not usually the kind of guy who runs to one girl after losing another. And of course, I have no history of having to deal with disappearance and murder. Believe me. I don't take what happened to Cynthia lightly. It did tear me up. I was inconsolable this morning when they told me they found her body.

And when they mentioned Joe's involvement, I was sent into all kinds of negative emotions."

"I can imagine."

"But, it's like I told you before, Angela," he continued. "Cynthia and I were headed for a breakup anyway. I had considered calling you before Karen's wedding, even without any interference or prodding by Jennifer and the girls."

"Is that so?"

"You don't sound like you believe me," he said. "But, it's true. That's what makes the girls' interference so detrimental. Their input makes it look as though they somehow inspired me to call you."

"It does seem that way a little, Neil."

"Not at all," he said. "In fact, all their continuous fanfare made it much harder to call you. I prefer working without an audience."

"That's understandable."

"And of course," he added. "Everything that's happened this past week only makes it worse. I know the timing seems dreadful."

"Yes. It does."

"Still," he said. "You agreed to go out with me. That makes me feel much better. And, you even let me pick you up at your place this evening. We're making progress."

"I wouldn't call it 'progress' just yet."

"What would you call it?"

She glanced back down at the table as she considered her reply.

"Right now," she finally said. "I'd just call it 'dinner'. Hey! A girl has to eat."

He watched the look in her eyes. It made him smile.

"Okay, fine," he allowed. "'Dinner' it is."

She used a fork to toy with her food.

After a few moments, she said, "You seem to be handling it well."

"Handling what well?"

She looked at him. She cautiously ventured, "Cynthia."

"Not really," he sighed heavily. "You forget. That's one of the reasons I asked you out. I'd prefer not to think about her. I'd rather not think about it."

"Sorry."

"That's all right," he said. "Of all people, you have the most reason to wonder how I'm taking it."

"Just curious," she said. "I do care… in my own way."

"It still hurts," he said. "That's why I won't be going to Karen's funeral tomorrow. I just couldn't face two of those things in one week. For Karen's sake, I had to put in an appearance at the wake. She was a sweet girl, and I worked with her for a few years. But I couldn't take the main ceremony tomorrow. I just couldn't."

"I don't blame you."

"I still want to kill Joe," he added. "I'm hurt. I'm angry. But, I'll move on. I have to. What's the alternative? Right?"

"I'm sorry I brought it up."

"That's okay," he said. "But, let me turn the tables on you. You've been grilling me pretty good so far this evening. But, let me ask you why you came here tonight, if you're so suspicious of me."

"I already told you," she reminded. "A girl's got to eat."

"And, I'm supposed to believe that's your only reason for being here?" he asked.

"Believe what you will," she said. "I think you've already made up your mind about what you want to read into this evening."

"Well," he pointed out. "Going by what Sarah told me at the wake today, I'd say your motives involved more than just food."

"Sarah does a lot of talking."

"And judging by that kiss last night," he pressed. "I'd say Sarah isn't so far off."

"Hey," she defended. "You kissed me. I can hardly be blamed for whatever you think that was."

"If you say so, sweetheart," he poked. "But the fact remains, you're here tonight."

She looked down at the table again. She moved some linguini around her plate with her fork.

"I'm sorry," he said. "This conversation took a wrong turn a long way back. We should get back on track. All of these questions are so pointless and counterproductive. We're both here because we both want to be. We should leave it at that."

"You're right," she said. "We're both behaving badly, aren't we?"

"Not that badly, really," he said. "This past week has taken a toll on all of us. I guess everyone at Blue Arrow has an increased urge to watch their backs."

"I guess."

"So, tell me, Angela," he asked. "How is it that a beautiful girl like you didn't already have plans on a Friday night?"

"I don't know," she shrugged. "I've only lived in town for about a month or two. I don't really know anyone in Thorn Ridge yet."

"Where do you come from?"

"Seattle."

"Seattle?" he asked. "What prompted you to move so far east?"

"My father got a job in Pittsburgh," she explained. "I live by myself. And sure, I had friends and a worthless office job out in Seattle. But, I had no real reason to stay."

"Was there a guy involved?"

"Why does everybody ask that?" she snipped. "Why can't a girl do something to improve her life without everybody asking if a guy is involved? If you move, it has to be because of a guy! If you change jobs or a hair color, it has to be because of a guy! Why does everybody think a girl can't just do something on her own? Why is that?"

"Whoa!" he said. "I'm sorry. I didn't mean to unleash some sort of beast here, honey. I was just asking a simple, innocent question."

"Sorry," she sighed. "I guess I did it again. I shouldn't be so defensive. I just hear that question way too often. I just moved here because I had nothing serious holding me to Seattle."

"Well," he said. "I, for one, am glad you're here."

"Thank you."

Later that evening, he dropped her off at her apartment.

"Well, dinner *and* a movie," he said. "I guess this counts as a real date."

"Maybe. Kind of."

"Thank you, Angela," he said. "I can't tell you how much I needed this tonight. You really made me feel better."

"Don't mention it," she said. "I should be thanking you, Neil. It was a wonderful dinner. And, the movie was great, too. I'm sorry for putting you through the wringer before. I know I need to lighten up a little bit."

"That's okay," he said. "I had a great time. Can I walk you to your door?"

"Sure. Thanks."

Her smile made the whole evening seem worthwhile.

He got out of the car. He circled around to the passenger's side. He opened the door for her and walked her up the steps to her building.

As they stood outside in the brisk autumn air, she looked up at him sweetly. "Thanks again, Neil," she said. "I really enjoyed myself."

"You're entirely welcome," he said. "By the way, now that I have your cell phone number, is it okay if I use it sometime?"

"I suppose so."

This kiss did not catch her by surprise. She knew it was coming. She closed her eyes. She willingly allowed this kiss to carry her on its destined course.

She may have even steered a little as she got swept up in the brief journey.

Afterwards, they said good night.

He made sure she got safely inside her building. Then, he went back to his car. He drove home through the dark, silent streets of Thorn Ridge.

When Angela was in her apartment, she sat in front of her television. She started watching the end of some cheesy movie on cable.

She didn't pay much attention. She was distracted. She was uneasy.

For one thing, how much would Jennifer and Sarah be able to guess without her saying a word? Once they suspected, how much would they torture her?

And, for how long?

❧ ❧ ❧

Earlier that evening, he was lying in bed. He winced with pain as he talked on the phone.

"How did you know I was in the hospital, Mr. Polopous?" he asked.

"Finding people is my job, Doctor," Polopous said. "I'm very good at what I do."

"Well, as you can tell," he said. "I had a very good reason for missing our appointment today."

"So, things didn't go so well for you, eh?" Polopous grinned. "I told you revenge is an ugly game. I told you to be careful not to dig your own grave."

"You were right," he said. "I should have listened. I let my emotions get the better of me. Obviously, I'll be laid up for a while. I'm very sorry, Mr. Polopous. You'll have to wait for your money."

"How long will you be in the hospital?" Polopous asked.

"They tell me a week to ten days."

"I'm not in the habit of giving extensions, Doctor!" Polopous grumbled.

"There's not much I can do about it," he explained sharply. "And of course, after the hospital, I'll be going straight to jail. But, don't worry. I won't let you down."

"Okay," Polopous sighed impatiently. "I know you're a good man. I'm sure you'll cover your debts. I'll be in touch, Doctor. Get well soon."

"Thank you," he said. "And, good evening."

He hung up the phone by his bed. He settled back down against the pillows with an aggravated grunt. Luckily, the nurse came in at that moment with the pain pills he had asked for. He thanked her before she left.

As he popped the pills into his mouth, two visitors entered his room.

"Hello, Detectives," he said. "To what do I owe the pleasure?"

"Good evening, Dr. Freitag," Sumaki said. "How are you feeling?"

"This pill will start working in a few minutes," he said. "I'll be feeling much better then. What can I do for you, gentlemen?"

"We found Cynthia Trott's body over near Joe McMahon's house," Sumaki informed. "You were right about him being the murderer."

"I told you he was the murderer?" he asked with surprise.

The detectives shared a glance.

"In a manner of speaking," Reynolds said.

"What we need from you now, Doctor," Sumaki explained. "Is any suggestions you may have concerning the whereabouts of Dylan Zeblonsky."

"We talked to his mother already," Reynolds added. "She didn't have anything to give us. Do you know where he might hide out?"

"I couldn't even hazard a guess."

"We figured he may have confided in you," Reynolds explained. "Since you're his psychiatrist. Maybe he has friends that nobody else knows about, or secret hobbies or something. We checked a store he mentioned called The Atomic Avenger. We got a few names of friends. We talked to those people, but none of them have heard from him. Are you sure you can't tell us anything?"

"I would if I could, gentlemen," he assured them. "Believe me. Frankly, I'm worried about him. I think he might be dangerous."

"I thought you told us he wouldn't hurt a fly, Doctor," Sumaki reminded. "What happened to that theory?"

"I'm afraid that's all my fault," he explained. "Dylan was a very introverted young man. It was my idea to use a new experimental technique somewhat similar to hypnosis in order to explore and express his true emotions. The idea is that if he feels free to express his emotions by circumventing his fears and going straight to the root of his most basic hates, desires and anger, he will no longer be afraid to express himself in the more normal every day situations like a typically well-adjusted person can."

"You're saying this is a form of hypnosis?" Sumaki asked.

"No," he said. "There are similarities, but there are also vast differences. I don't want to go into a long, complicated explanation. But, expanding into a mindset whereby he was able to release a short burst of the rage he felt towards people he disliked was meant to open his consciousness to the concept of acting in a normal way to the public. It was supposed to bring him out of his shell."

"So, you used your wife and her lover as victims in this ugly little experiment of yours," Sumaki said. "Is that right?"

"Yes," he begrudgingly admitted. "And, I know now that it will cost me my career. But, it was supposed to be a quick release of aggression. It should have been over as soon as he walked away. But, I've talked to him on the phone today. He won't tell me where he is. But, I get the feeling he hasn't snapped out of it. I have the distinct impression he means to hurt someone else."

"Who do you think he wants to hurt, Doctor?" Reynolds asked.

"Joe McMahon, for one," he replied. "Maybe a few more people in his office. There's a good chance he may be dangerous. And, it's all my fault. I tried to convince him to turn himself in. He wouldn't listen. He's not himself, gentlemen."

"If he plans on hurting anyone," Sumaki stated. "We'll have to stop him."

"He's a good young man," he said. "He has his problems, but he's a decent person. This is just a misdirected exploration that somehow went wrong. And I'm not sure how to fix it. It's all my fault!"

"Well, I hope you are aware, Doctor," Sumaki informed him. "That your misdirected exploration is going to cost you more than just your career. We have officers posted outside your room. As soon as you are well enough, you'll be going to jail for your role in the assault on your wife and Grant Langley."

"I know," he sighed with resignation. "I've been told. I deserve it, I suppose. Looking back on this incident, I wish I had done things differently."

"At least you learned your lesson," Reynolds commented.

"Not that it does me any good now," he muttered.

"Try calling Dylan again," Reynolds suggested. "Let's see what his present state of mind is."

"I know I shouldn't be using my cell phone in the hospital," he said. "But, this is an emergency."

He dialed. He listened to the ringing of Dylan's phone until his voice mail came on.

He hung up.

"It's no use," he said. "Dylan's not answering at the moment."

"Is there anything else you can tell us?" Sumaki asked.

"Only that he mentioned something about painting over the design on the side of his SUV," he said. "So it wouldn't be so easy to identify. I can't remember what color he told me precisely. But, black would be the most logical option."

"That's nice to know," Sumaki said. "By the way, we made some inquiries. It turns out Joe McMahon did show signs of having a crush on Karen Broderick. There were various reasons people didn't mention it before. Either people forgot because no action occurred on the subject for a few years, loyalty or fear of reprisal at the workplace. Most people just didn't think he was capable of such an act of hostility."

"That's often the case," he said. "It's hard for most people to imagine someone we know is capable of that kind of violence."

"We also heard rumblings that McMahon was not very fond of women as a whole," Reynolds added. "I think you mentioned we might be dealing with a misogynist. A few of his coworkers reinforced your theory, Doctor."

"I'm not surprised."

"So far, he's killed two women after killing Karen," Sumaki said. "Both women had a brief affair with Karen's husband. We don't know what other trait they may have shared, except that they may have had information on Karen's murder. Is there any reason to believe McMahon will go on killing?"

"I couldn't even guess," he said. "I never met the man. I have no idea what his motives are. I'm more concerned with Dylan. He's more of an immediate threat."

"Okay," Sumaki said. "Thanks, Doctor. I hope you're feeling better. We'll let you know how things progress."

The detectives left the room.

The doctor was glad they were gone. His pills were starting to kick in.

He was very tired... and very upset.

As they walked to their car, Reynolds said, "You almost have to feel sorry for the old guy. He got into all this just because his wife was cheating. His whole world is just about finished now. Still, you'd expect more mature behavior from a psychiatrist."

"It just goes to show you," Sumaki said. "Women can screw up anybody. However, our main concern is Zeblonsky. That's one messed up kid that we have to catch before anyone else gets hurt."

"Or even worse," Reynolds added. "Killed!"

❧ ❧ ❧

Saturday morning was gray and dismal. It was the sort of day that should be reserved for funerals.

It was just after 11:00. People were gathered at the cemetery near a freshly dug hole in the earth. Heavy jackets were worn over respectful dark suits and black dresses. Umbrellas were opened against the cold rain.

"Oh, John," she said with sympathy. She offered a hug. "How are you holding up?"

"As well as any man who's about to bury his daughter, I suppose," he muttered. "It's been a difficult week. I still can't believe this is happening."

"I know," she said. "Nobody can."

"Thanks for coming, Rachel," he said. "It means a lot to us."

"Think nothing of it," she said. "I'm sorry I didn't see you before the funeral. I've been running late this morning. I'm such a scatter-brain."

"We're just glad you made it," he said.

"Oh, Yvonne," Rachel said. "This has got to be killing you."

The two women hugged.

"It is, Rachel," she sniffed as she wiped her eyes. "You never think this can happen to you. A mother should never have to bury her child. She was so young and pretty and so intelligent. Her whole life was in front of her. God! I feel so guilty!"

"Guilty?" Rachel said. "What do you have to feel guilty about?"

"The police told us her boss is the main suspect," Yvonne said. "That bastard killed my little girl! I remember Karen telling me about a harassment issue a few years ago. I told her to stay with the company. I told her it would pass. The salary she was making, and the benefits. I told her it would be stupid to throw it away. Oh, God! I killed my little girl!"

She began to cry uncontrollably.

"Of course you didn't," Rachel consoled her. "It wasn't your fault."

"Of course not," John said as he took his wife into his arms. "Don't blame yourself, sweetheart. You had no way of knowing. It wasn't you, dear. There's only one person who's responsible for this. It wasn't you."

He did his best to stop her tears.

A closed casket was set on two supports over the open grave.

An elderly priest waited patiently as the last few cars stopped near the gravesite. Mourners exited their vehicles. Two young men in their twenties approached the grieving parents of the dearly departed.

"Mr. and Mrs. Ryland?" he addressed. "I'm sorry to disturb you. I know how you must be feeling."

"That's alright, Scott," John said. "It was nice of you to come. You too, Brady."

"Well, Karen was a friend," Scott said. "She was a good girl. I wanted to pay my respects. And, I wanted to offer my sincere condolences for your loss."

"Me, too," Brady said. "I'm very sorry for your loss."

"Thank you, gentlemen," John said. "We appreciate it. Feel free to stop by the house after the service. We'll be having a buffet for family and friends."

"Thanks," Brady said. "We'd love to."

"Yes," Yvonne agreed as she wiped her eyes. "You boys are welcome to come to the house. We appreciate your coming today."

"Thank you, Mrs. Ryland," Scott said.

"Rachel Carver," John introduced. "This is Scott Tribbau and Brady Hathaway. They are friends of Karen and Peter."

"Nice to meet you," Rachel said.

"The pleasure is ours," Scott said.

"By the way," John added in an irritated tone. "I noticed Peter couldn't be bothered to show up to his own wife's funeral. What's the matter? Is he too busy having sex to notice that today they were going to bury his new bride?"

"I'm sure it's nothing like that, sir," Scott said. "I'm sure there's a perfectly good reason why Peter isn't here."

"I know Karen, Cynthia and Michelle are dead," John continued. "But, I'll bet there are plenty of other women in Thorn Ridge that Peter hasn't gotten to yet."

"I'm sure he's not doing anything like that, sir," Scott assured. "He was devastated when Karen died."

"Then, what was he doing with that slut, Michelle Dorsett?" John grumbled. "If he gave a damn about my daughter, where the hell is he now?"

"Don't do this, John," Yvonne urged. "Please. Not here. Not now."

John saw the tears in his wife's eyes.

"You're right," he said. "This isn't the time."

"I'm sure there's a logical explanation," Brady said.

"Just drop it," John said calmly. "You're very kind to defend your friend. But, you don't need to bother. You boys came, and that's all we care about. My wife and I appreciate your support."

"Thank you, sir," Brady said.

As Yvonne began to cry again, John took her in his arms.

Scott took the opportunity to pull his friend aside.

"It is kind of strange," he observed. "Isn't it, Brady?"

"What?" Brady asked. "The fact that Peter's not here? Yeah. It struck me as being kind of odd, too. Why?"

"Well, aren't you curious?"

"Sure," Brady nodded. "I can't imagine Peter missing this for anything."

"Maybe we should go check on him after this is over," Scott suggested.

"I'm with you," Brady agreed. "I called him when we were driving over here. I got no answer. I'll call him again after we get to the Rylands' place. If I can't get through, we can go over to his place this afternoon."

"Sounds good," Scott concurred. "I know he was planning to attend. Hey. Look. I think they're getting ready to start this thing."

They looked on respectfully as the priest called for everyone's attention.

It was time to say the final farewell to Karen before lowering her into the ground on a rainy Saturday.

❧ ❧ ❧

She sat in a booth at The Ruby Red Diner. It was her favorite greasy spoon eatery in the downtown area.

The lunch rush was nearly over. It was closing in on 1:30. Only half of the counter and tables were occupied. Those that were empty were still littered with the dirty dishes of the customers who had just left. Uniformed waitresses rushed around cleaning up the mess.

She paid no attention to the chaos going on all around her. She sipped her iced tea and watched the rain outside her window.

An attractive brunette in glasses took a seat across from her in the booth.

"Hi, Angela," she said as she sat. "How are you?"

"Hi, Barbara," Angela said. "I'm fine. And you?"

"Not bad," Barbara said. "Your arm looks much better. That's a much smaller bandage than you had the last time I saw you."

"Thanks," she said. "I told you they overdid it when they first bandaged me up. It wasn't nearly as bad as they made it look."

"So, you're healing nicely?" Barbara asked. "That's nice to see. Did you order yet?"

"No," she said. "I figured I'd wait for you. I'm not that hungry."

"Why not?"

"I don't know," she said. "They're supposed to be burying that girl who got murdered at work today. It's a bad day for a funeral. It seems to me the rain would just make everyone feel worse."

"You do seem a bit down today," Barbara observed. "I didn't think you knew her all that well. Is it really bothering you?"

"I don't know," she shrugged. "I did know her. I guess that sort of thing always gets to me."

"Well, try not to think about it," Barbara advised. "Think about something happier. Didn't you have a big date last night? How did it go?"

"It wasn't a big date," she corrected. "It was dinner and a movie."

"Fine," Barbara said. "Whatever you call it, how did it go?"

"It was good," she said. "I had a great time."

"What movie did you see?"

"Some action flick," she said. "'Hero in ripped T-shirt with machine gun single-handedly wipes out army of terrorists', or something like that. Lots of explosions and people getting shot out of palm trees and hotel windows. Car chases galore. Jeeps chasing tanks and vise versa."

"Sounds good," Barbara said. "I think I saw the commercial for that. I kind of wanted to see it. Did the hero have a tank or a jeep?"

"It depends on what part of the movie you're up to," she said.

291

They shared a laugh.

"So, this date," Barbara said as she saw the opportunity. "It was with that guy from work? The one you don't have a thing for?"

"Yes," she sighed. "And, don't you start. I get enough of that at the office."

"I'm not starting anything," Barbara said. "I'm your friend. I'm just asking you how it went."

"Fine," she said. "I really enjoyed it."

She paused for a moment.

"To tell you the truth, Barbara," she confided. "I really do like him a little. And our times together have been great. But, there's a reason why I hate to admit it. Well, two reasons, actually."

"I'm glad to hear you say it," Barbara smiled. "It is kind of obvious when you talk about him. I'm sure those girls at the office pick up on it, too. That's why they tease you. I'm sure they don't mean any harm."

"I know," she said. "In their own way, they're probably trying to help. They seem to want to include me in their little circle of friends. And this thing with me and Neil gives them something to gossip about. They're nice girls and all, but I just don't like feeling like I'm going to see my picture in the office tabloids just because I'm talking to some guy."

"I know how you feel," Barbara said. "Especially at this early, delicate stage of the game. You need some privacy. Just to see how and if anything develops."

"Exactly."

"So," Barbara deduced. "The girls at the office are one reason you hate to admit that you like this guy. What's the other reason?"

"His last girlfriend was just killed," she said. "They were still together when all this started. He swears they were over, but how do I know it's true? I don't want to be just some meaningless rebound affair he has while he's getting over someone else. I don't want to do this unless it's for real."

"I don't blame you."

"I'm not going to be some disposable bimbo that he can use and then throw away when he's done," she declared. "If he's not serious about this, I don't want to waste my time."

"So, what does your heart tell you?" Barbara asked.

"That's just it," she said. "I'm not sure yet."

"Then, tell him, Angela," Barbara advised. "Don't rush into anything you're not ready for. Be certain. You deserve the best, Angela. Don't put yourself out there until you know what you're 'out there' for."

"You're right," she said. "I'll be careful. But, I really do like this guy."

"There are plenty of guys out there that you could really like, if you wanted," Barbara said. "But hopefully, you're only going to end up with one of them. Make sure this guy's the one. That's all I'm saying."

"Thanks, Barbara," she smiled. "You always know how to make me feel better."

"I aim to please," Barbara said. "Now, if I just knew how to get someone to come over and take our order, we'd be in business."

She looked around at the various waitresses scurrying by with more important things to do.

"I hear you," Angela said. "My appetite's coming back already."

There was a beautiful spread laid out across the dining room table. Platters displayed a wide variety of cold cuts and cheeses. There were trays of fruits, vegetables, crackers, chips and dips. Everything looked expensive and fresh from the deli.

"My daughter's funeral is costing me almost as much as her wedding only a week before," John was heard to say to a friend. "Eat up. I'm relatively sure she's only going to have one of these funerals. That's more than I could've said about her wedding."

"Poor Mr. Ryland," Scott confided to his buddy. "This thing is really tearing him up. He's trying to hide it under a gruff exterior, but Karen's death is hitting him hard and deep."

"You can't blame him," Brady replied. "I can't imagine what it must be like. And, look at Mrs. Ryland. She's trying so hard to be strong, but you can tell she's almost ready to break down and cry again."

"Yeah," Scott nodded. "It makes me wonder about Peter. What the hell could he be doing? You don't suppose he was afraid to show his face in front of Karen's parents, do you?"

"It's not too likely," Brady said. "He was at the wake yesterday."

"You have a point," Scott said. "That reminds me. I talked to him for a while at the wake. He had a few interesting stories to tell."

"Like what?"

"He told me something that happened on the night he had sex with Michelle," Scott explained. "The day before she was killed."

"What happened?"

"He told me Michelle saw Karen," Scott said. "Wearing the bloody bridal veil and everything!"

"I heard that rumor," Brady admitted. "But, that same rumor went around about Cynthia Trott when she disappeared. Now they're claiming her boss killed Karen. And probably Cynthia, too. You can't be trying to say Karen's going around murdering every girl who slept with Peter, are you?"

"Well, it's a bit of a stretch," Scott admitted. "But, there are coincidences."

"There are tall tales," Brady corrected. "There are rumors. That's all there is. There's no such thing as ghosts! Karen's not going out there killing everyone she was mad at in life! It's just not possible!"

"But, there's something I didn't tell you," Scott added.

"And what's that?"

"Peter saw Karen, too," Scott confided. "That's how he knew something was wrong with Michelle. That's why he went looking for her on the day she turned up dead!"

"So, what are you saying?" Brady asked. "Peter didn't come to Karen's funeral because her ghost murdered him?"

"Of course not," Scott said. "I wouldn't say such a thing. I don't believe in ghosts either. I'm just wondering what happened to him. He wouldn't have missed the funeral. I'm just worried. That's all."

"Well, I should give him another call," Brady said. "It is kind of strange that we can't get in touch with him."

"That's what I'm saying."

They made their way past a few rooms filled with Ryland family members and friends. They stepped outside.

The rain had stopped. It was still cold and damp.

Brady took out his cell phone. He called Peter.

On the third ring, a machine came on. Peter's voice told the caller to leave a message at the beep.

"Still nothing," Brady said as he hung up. "He's still not answering."

"It makes you wonder," Scott said. "Doesn't it?"

"Karen didn't kill Peter!" Brady insisted.

"Wouldn't you feel better if we went over and took a look?" Scott suggested.

They shared a concerned glance.

"Yeah," Brady said. "I guess."

They went inside. They said their good-byes. They expressed their thanks and sympathies. Scott told his wife he wouldn't be gone long. Then, they left.

Scott drove them to Peter's home.

It was still dark and gloomy outside. No rain was falling. However, it seemed as though the threat of precipitation had yet to vanish.

A cold wind blew by as they parked in Peter's driveway. It slapped against their faces as they got out of the car.

They walked up to the front door. Scott rang the doorbell.

There was no answer.

He rang again. He also knocked loudly, just to be sure.

The door creaked open just a crack.

Scott and Brady looked at each other with a touch of worry.

"That don't look good," Brady commented.

They quickly entered the domicile. They glanced around anxiously.

"Peter?" Scott called out.

There was no reply.

Scott called out again. So did Brady.

Only an eerie silence rewarded their efforts.

They spread out to cover more ground.

Brady was in a hall when he called out, "Oh my God! Scott! Come quick! There's some blood in the hall!"

It only took a few seconds for Scott to catch up to his friend. They looked down at the spatters and smears of blood on the floor.

They followed the smears a few feet down the hall to the bedroom.

Scott opened the bedroom door. He turned on the light.

Peter was laid out very neatly on the blood-stained bed. His arms were folded across his chest as if the mattress was meant to be his coffin.

His eyes were closed. His head rested nicely on the red-soaked pillows.

He was wearing the suit he had planned to wear to his wife's funeral. It would have been a snappy, smart-looking suit had it not been sliced, torn and caked with blood.

The well-tailored, horrifying sight was complimented by the word "BETRAYER", which had been carved angrily into the wooden headboard of the bed.

Chapter 12
The Mind of a Predator

They were getting used to these halls in the hospital. They recognized many of the staff as they passed by in blue scrubs or white lab coats.

They didn't need directions. They knew which room they had to visit.

Each corridor took them past a different group of patients in bandages, wheelchairs or on crutches. It was easy to ignore the many wounded individuals that traveled through the halls like a scattered herd of damaged antelope on a sterilized, linoleum prairie.

The elevator door was open when they approached. Four other people entered along with them. They got out on their floor and walked to the room with the officer posted outside.

The officer acknowledged them. He allowed them to pass.

The patient was sitting up in bed when they entered.

"Good afternoon, Detectives," he said. "Or is it evening already?"

"It's early evening, Dr. Freitag," Sumaki informed him. "How are you feeling?"

"I'm getting a little better every day," he said.

"Good," Sumaki said. "We have a few matters to discuss with you. To begin with, it has come to our attention that you have made arrangements for a Mr. Paul Shapiro to pay a sum of money nearing $6,000.00 to a sleazy private investigator named Donald Polopous on your behalf. Why is that, Doctor? It wouldn't have anything to do with the reason you, your wife and Grant Langley are in the hospital, would it?"

"Certainly not," he said. "I'll admit I hired him to follow my wife when I suspected she was having an affair. That's perfectly legal, isn't it? I owed him for his work, and I wanted him to get paid. That's all."

"Okay," Sumaki said. "We don't really need to pursue that issue, although I wonder what would turn up if we did. Still, you could help us in our current investigation."

"I'd be glad to help in any way I can, Detective," he said. "You don't need to resort to idle threats and strong arm tactics to gain my cooperation."

"I'm sorry, Doctor," Sumaki said. "This case has everyone on edge. Just when we think we're getting a handle on it, everything takes a turn for the worse."

"What's the matter?" he asked.

"Karen Broderick was buried late this morning," Sumaki explained. "Her widower never made it to the funeral. His body was found in his bedroom this afternoon. It looks as though he was murdered while preparing to attend his wife's funeral."

"I'm sorry to hear it," he said. "Are you suspecting Joe McMahon as the killer?"

"We've considered a few options," Sumaki said. "The most troubling piece of evidence is the fact that someone carved the word 'BETRAYER' very sloppily deep into the headboard of his bed. Our first thought was that Karen's father may have been taking advantage of the oddities in this case to get away with murder. But, there are a hundred witnesses to the fact that he has been either home or at his daughter's funeral all day."

"Which brings you back to McMahon," he theorized.

"Of course, the carving in the headboard is the thing that worries me the most," Sumaki said.

"I've heard the rumors," he said. "That Karen's ghost is out for revenge."

"Well, look at the victims," Sumaki pointed out. "After Karen, there was Cynthia, then Michelle, and now Peter. Karen's husband and the two women he cheated on his wife with. And with 'betrayer' carved in his deathbed, it makes you wonder. Could Joe McMahon's guilt over killing Karen lead him to think she's forcing him to act on her behalf? Especially with his suspected misogynistic tendencies, is that possible?"

"Sure," he said. "In fact, it's quite probable. A misogynist's hatred of women can often be attributed to the belief that women are evil. This belief can stem from many factors including being taught by word, treatment or behavior through parents. General mistreatment by women can cause it as well. But as I understand McMahon's condition, if his love for Karen caused him to contradict his negativity toward women, he may well have thought Karen (in her evil nature) forced him to do things against his will such as stalking or even killing her. The resulting guilt of her murder could easily drive him to think she is now forcing him to do her evil bidding."

"Thank you, Doctor," Sumaki said.

"A conflict already existed inside McMahon," he continued. "The guilt over Karen's murder can only complicate a preexisting condition. Not only guilt, but self justification over behavior he always found unsuitable and beneath him could be a factor."

"Of course, that still doesn't explain why everyone who dies," Reynolds added. "Claims to have seen Karen's ghost shortly beforehand."

Sumaki gave him an exasperated look.

"The victims all had their own guilt to wrestle with," Freitag reasoned.

"Not to mention," Reynolds said. "Michelle and Peter had the rumors of what Cynthia claims to have seen."

"That's true," Freitag agreed. "Rumor can be a powerful stimulant to the mind in cases such as these."

"Well, not to change the subject," Sumaki said. "Have you had any luck in contacting Zeblonsky, Doctor?"

"No," he said. "I've called him a few times. He never answers. And, he doesn't return my calls. That's not a good sign."

"Didn't you say the technique you used on him was supposed to be temporary?" Sumaki asked.

"It was," he said. "He should have snapped out of it as soon as he released the aggression that triggered his explosive episode. That's supposed to be the beauty of this psycho-therapeutic method. Due to pure shock value, it's supposed to control and contain itself and the patient. I promise you, Detective. Despite my selfish motives for choosing Dylan's target, this procedure was carefully planned and should have concluded on cue."

"So, what went wrong?" Sumaki asked.

"It's hard to say," he replied. "I must've misread the depth of his rage."

"It sounds like you could have been a bit more careful," Reynolds commented. "Is there any way he could still snap out of it?"

"Sure," he said. "He could come back to normal at any time. Although, it's most likely that some sort of emotional shock will be the trigger."

"Can you try calling him again please?" Sumaki asked.

"If you wish," he said.

He took out his cell phone. He dialed a number.

The detectives waited anxiously as he listened for a response.

After a time, he hung up. "I'm sorry," he said. "Still no answer."

"Well," Sumaki muttered. "I guess we still have two lunatics to hunt down."

"Please remember, Detectives," Freitag reminded. "Dylan is basically a good young man. What he's going through now is not his fault. He could still come out of this as a decent, worthwhile, productive human being."

"We'll keep that in mind, Doctor," Sumaki said. "Thanks for your help."

"Anytime, gentlemen."

When the detectives were gone, he settled back down in his bed. He closed his eyes.

Nearly half an hour passed. He was almost asleep when the phone on the nightstand beside his bed rang.

He answered with a groggy, "Hello?"

"Hi, Dr. Freitag," said the caller. "I see you've been trying to reach me."

"Dylan?" he said anxiously as he sat up. "How are you? Where are you?"

"I'm just fine, Doctor," Dylan said. "That's all you need to know."

"Are you in the general area?" he asked. "Why don't you come back? Let me help you. You need to snap out of this."

"I've never felt better in my life," Dylan said. "I don't need to snap out of anything."

"Are you still planning on going after those people from work?" he asked.

"Of course," Dylan said. "They haven't paid yet."

"This isn't right," he begged. "Please agree to meet with me, Dylan. This is all my fault. What you're feeling right now isn't natural. Your perceptions have been altered. This isn't you, Dylan!"

"Well, whoever it is," Dylan grinned. "I like it! I've been afraid to express myself all my life! I've never been allowed to feel anything! Anger! Pain! Want! Love! Do you know what that's like, Doctor? Do you know what it's like to feel nothing? Do you know what it's like to not be allowed to feel anything? Do you?"

"No, but..."

"'You have no right to be angry, Dylan,'" Dylan said in a voice that mocked his mother's. "'What makes you think you have the right? Pain? You're not allowed to feel pain, Dylan! You're three years old! Grow a pair, for Christ's sake! Why do you think you should be allowed to want something, Dylan? Why do you deserve to have anything, you insignificant little butt hole?'"

"We can work through these issues in therapy," he offered. "Give me a chance."

"And, love?" Dylan fumed. "I didn't deserve love! Not from my mother! Not from anybody! Maybe those girls at school could have loved me! If they stopped laughing at me long enough to even look at me! But they never did!"

"Dylan!" Freitag implored. "Please listen to me..."

"They never did, Doctor!" he snarled. "And, why should they? Why did *I* deserve their attention? Why should *I* get to be human? They just laughed! They avoided me! They feared me! Just like Angela Pierce!"

"Let's discuss this, Dylan..."

"Just like Angela, Doctor!"

"You seriously need..."

"Don't tell me what I need!" Dylan demanded. "I used to know what I needed! The same things as everybody else! But apparently, *I didn't deserve it*!"

"That's not true..."

"You know, Doctor," Dylan sneered. "In the mind of a predator, prey is just prey. It has no identity, and no reason to believe it deserves to survive. It's just prey! Well, I've been the prey for too damned long! Now it's *my* turn to be the predator!"

He hung up.

He stood outside for a minute. The sun had disappeared behind the horizon. Darkness settled like a mother space eagle sitting on a nest. He found it comforting, reassuring and protective, despite the accompanying chill.

He enjoyed the sting of the breeze on his face for another minute. Then, he climbed back up into his SUV.

He sat in the driver's seat and looked out into the woods that surrounded him. The vacant trees seemed so dark and bare with no leaves on their shuddering branches. They appeared to be exposed and vulnerable in a darkness that grew deeper as he watched.

The headlights showed the path that would lead back to civilization. He turned the lights on inside his vehicle. He looked in his rearview mirror.

He saw a shadow. It was the shadow of a woman's head. She must have been sitting behind him. He couldn't make out her face. The shadows were too dark.

However, she appeared to be wearing a bridal veil on her head that had been soaked in a puddle of blood.

He gasped!

Then, he spun quickly around to see what was behind him. Nobody was there. Nothing appeared to be out of place.

He heaved a sigh of relief.

But, he remained vigilant. He continued scanning the back of his vehicle for signs of the eerie intruder.

"I don't believe in ghosts!" he loudly assured himself.

Still, he kept glancing around. He remembered the rumors he'd heard.

"But just in case," he continued. "If that's you, Karen! I want you to know I had nothing to do with it! McMahon paid me to hack into that security system! I didn't know what he was going to do! I had no way of knowing he was going to kill you! I'm innocent! I never meant you any harm!"

His eyes kept searching the back of the SUV. There was no sign of any ghost.

He spun around again to face the dashboard. Suddenly, he was filled with the urge to move away from this location. He put the key in the ignition and turned it.

The engine sputtered, but didn't catch.

He tried again. Once again, the engine wheezed and sputtered. But, it didn't turn.

Then, he heard a female voice whisper softly in his ear.

"Sunday brunch at The Sandalwood," she whispered. "Tomorrow at 11:00."

He nearly leapt out of his seat. His heart was pounding. He was trembling. He was afraid to move.

"The Sandalwood?" he asked nervously. "But, that's too public! I can't be seen in town! I'm wanted by the police!"

"You love Sunday brunch at The Sandalwood," she softly insisted. "And, you'll definitely love it tomorrow at 11:00."

"I do love their Sunday brunch," he admitted shakily. "But, I can't be seen in public!"

"Be there. Trust me."

"But, I can't!"

There was no other response.

After a minute of quaking in his seat, he found the nerve to slowly turn around.

No one was there. Everything appeared as it should.

He quickly turned to face the front of the vehicle. The urge to leave this location grew immediately stronger. He tried the key in the ignition. After a few attempts, the motor finally turned over.

As soon as possible, he started his SUV down the bumpy path out of the woods. Without hesitation, he sped off into the fresh darkness of a crisp, new night.

❧ ❧ ❧

"I'm glad we came back to Taylor's Restaurant," she said. "I really liked this place the last time."

"I figured as much," he said. "You seemed to enjoy it the other night."

"It's more crowded than it was the last time we were here," she said.

"Well, it's Saturday night."

"That would explain it."

"It's nice to see you relax a little," he observed. "You have a more conciliatory attitude than you've had the first few times we were out. That's nice to see."

"Well, I am here to enjoy myself," she said. "But, don't get too excited. I still plan to take it slow. I know we've been out three nights in a row now. But, it is the weekend. It's nice to have something to do on a Saturday night. And, I appreciate all you've done. But, I'm not going to make a habit out of going out every night with you."

"It's just as good," he smiled. "I can't afford going to places like this all the time."

"Why are you bothering with fancy restaurants like this so early in the proceedings?" she asked.

"To make a good impression, of course."

"This kind of 'good impression' only tends to make me suspicious," she said.

"I know," he said. "That's a popular subject with you. We talk about it every time we go out."

"And yet, you keep taking me to places like this," she said.

"Well, I figure sooner or later you're bound to get sick of being suspicious," he said. "It's already working. You're starting to lighten up."

"Maybe a little."

"See?" he said. "So, it was all worth it."

She watched him for a moment. She wanted to believe.

"Not to bring up a sore subject," she began. "But, is this how you started with Cynthia?"

"No," he said. "I wasn't making as much money as I am now."

"Oh."

"Can we please stop talking about Cynthia?" he asked. "Yes, it hurts that she's dead. I cried when I found out. And yes, I'd still like to slaughter Joe for killing her. But, this has nothing to do with any of that. What do I have to do to convince you, Angela? I'm only going out with you because of *you*!"

"I'm just protecting myself, Neil," she said. "I will not be a meaningless rebound relationship for you. I just won't!"

"I understand that, Angela," he said. "I promise."

"Okay," she sighed. "I'm sorry. I guess you probably don't deserve to have me doubt you all the time. I do appreciate everything. You've been wonderful."

"Thank you," he said. "It's been a pleasure."

"Anyway," she continued. "It's easy to get paranoid working in a place like Blue Arrow. Look at the people we work with."

"Are you talking about McMahon?" he asked. "Or do you mean the girls?"

"Both, actually," she smiled. "Joe, Jennifer, Sarah and Lorraine are all enough to drive you nuts. But, I was really talking about the new story I saw on the news today."

"What new story?"

"Evidently," she explained. "The cops are looking for Dylan Zeblonsky now, too. It seems he attacked and stabbed his psychiatrist and a couple other people in a fit of rage. They say he is believed to be armed and dangerous."

"Zeblonsky, huh?" he said. "That's not a surprise. I told you that creepy little freak was dangerous. I should've killed him when I had the chance."

"I meant it when I said he almost scared me to death the other day in the archives room," she reminded. "No kidding! He claimed he just wanted to talk. I knew he was just about to go off the deep end."

"No one questioned your version of that incident, Angela," he assured her.

"Joe did," she argued. "He tried to tell Steve I was blowing it out of proportion."

"That's just Joe," he said. "We know what he's like. Especially after what he's done now. Steve knows better. He'll stand by you."

"He didn't fire Dylan," she persisted. "That little creep is still working there."

"Not any more," he said. "Not if he's running from the police for stabbing his shrink. You'll never have to worry about that little freak ever again."

"Joe and Dylan are both running from the cops," she muttered. "For two separate violent incidents. I've only been working in that place for two weeks, and I'm already sick of all the insanity and crazy people. I'm thinking of leaving The Blue Arrow Agency for good."

"Please don't, Angela."

"I can't take it, Neil," she said. "I can't work with these people!"

"Dylan and Joe are history," he said. "They'll never be allowed to work there again. You have no one left to worry about. You like most of the people, don't you?"

"I suppose."

"You like the girls, don't you?" he continued. "Aren't they your friends?"

"Jennifer, Sarah and Lorraine?" she asked. "Yeah. They're nice enough, I guess."

"And, Steve?"

"Steve's a good guy to work for," she admitted. "Most of the time."

"And, what about me?" he pressed. "You like me, don't you?"

She paused for a moment... mostly to tease him.

"Kind of," she finally said.

"Well, there you go," he summed up. "Where else are you going to find a package like this? All these great people to work with, plus benefits. You can't beat it."

"Well... maybe."

"Give it a chance, Angela."

"We'll see," she said. "Don't panic. I haven't made any final decisions yet. I have plenty of time to think about it."

"Okay," he said. "Just don't make any sudden, rash decisions."

"I won't," she said. "I promise."

"That's good," he said with a sigh of relief. "You had me so worked up, I thought I wouldn't be able to finish my steak!"

"How terrible for you," she smiled.

"And, there really is no way to sound masculine when you ask the waitress for a doggy bag," he added. "I'm sorry. There's just no way."

"Maybe I should ask the waitress for you," she joked.

"That's okay," he said. "I'm fine now. I shouldn't have any trouble finishing my dinner."

"I'm glad to hear it."

Later that evening, he drove her home. He found a parking space right outside her building. He walked her to the door.

"Thanks again for everything, Neil," she said. "I had a great time."

"I'm glad you enjoyed it."

"But, I have to say," she commented. "Two movies in a row? That doesn't say much for your imagination."

"You were the one who was complaining at dinner," he reminded. "That I'm trying too hard to make an impression. You're the one who wants to take it slow… the one who's telling me to take it easy."

"So, it's all my fault?"

"That's right."

"Well, in that case," she teased. "Next time I'll make you sit through a nice love story. In fact, I have just the movie in mind."

"Please spare me," he said. "I'd love to keep seeing you, Angela. But, I do have my limits."

They shared a quick laugh.

Then after a pause, she looked at him. "Part of me would like to invite you upstairs," she explained. "But, I'm not ready yet. I meant what I said before. I'm going to take this slow. I do like you, Neil. But, I'm not going to be a quick rebound fling for you. I hope you can understand."

"Of course," he said. "And, it'll be fine. I'll be seeing you at work. I can always call you. And, I can take you out again next Friday, right?"

"Sure," she said. "I'll look forward to it."

"Well then," he said. "I guess I can let you go under one condition."

"And what's that?"

"That you agree to have Sunday brunch with me tomorrow at The Sandalwood," he said.

"Sunday brunch?"

"The Sandalwood is kind of a landmark in Thorn Ridge," he explained. "And one of the things they're famous for is their Sunday brunch. We actually had an office party there once. That's how I first heard of it. It's unbelievable! They have a buffet with everything you could possibly think of. The menu items are just as fantastic. Trust me. You shouldn't miss it."

"It does sound intriguing."

"Can I pick you up tomorrow morning at 10:30?" he asked.

"Well..." she said as she thought. "Okay. I guess it couldn't hurt."

"That's my girl!"

"Thanks again, Neil."

"Don't mention it."

Their kiss was long and sweet. It was a tantalizing reminder of why she had agreed to go out with him this evening. And, it was a dangerous reminder of how difficult it was going to be for her to take it slow.

She looked into his eyes and smiled when she said, "Good night."

Still, she managed to leave him standing out in the cold of this frosty night.

When she was safely inside, he turned and went back to his car. This was the best he'd felt in a long time.

His car started right away. The darkness didn't phase him. He smiled as he drove home. He finally had a reason to feel optimistic.

Somehow, he just knew that his upcoming Sunday brunch at The Sandalwood was going to be a memorable experience.

🌿 🌿 🌿

Everything seemed all too familiar. The tight feeling in his stomach, the pain in his heart and the boorish decorations in The Presidential Room at The Classico Elegante were vividly etched into his brain.

He hadn't been invited to the wedding or the reception. It seemed like a blatant, heartless slap in the face after all he'd been through and all he'd done.

But, that's women for ya!

He wore his best suit. It was easy to blend into the crowd. The room was filled with people. Most of them would have no way of knowing he had no right to be there. He was aware of the security cameras.

They were no problem.

He could stay low and keep out of sight. And he'd taken care of the important timing. He paid good money to make sure those cameras would not be a problem when the time was right.

He still wasn't sure what he was going to do.

He didn't have a specific plan written in stone.

Sure… she had just married that philandering roach stomper. But, all was not lost.

Not necessarily.

If he could talk to her, he could still get through to her. Possibly.

He just had to get her alone. Maybe a short drive.

If she wouldn't listen to reason, he would simply have to insist. The knife in his pocket was only there as a bargaining chip. She would be less likely to be disagreeable with that knife in his hand.

He hoped he wouldn't have to use it.

But, let's face facts. The chances of convincing her that they were meant to be together were getting slimmer with each passing second!

She wasn't far away. It was easy to see her from where he was standing. She looked so beautiful in her wedding dress.

She was talking to some guests. She was laughing.

Look at how easily she could laugh... even after what she'd done to him!

It was disgraceful! Gorgeous... but, absolutely disgraceful!

He'd called Dylan a few minutes earlier. The little goon promised he'd be on standby. He would be at the ready.

Now, all he had to do was figure out how to get her alone.

How? Where?

It was difficult to remain patient. Time was his enemy. Still, he had to wait and watch as this delectable little demon mocked his very existence with every move she made.

Every smile. Every giggle. Every gesture. Every step.

All she did was meant to humiliate him and disregard his feelings.

Then, she caught his attention. She excused herself to go to the ladies' room. She went down that back hall that was so close to where she stood. Not many people knew about the rest rooms down that poorly lit back hall to the exit.

This was his chance!

He took out his cell phone as he snuck into a back corner. He dialed.

"Dylan?" he said into the phone.

"Yes."

"This is Joe," he said. "I want those cameras down now."

"Okay," Dylan said. "This won't take long. I've cracked their code. I just need to type in the authorization number. Here we go. Then, we get the clearance code. Now I type in the command, and..."

"Hurry up!"

"Give it a second," Dylan snipped. "Okay. There you go. We're done. The cameras are scrambled."

"Thanks."

He hung up.

He slipped unnoticed into the back hallway. He quietly rushed down the corridor. Then, he burst into the ladies' room.

She was fixing herself up by the sink. She gasped when she saw him in the mirror.

She spun around to face him.

"Joe!" she demanded. "What are you doing here?"

"I have to talk to you, Karen," he said.

"There's nothing to talk about," she said. "I just got married, for God's sake! Get out of here!"

"You married a termite swatter," he said. "Who will always smell like rat poison as surely as he will always cheat on you."

"Peter made one mistake," she said. "And, I forgave him. How is that any of your business?"

"It's my business," he replied. "Because I love you, Karen."

"Not this again," she sighed while rolling her eyes. "We've been through this, Joe! You're too old for me. You're my boss! I could never have feelings for you! I'm sorry. I promise I never meant to hurt you, but that's the way it is."

"You look breathtaking today, Karen," he said. "Absolutely stunning in white."

"Please don't, Joe," she said. "You promised. You told me that if I kept working for you and didn't press charges, you'd stop this crap. I overlooked a few of your slip-ups, but now you've stepped way over the line!"

"I've tried to be good, Karen," he explained. "I thought I could handle it if I just had you near. But then, you started seeing that cockroach stomper! I couldn't stand to see you throwing your life away like that!"

"I don't need to justify myself to you!" she argued. "It's none of your business who I marry! This is my wedding day, and you're not going to ruin it, Joe! Now, get out of here, or I'll have you thrown out!"

"You're not going to do that, Karen," he said.

Suddenly, the look in his eyes scared her.

He took a step toward her.

"What do you think you're doing, Joe?" she asked.

"I love you, Karen."

"If you don't leave, I'll scream!"

"You know I love you," he said with quiet assertion. "You've always known, and you've never cared."

"I mean it, Joe," she sputtered. "I'll scream!"

"You want to scream?"

He didn't remember grabbing the knife. He didn't remember stabbing again and again. Still, he could remember the look in her eyes.

"Do you like to scream, Karen?" he asked. "Do you enjoy it as much as you enjoy tearing out my heart? Isn't that just part of being a woman, Karen? Isn't it? Well? Isn't that part of being a woman?"

When he was done questioning her, he stood silently.

He was stunned. Why was Karen dead on the floor? Why was he holding that bloody knife?

This isn't what he wanted!

He just wanted to take her for a ride... whether she liked it or not! How did she end up dead? Wasn't this just like a woman? She couldn't even get *this* right!

What had he been thinking? How had he let her screw up his head for so long?

How had he allowed himself to be sidetracked by this insignificant incarnation of evil?

She remained motionless on the floor. She finally looked harmless.

Now he was finally rid of her. Still, he needed closure.

He needed a lasting symbol of what she really meant to him.

No one used this back hallway. And, her body was so light and easy to drag. It took no effort to get her all the way to the secluded exit.

No one at that party of fools would notice.

He got her outside and down the stairs without even working up a sweat.

Just as he suspected, there was a dumpster out back. That's where she belonged! This devil in white! This harbinger of pure evil! She should be taken out with the rest of the trash!

He hated getting her blood on his suit. It had been so easy to avoid up until this point. But now, he would have to just deal with it.

He lifted the lid of the dumpster. He picked up the limp, weightless body in his arms. Then, he put her right where she deserved to be.

He looked down at the glorious sight. He smiled.

Then, she opened her eyes.

He gasped with shock.

"So, it was easy to murder me," she sneered. "Wasn't it, Joe? It was just so easy!"

He stared in disbelief.

"Now it's my turn, Joe," she continued. "Now *I'm* calling the shots!"

"But… I…"

"Sunday brunch at The Sandalwood tomorrow," she said. "Dylan Zeblonsky will be there. You're going to kill him for me, Joe. You're going to kill him for his role in helping you murder me!"

"Dylan?" he stammered. "But, I can't…"

"You had no trouble murdering me," she reminded coldly. "Now you will have no trouble murdering Dylan! Sunday brunch at The Sandalwood tomorrow at 11:00! Be there, or you're next!"

He sat up suddenly in his bed. He was sweating. He was trembling. He was short of breath.

He looked around in the darkness. It took a minute to recognize his bedroom.

It had been just another bad dream. A dream like all the others!

He sighed with relief. Then, he leaned back against his pillows. He closed his eyes.

He tried his best to relax.

Outside, the all-embracing darkness seemed a chilling omen for what was to come.

Chapter 13
Fate

The sunlight burned too brightly through his windows. There was a warming effect that was easy to appreciate. Still, he found this natural wake-up call to be extremely obnoxious.

He rolled over in the cramped, confined space. He put a pillow over his head.

It didn't help.

After a minute, he sat up. He stretched. There was a pain in his back and neck. It occurred to him how much he was beginning to hate sleeping in the back seat of his SUV.

The previous night seemed like a distant, bad memory. He'd had a few beers. Not too many, though. He'd only had just enough to calm himself a little.

As he rubbed his neck, he wondered.

Why was he here? Why was he sleeping in his vehicle?

What was going on? What had he done?

He opened the door. He stepped out into the dirt.

The cold air hit him with a solid blast to his hands and face. It wasn't frigid. But, it was cold enough to snap him into total consciousness. He stood in place for a minute.

He found the brisk air to be refreshing and exhilarating.

He still wasn't sure why he was here. He only knew one thing.

Angela, Neil and Joe were responsible!

Somehow, they would have to pay!

He recalled the vision he'd had the night before. He remembered the voice in his ear. It was all so spooky, so frightening...

And so real!

Had it really been Karen?

It couldn't have! Could it?

Even if it was, why would she want him to go to The Sandalwood for Sunday brunch? It didn't make any sense!

Either dead or alive, since when did Karen care about his happiness or his health?

He checked his watch. It was still kind of early. But, his stomach was growling. It had been days since he'd eaten a decent meal. And, he was getting sick of living like a fugitive. He still wasn't sure what he was doing.

He still wasn't sure what he wanted to do. Even in the immediate future.

However, no matter what was going on, brunch at The Sandalwood felt like a good idea. Somehow, it seemed like it would be just the thing to perk up his spirits.

A few hefty, white clouds floated by the sun in a blatantly blue sky as if they had nothing better to do. Rotting leaves were matted down at the bottom of puddles like decaying brown swimming pool liners against the curb.

The morning was growing warmer. Still, it was becoming obvious that the sun was finding it more difficult to hold off the upcoming inevitability of winter.

It was precisely 10:37 when he rang her doorbell. She was wearing a long coat and an endearing smile when she greeted him at the door.

"Hi, Angela," he said. "You look gorgeous in that hat. I don't think I've ever seen you in it. It goes well with that coat."

"Thanks," she said after a quick kiss. "It's a fall hat. I only wear it in October. And maybe November, depending on the weather."

"Are you ready for brunch?" he asked as they walked to his car.

"I sure am," she said. "I'm kind of hungry, too. I hope this place is as good as you say. I'm kind of in a waffle mood today. Waffles and fruit."

"Best waffles in Pennsylvania," he proclaimed. "And the gods hand-pick these fruits from the best gardens in Heaven."

"Wow!" she laughed. "It sounds too good to be true."

He opened the car door for her. When she was seated, he closed the door and circled around to the driver's side. A few moments later, they were on their way to The Sandalwood.

"So, this is another place you heard of through some celebration at work?" she asked. "You guys seem to go to a lot of great places when you have an occasion. Who plans all these things?"

"Who knows?" he said. "Sometimes it's Steve, Rick or Joe. It could be their secretaries. I think Alex has chosen the location a few times. He's one of the owners of the company. We almost never see him down on our level."

"Well, whoever organizes these things must have great taste," she said.

"That's another reason why you shouldn't leave Blue Arrow, Angela," he said. "We have fantastic events for all sorts of occasions. Birthdays, anniversaries, retirements, you name it. If there's a reason to shut down the office, we do it in style."

"Then, how do so many people get...?" she began. She stopped. She glanced down at her lap.

Sensing a mood, he replied with delicacy. "It's a big, nasty world out there," he said. "No matter where you go, you're going to run into some crazy people. That's just how it is. You can't avoid them unless you plan on hiding under a rock. I'm sorry you saw the worst we have to offer in such a short time with us. But, don't take it too hard. There are a lot of nice people working at Blue Arrow. You just have to give us a chance."

"I know," she sighed. "You're right. I've just had a lot thrown at me in just two weeks. It's hard to take it all in."

"That's certainly true," he concurred. "You've been through a lot. And you've seen a lot of crap too. But, don't take it to heart. I've been working here for years, and I've never seen anything like this happen. It's usually not like this, honey. Trust me. Usually, we're a great bunch of people."

"I believe you," she said. "I should give Blue Arrow a chance. I just wish I didn't have to start my employment with such a 'trial by fire.'"

"Well, the worst is over now," he said. "Joe and Dylan are gone. They won't be coming back after what they've done. It's nothing but sunshine from here on in. You're on your way to a nice brunch. Nothing could be safer than that, right?"

"I guess."

"Then next week," he said. "Everything will go back to normal."

"I sure hope so," she said. "That's what I need. A nice, normal place to work."

"That's the least you could ask for," he smiled.

Five minutes later, they pulled into the parking lot of The Sandalwood. It was already getting crowded. He needed to look for a parking space.

Eventually, they had to walk a fair distance to the restaurant.

"You see?" he said as they approached the front door. "This place is a Thorn Ridge tradition on Sundays."

"Well, I'm glad I get to share in the experience," she replied.

They smiled at each other as he opened the door for her. Neither one of them noticed an SUV covered in a thick, sloppy coat of black paint pull into the parking lot as they entered the building.

The young man in the SUV squinted at the restaurant as he drove between cars. His eyes narrowed with recognition.

"Was that Neil Worthington?" he asked himself. "Who is he with? That girl in the hat. Is that Angela? Are they dating now? That figures! Sunday brunch? I should've known! Damn it! Damn the both of them!"

He took his time finding a parking spot.

Inside the restaurant, the young couple was seated at one of the last open booths.

"This place is much bigger than I expected," she commented. "And much nicer. I'm glad we came."

"Wait 'til you taste the food," he said. "Would you like to order something, or would you prefer to try the buffet?"

"I'd rather get something off the menu," she said. "If that's alright with you. I definitely know what I want."

"That's fine," he said. "I already told you they have the best waffles in Pennsylvania. This promises to be a meal you'll never forget."

She smiled at him.

"Would you like to do something together after we eat?" he asked. "I assure you I can think of something more imaginative than going to a movie."

"No," she said. "Thanks for the offer, but I already promised Jennifer and Sarah we could go shopping this afternoon."

"Jennifer and Sarah?"

"Yes," she said. "I was supposed to have lunch with them, too. I almost declined your offer for this brunch because of that. But I knew if the girls found out I passed up an invitation to have brunch with you, I'd never hear the end of it."

"I can believe that," he chuckled.

"They would have insisted that I go with you instead anyway," she said.

"So, how did they take the news that we were having brunch?" he asked.

"As you might well imagine," she explained. "They were positively giddy. It took me forever to convince Sarah I didn't spend the night with you."

They shared a laugh.

"That's our Sarah," he said.

"I'm still not sure she believes me," she said.

"Don't worry," he said. "I'll back up your story."

"Thanks."

"So, you're actually getting friendly with the girls?" he asked.

"I suppose so," she sighed. "They're basically good people. They just get a little carried away sometimes. They seem to be making an effort to let me into their circle of friends. That's awfully nice of them."

"Well, you're a very likable person," he said.

"And I'm sure my stock's been rising since I've been seen dating you," she added.

"Well, *I'm* a likable person, too."

"It certainly seems that way at the start," she admitted.

"I guess it's up to me to see that perception doesn't change," he said.

328

"See that you do."

Outside, a young man in a black SUV decided to stay in his vehicle. His stomach was growling. He desperately wanted to eat. However, he didn't want to be seen.

And, it occurred to him that he may have an opportunity to get revenge on two of the people on his list.

It almost seemed like poetic justice that he would find them both together on a date. He still wanted Angela. He wondered if it would be worth trying to talk to her.

What was he thinking? She wouldn't talk to him in the office. Why would she talk to him now? She must have heard something of his recent exploits on the news by now.

Maybe if she saw what he was going to do to Neil…

No! Probably not!

The time for talking was over! Now it was time for revenge!

He took out the knife. He inspected the long, sharp blade.

It was so sharp! It was so shiny!

Even though he hadn't anticipated getting such an opportunity so quickly, he had prepared the blade with particular care.

He knew this chance would come eventually. He had looked forward to it! He had yet to formulate a plan of action.

All he knew was that he couldn't let this chance pass without taking advantage of the situation. He just had to act!

Neil and Angela together? On a date? It was all too perfect!

He grinned as he regarded the flash of light against the long, sturdy blade in his hand.

He would have to wait here in the parking lot. He would have to be patient. But, he could do that.

Still, he had to wonder if there was some sort of divine intervention when he thought Karen had suggested brunch at The Sandalwood the previous evening.

Had he really seen Karen? Or was it just fate?

As the delightful feeling of rage rose in his blood, it didn't matter anymore.

All that mattered was the blissful expectation of total release!

After ordering their food, the young couple resumed their casual conversation inside the restaurant.

"So, where are you girls going shopping?" he asked.

"I don't know," she said. "I'm sure Jennifer and Sarah plan on showing me all the hot spots for fashion in town."

"See?" he said. "For all your complaining about working at Blue Arrow, you seem to be getting along with everyone."

"That's true," she agreed. "People have been wonderful."

"Everybody seems eager to show you around town," he pointed out. "Befriend you and show you all that Thorn Ridge has to offer."

"I must admit," she said. "Most of the people I met have been great. And this is a pleasant town. I could grow to like it here."

"Of course you could," he said. "Don't let a few bad apples like Zeblonsky and McMahon ruin it for you."

"You're right."

"Aside from anything else," he reminded. "They're out of the picture now. They won't be bothering you anymore."

"I know," she said. "It's just that this last week has kind of left a bad taste in my mouth. I'll get over it. It might take some time, though."

"Take all the time you need," he said. "You have all the time in the world. And, a growing list of friends to help you."

"I might be a little homesick too," she said. "I miss Seattle."

"That's only natural," he said. "Your growing list of friends can help you there, too."

"I'm sure they can."

"Not to mention the waffles you just ordered," he said. "You'll forget all about Seattle after you sink your teeth into those babies."

"We'll see about that."

He found her smile rather engaging.

"Thanks for coming to brunch with me, Angela," he said.

"That's okay," she said. "Thanks for inviting me."

"It was my pleasure."

"And, these better be mighty fine waffles," she added playfully. "I have a lot of shopping to do this afternoon."

"Trust me," he said. "After these waffles, your shopping trip will be a big let-down."

"Get a hold of yourself," she said. "They're only waffles."

They shared a laugh.

"And, I must say," she added. "I'm proud of you for taking me to a nice, normal restaurant instead of those fancy, romantic places where you've been taking me to dinner. This makes you look more like a regular person instead of someone who's making too much of an effort to make a definite impression."

"Well, I do have many sides," he informed her. "And, I'm full of surprises."

"There's that 'definite impression' again," she pointed out.

"Are you surprised?"

"Not really."

"Well, keep yourself braced anyway," he said. "I promise you I'm full of them. Surprises, that is."

"You're full of *something*, alright."

They shared another quick chuckle.

When the meal was over, she admitted, "You were right. The food here is excellent. Thank you, Neil. I really enjoyed it."

"I'm glad," he said. "We'll have to do this again sometime."

"I'd like that."

"Is there anywhere special I can drop you off?" he asked as he stood. "Are you supposed to meet the girls somewhere?"

"They're going to meet me at my place," she said while glancing at her watch. "In about 45 minutes. Oh God! I'd better get home!"

"No problem," he said as he helped her on with her coat. "We'll get you there in plenty of time."

They walked out to the parking lot.

As they approached his car, she gasped, "Oh no! I forgot my hat! I think I left it back in our booth."

"Wait here," he offered. "I'll get it. I'll be back in a jiffy."

"Thanks."

She waited by the car as he ran back into the restaurant.

He located the hat right away. He excused himself to the people who were taking their seats in the booth. Then, he hurried out to the parking lot. But as he walked up to his car, he saw no sign of Angela.

He quickly glanced around the parking lot.

It didn't take too long to spot a man who looked like Dylan Zeblonsky. He was putting something in the back seat of a black SUV. It looked like a body. It could have been Angela.

But, she wasn't moving!

Dylan slammed the door closed. Then, he ran around to the driver's side.

"Dylan!" Neil shouted as he ran toward the SUV. "Dylan! Wait! What are you doing, you little bastard! Stop!"

Dylan locked his door. He tried the key in the ignition. The engine chugged a few times, but didn't catch.

Neil caught up to the side of the black vehicle. He tried to open the back door where Dylan had placed Angela. The locked door wouldn't open.

Dylan was trying to start the engine again as Neil punched the side of the SUV with frustration.

Luckily, the engine still didn't start.

Neil quickly ran around to the driver's side. "Zeblonsky!" he shouted. "Stop, you little asshole! Get out of the fucking vehicle, or I'll rip your head off!"

Dylan glanced over at the man who was angrily banging on his window with his fist. Then, he turned the key in the ignition again. This time the motor roared into action.

"Zeblonsky! You son of a bitch!" Neil warned. "Open the fucking door! Let Angela out of there, or I'll kill you!"

With complete confidence, Dylan shifted the vehicle into reverse. Neil was still pounding on the window as the driver backed out of the parking space.

"Zeblonsky! You psycho!" Neil threatened. "Stop the damned car! Let Angela go! I'm warning you!"

Dylan glared down at the man who was now standing only three feet in front of the SUV. He shifted into gear with authority.

Suddenly, Neil's gaze turned from angry to scared. The look in Dylan's eyes told him that the little freak had dangerous thoughts on his mind.

The screeching of tires drove Neil to jump up on the hood of the nearest car as the SUV headed straight for him. Dylan turned in time to miss the car. Still, he sped to the end of the parking lot.

Neil rolled off the hood of the car as he watched the back of the SUV. "That's it!" he grumbled to himself. "I'm going to kill him! If he hurts Angela, I'll skin him alive!"

His car was only a few spaces away. He raced over as quickly as possible. There was a cell phone on the ground near the front tire. Either by instinct or on a hunch, he picked it up. Then, he unlocked the door and quickly jumped in. With careless disregard, he tossed Angela's hat and the cell phone on the passenger's seat.

He swore under his breath when his first attempt to start the car failed.

His second attempt brought the car to life. He immediately backed out of his space just in time to see the SUV pull out into traffic.

He sped across the lot. Then, he plunged out onto the main road without allowing for a break in the traffic. He ignored the sound of screeching tires and an angry car horn as he focused on following Dylan.

The black SUV was nearly a block ahead of him. Still, he managed to keep it in view as he tried to maneuver into a lane that could bring him closer to his target.

The cell phone beside Angela's hat began to ring. Out of sheer desperation, he decided to answer it. He tried to keep his eyes on the SUV up ahead of him as he grabbed for the noisy instrument.

He opened the phone, put it up to his ear and said, "Hello?"

"Hi," the caller said curiously. "Who's this?"

"It's Neil," he said. "Who are you?"

"Oh hi, Neil," she said. "It's Jennifer. I heard you were having brunch with Angela. Where is she? We're supposed to go shopping this afternoon."

"She's been kidnapped," he said. "By that little turd Zeblonsky!"

"Dylan?" she gasped. "Dylan kidnapped Angela?"

"Yeah," he said. "She must have dropped her cell phone when he grabbed her. I picked it up in the parking lot. I'm about five cars behind him. He's moving pretty fast going east, but I've got my eye on him."

"You're following them?" she asked. "But, how? I mean, how did he even know where you two were?"

"How the hell should I know?" he snapped. "We were leaving the restaurant. Angela left something behind. I went back in to get it for her. And when I came back out, Dylan was putting her in the back of his car. He took off before I could get to him."

"Is there anything I can do?" she asked.

"Call the cops," he instructed. "Get that Japanese detective. What was his name? Sumaki! That's it! Tell him it looks like Dylan painted his greasy Ford Explorer black. He's going east on Chandler Rd. I think he's heading out of town."

"Okay," she said. "I'll call him right now."

"And, Jennifer?" he suggested. "Keep in touch."

"Will do."

In the back of the SUV, Angela began to stir. She had a headache. She was groggy. The side of her face felt as if it had been hit by a truck. She couldn't move her arms. Her hands seemed to be tied behind her back.

She moaned from the dull pain that filled her head.

"Hello, Angela," said a vaguely familiar voice.

"W-what?" she muttered. "What's going on? Where am I?"

"You're in the back seat of my sweet ride," the driver explained. "Incidentally, I'm Dylan... in case you didn't recognize me. God knows you've never looked at me or paid the slightest bit of attention to me."

"Dylan?" she asked as she finally opened her eyes. "What am I doing here?"

"I grabbed you in the parking lot of The Sandalwood," he informed her. "You were on a date with your new boyfriend. By the way, I'm sorry I had to hit you. I don't usually hit girls. But, this operation was not exactly planned out. It was a stroke of luck that I found you. I only went there for brunch. But, when I saw you were dating that shallow little pretty boy, I knew I had to do something. And, I had to act quickly. There wasn't much time."

"You're kidnapping me?" she asked. "But, why? Where's Neil?"

"Oh, I suspect pretty boy is following us," he said. "Or trying to, at least. I doubt he'll have much luck. Oh. Also, I want to say I hope I didn't tie your hands too tightly behind your back. There again, it was done on the spur of the moment. I didn't have much time to think about it. I just acted on instinct."

She tried to free her hands from behind her back. They were tied too tightly. The restraints were beginning to hurt.

"Why are you doing this, Dylan?" she asked. She tried to mask her fear.

"Apparently," he said. "It's the only way I can get you to talk to me."

"What are you talking about?" she asked.

"The last time I tried to talk to you," he reminded. "You refused to speak to me. All you did was scream and cause a big, unnecessary commotion for no reason."

"You were scaring me!"

"So, if I talk to you," he deduced. "I scare you. Then, you organized a big meeting designed to get me fired."

"I'm sorry things got so..." she began.

"Next thing I know," he interrupted. "I'm talking to my shrink. He tells me he has a great new technique that can help me work through my anger, so I can deal with people a little better. All I have to do is stab three people. Two of those people I never even met. One of them was his cheating wife. So now, I'm running from the cops. But at least, my shrink took care of his personal problems. And, it's all because I tried to talk to you, Angela."

"What?" she asked in shock. "Your shrink told you to stab three people?"

"Pretty much."

"And, you're blaming that on *me*?"

"Who do you suggest I blame, dear?" he asked. "The people who don't refuse to talk to me didn't cause my problems."

"Please don't do this, Dylan," she begged. "If you let me go, I promise I won't press charges. And if you want to talk, we can talk. You don't have to kidnap me to make me talk to you, Dylan. I never meant to be a jerk."

"You never meant to be a jerk?" he asked. "It's funny. Nobody ever means to be a jerk. They just won't talk to you. They laugh at you behind your back. They make up names they can call you when they think you can't hear. They spread rumors. They tell the cops, 'Dylan must have killed Karen. Dylan's a creep.' If you try to talk to them, they scream and try to get you fired. But, *nobody* ever means to be a jerk!"

"I've only been working there two weeks," she explained anxiously. "Maybe I shouldn't have listened to what people said about you. But, I'm new in that office. I was scared. I was still trying to find my way and fit in."

"Two weeks?" he scoffed. "I've been trying to find my way and fit in for *years*! But, people won't even let me! Two weeks and you're best friends with people like Jennifer Cibello and Sarah Krause! You go shopping with them on weekends! I've seen you in stores together. But, God forbid I dare to say hello!"

"You could've…"

"Two weeks," he continued. "And, you're dating the shallowest pretty boy in the whole building. So shallow and pretty, all the girls want him. And you're having brunch at The Sandalwood with him after working at Blue Arrow for only two weeks! I wish I could say I'm surprised, Angela. But, I'm not! I'm very disappointed in you, Angela. But, I'm not surprised!"

He didn't notice who was driving the expensive car behind him. It was a familiar older man from The Blue Arrow Agency.

It was a man with anger in his eyes. It was a man with a purpose.

It was a man who had paid Dylan to hack into the security cameras at The Classico Elegante.

Three cars behind him, a young man was still struggling to keep the black Explorer in his sights.

The cell phone in the passenger's seat rang.

He picked it up and answered, "Hello?"

"Hi, Neil," she said. "It's Jennifer again. Where are you now?"

"We're still heading east," he explained. "We're about at the outskirts of town. I still have my eyes on him, but I haven't been able to gain much ground. The traffic is murder today."

"Please don't say, 'murder', Neil."

"I'm sorry," he said. "I'm worried about losing him. Chandler St. is going to be turning onto the highway soon. That could be dangerous."

"I called Sumaki," she said. "He must be headed in your direction by now."

"I can hear a siren coming up behind me," he said. "That's probably him."

"Most likely," she said. "I can hear the siren, too. We can't be that far behind you."

"You're following us, too?" he asked. "Are you insane?"

"Sarah thought I was crazy too," she informed him. "But, I couldn't just leave Angela behind. Not with that perverted little scuzz bucket. I had to make sure she's okay."

"Don't you realize what's happening here?" he questioned. "Zeblonsky's obviously gone off his rocker. He's driving like a lunatic! God only knows what he's capable of! You could get killed!"

"I can't just sit by and watch that little creep hurt Angela!" she insisted.

"Well," he sighed. "We just passed the intersection of Foster Ave. about a mile back. We'll be hitting the highway soon. I have to get off the phone so I can watch him. If he's going to make a move, he's going to have to do it soon. Be careful."

"You too."

Back in the Explorer, Angela was practically in tears.

"Please stop, Dylan," she begged. "You're driving like a maniac! You're going to get us both killed!"

"It's a shame I had to do this to get you to talk to me," he said. His tone was getting dark. "Isn't it, Angela? It's a fucking shame that it had to come to this."

"Please don't!" she implored as the first few tears trickled down her cheeks. "Stop the car! I promise I won't press charges. We can talk all you want. Just please don't do this!"

"Do you hear that siren, Angela?" he asked in a tone that reminded her of their talk in the archives room. "They're coming for us. I finally got someone's attention. The cops are paying attention to me, just like you are. And all I had to do was grab you in the parking lot. I didn't want this, Angela. You made me do this!"

"I didn't mean to!" she sobbed. "I never meant any harm!"

She desperately tried to free herself from the rag that bound her hands too tightly behind her back.

"Fate is a funny thing," he said. "Isn't it, Angela? Fate can be so sweet for some people. But, it can also be so cruel and brutal to others. Do you believe fate brought us to this moment, my dear?"

"I don't know," she wept.

"I truly fell in love with you, Angela," he said.

"You did?" she wept. "I'm sorry. I didn't know."

"I tried to tell you," he grumbled. "But, you wouldn't talk to me. I tried to tell you. I tried to talk to you. But, you refused. You just screamed. You caused a big commotion for no reason at all. Then, you tried to get me fired. That's why you didn't know."

"Please just stop," she begged. "We'll talk about it! I never meant to hurt you!"

"Of course you didn't," he said. "I could've made you happy, Angela. We could've been good together. Fate brought us to this moment, my darling. And now, you're going to be mine! Now it's your turn to make me happy. Can you do that, Angela? Can you make me happy?"

"What do you mean?"

Her sense of fear was greatly renewed. She tried again to free her hands.

"You bled so sweetly for me in the archives room," he explained. "The way the blood ran down your arm. It was more than beautiful. It was exquisite!"

"Oh, my God!" she muttered to herself.

"If you could have been bothered to talk to me before," he continued. "I never would have asked you to bleed for me again. But since we had to do this..."

A fresh wave of tears ran down her face as she desperately tried to pull her hands free from their bonds.

"Now that you're mine," he informed her. "You're going to bleed for me, Angela. You know how to bleed. Don't you, my dear? You know how to bleed so sweetly!"

"No!" she screamed. "Please don't, Dylan! Please don't hurt me!"

"Don't worry, darling," he said. "I have no intention of killing you. I love you. Remember? I just want you to bleed in that divine way you have, to show me that you love me too."

He could hear more than one siren. Apparently, more cops were joining the chase. He touched the blade of the knife in the passenger's seat.

"Sometimes love hurts, my darling," he explained. "Believe me. Nobody knows that better than I do. And sometimes, love even bleeds. That's right, Angela. Love bleeds. And in your case, that can be such a beautiful, gorgeous thing."

"No!" she sobbed. "Please no!"

"Oh, don't make such a fuss," he said. "I won't cut you that deep. Just enough to make your blood run free."

She couldn't say any more. She was crying uncontrollably in the back seat.

The sirens didn't sound any closer. However, they still seemed too close for Dylan to feel comfortable.

He glanced over at the knife.

Then, he heard a ringing in his pocket. He heaved an impatient sigh as he reached for his cell phone.

He answered it with an angry, "What?"

The female voice on the other end frightened him. "Hello, Dylan," she said. "Remember me?"

"Karen?" he gasped. "It can't be! You're dead!"

"Check your mirror, Dylan," she said. "Look in the car behind you. I'm right on your bumper, my friend."

He looked in the rearview mirror. His eyes grew wide as he noticed who was driving the car behind him. It was difficult to make out her face. But, there was no mistaking the blood-soaked bridal veil she was wearing.

"I'm coming to get you, Dylan," she warned. "You're going to pay for what you've done!"

A chill went up his spine. In his fear, he dropped the phone between his legs. He was still staring at the bloody sight in his rearview mirror.

The SUV sped through the red light and into the busy intersection.

A red sports car plowed into the front corner of the Explorer on the driver's side. Dylan's head banged against his side window as his vehicle spun around. And when Joe's car smashed into the back of the vehicle, it whirled around to complete a full circle.

What had once been The Space Eagle was facing east again when it came to a stop.

Dylan felt a little foggy as his head throbbed. It took a few seconds to realize what had happened. However, when he saw a chunky man in his forties leap out of a crumpled sports car, he came back to life.

"Hey, asshole!" the man shouted. "What the hell's a matter with you? Look what you did to my car! Don't you know what a red light means?"

Dylan's eyes narrowed as he reached over and grabbed the knife.

He quietly... slowly exited his vehicle.

As the man approached, Dylan displayed the knife and glared. "You got a problem, bitch?" he growled.

The man's jaw dropped when he saw the size of the knife. He froze.

"N-no," he stammered. "No problem!"

He slowly backed away.

Then, Dylan turned to face another angry presence. This antagonist was wearing a bloody bridal veil.

"Karen!" Dylan gasped. "How can this be?"

Angela managed to sit up while leaning against the door and look out the window.

"Why is Dylan acting as if he's talking to Karen?" she asked herself. "That's clearly Joe McMahon. My God! Check out that knife Joe's carrying!"

Dylan froze as he stared in disbelief at the image of the dead bride.

"Karen wants you to pay for your part in her murder," Joe declared.

Dylan only heard Karen's voice. His back was pressed against the side of his vehicle as the veiled figure raised her knife.

"Karen!" he begged. "Please! It wasn't me! I didn't..."

Dylan gasped as Joe's knife sank deep into his ribcage. The pain was intense.

Everything grew cloudier.

"Karen wants you to die!" Joe asserted.

Dylan watched the bloody bride raise her knife again. He feared for his life. He was bleeding from a deep chest wound. He felt a bit weak. His vision was faltering.

In sheer desperation, he lunged forward with his own knife.

The long, shiny blade sliced clean through Karen's throat. It then came out through the back of her neck.

Suddenly, Dylan saw everything much more clearly.

That wasn't Karen who was confronting him! It was Joe!

Dylan let go of the knife that was protruding out the back of Joe's neck.

Joe dropped the knife he was holding. His eyes rolled back up into his head. Then, he dropped like a bag of bones at Dylan's feet.

Dylan looked down at the body with the knife in its neck. He was confused. He glanced around as if he had no idea where he was.

"Where am I?" he muttered. "How did I...?"

Suddenly, Neil ran up and grabbed him by the collar. "Where's Angela, you little freak? What did you do with her?"

"What?" he stammered. "How should I know?"

"Don't lie to me, you pathetic bag of puke!" Neil threatened. "If you hurt that girl in any way, I'm going to slaughter you!"

He punched Dylan in the stomach. Dylan grunted as he doubled over in agony. Then, he fell to the ground near the motionless body of Joe McMahon.

Neil tried to open the back door of the damaged SUV. It took some effort to get the door open. After a few yanks, it gave way.

"Angela!" he cried. "Are you alright, sweetie?"

"I think so," she said. "I bumped my head a little in the crash. But, I think I'm okay."

Neil quickly untied her hands as he said, "Maybe we should get you to a hospital, just to be safe."

"That sounds good to me," she agreed.

As she freed her hands, Neil took her in his arms. They held each other tightly in the middle of the road.

"My God!" Neil muttered. "If he'd hurt you, I don't know what I'd do!"

"I'm okay, honey," she whispered as she clung to her man. "Thanks."

The nearest siren stopped right behind the crash.

"Oh, Christ!" Sumaki sputtered as he jumped out of his car. "Look at this mess! Are you alright, Miss Pierce?"

Angela never let go of Neil. "I'm fine," she answered. "Now."

"Dave," Sumaki ordered. "Keep an eye on Zeblonsky. I'll call for an ambulance and some officers to take care of all this."

"You got it," Reynolds said.

He drew his gun. He cautiously approached Dylan, who was still lying on the ground near Joe's motionless body. One knife was still on the street between Dylan and Joe. Reynolds kicked it off into the grass, so Dylan couldn't grab it.

Two patrol cars that had been following the detectives stopped. Three officers immediately started dealing with the accident. One officer joined Reynolds. He knelt down and checked Joe's wrist for a pulse.

He looked up at Reynolds and said, "This guy's gone."

"What happened here?" Reynolds sharply asked Dylan. "Are you responsible for all this? Did you stab Joe McMahon?"

"I... I don't know what's going on," Dylan stammered. "Last thing I remember is talking to Dr. Freitag. He was supposed to help me. Then, Karen was trying to kill me. Then, Karen was Joe! I was just defending myself!"

"Bullshit!" Reynolds barked. "You kidnapped Angela, you caused this crash and then you killed McMahon!"

"I don't remember!" Dylan averred. "This is all Freitag's fault! I would never hurt anyone! Tell him, Angela!"

"You're a real piece of work, Zeblonsky!" Reynolds spat. "My partner's calling for back-up and an ambulance. But, I don't know why we should bother! I can't imagine why we shouldn't just let you bleed to death right here!"

"I would never hurt anyone!" Dylan insisted. "I couldn't hurt Angela! She knows I would never hurt her! Tell him, Angela! Tell him I would never hurt you!"

Angela didn't even hear him. She and Neil were still holding each other near the back of the mangled SUV.

The officer tended to Dylan's wounds. Reynolds kept his gun trained on the bleeding kidnapper.

Another car stopped by the side of the road. However, Jennifer and Sarah never exited their vehicle. They watched the scene play out from the safety of their seats.

"Oh, God!" Jennifer gasped. "I don't believe it! Look at that crash! What a disaster! I hope Angela is okay."

"It looks like she and Neil are doing fine," Sarah pointed out. "Oh, gross! Is that Joe McMahon over there with a knife through his neck?"

"Well," Jennifer said as she refused to look. "At least, he won't be ruining any more weddings."

Sarah followed Jennifer's gaze.

"Are you talking about Neil and Angela?" Sarah asked. "You must be kidding! They've only known each other for two weeks. They've only dated a few times."

"It's fate," Jennifer stated. "Believe me. It'll happen eventually. I know it'll happen when the time is right. Trust me. I have a special sense about these things."

Sarah and Jennifer smiled as they watched the young couple holding each other silently amid the chaos.

Dylan was still lying down in the street. As the detectives watched, he propped himself up on one elbow. A makeshift bandage covered his wound.

"Angela!" he shouted. "You know I would never hurt you! Tell them, Angela! You know I couldn't even hurt a fly! Tell them, Angela! Please! Angela!…

…ANGELA!!!…"

About the Author

Donald Gorman was born on September 25, 1961 in Albany, NY. He grew up in the nearby small town of East Greenbush, where he graduated from high school in 1979. He has attended a few local colleges, although he has never earned a degree. His extensive travels in the northeast also include Montreal, Chicago and Milwaukee. He currently resides in upstate NY and works for The State in Albany. His love for the horror genre began while reading Stephen King novels and watching slasher movies in the 70s and 80s. His first five novels: "The Brick Mirror", "The Waters of Satan's Creek", "Macabre Astrology", "A Grave in Autumn" and "Deliciously Evil: A Cookbook for Killers" are all great examples of his work as well.

Printed in the United States
77919LV00001B/7-24

9 781434 304063